Acclaim for MICHAE

THE ENGLISH PATIENT

"A magically told novel…ravishing…many-layered."
—*Los Angeles Times*

"Profound, beautiful and heart-quickening." —Toni Morrison

"Lyrical…dreamlike and enigmatic…*A Farewell to Arms* drenched in spooky ennui. It is also a difficult novel to leave behind, for it has the external grip of a war romance and yet the ineffable pull of poetry…An exquisite ballet that takes place in the dark." —*Boston Sunday Globe*

"A tale of many pleasures—an intensely theatrical tour de force but grounded in Michael Ondaatje's strong feeling for distant times and places." —*The New York Times Book Review*

"A poetry of smoke and mirrors." —*Washington Post Book World*

"In this masterful novel, Michael Ondaatje weaves a beautiful and light-handed prose through the mingled histories of people caught up in love and war. A rich and compelling work of fiction."—Don DeLillo

"It seduces and beguiles us with its many-layered mysteries, its brilliantly taut and lyrical prose, its tender regard for its characters…. On every page *The English Patient* pulses with intellectual and aesthetic excitement." —*Newsday*

"A narrative of astonishing elegance and power…one of the finest novels of recent years—large, rich, and profoundly wise."—*Mirabella*

"It is an adventure, mystery, romance and philosophical novel in one…. Michael Ondaatje is a novelist with the heart of a poet." —*Chicago Tribune*

MICHAEL ONDAATJE

THE ENGLISH PATIENT

Michael Ondaatje is a novelist and poet who lives in Toronto, Canada. He is the author of *In the Skin of a Lion, Coming Through Slaughter*, and *The Collected Works of Billy the Kid*; three collections of poems, *The Cinnamon Peeler, Secular Love*, and *There's a Trick with a Knife I'm Learning to Do*; and a memoir, *Running in the Family*. He received the Booker Prize for *The English Patient*.

INTERNATIONAL

THE
ENGLISH
PATIENT

THE
ENGLISH
PATIENT

a novel by

MICHAEL
ONDAATJE

Vintage International

VINTAGE BOOKS

A DIVISION OF RANDOM HOUSE, INC.

NEW YORK

FIRST VINTAGE INTERNATIONAL EDITION, DECEMBER 1993

The chapter here called "In Situ" appeared in somewhat
different form in *The New Yorker*.

Owing to limitations of space, all other acknowledgments
for permission to reprint previously published material
can be found on page 304.

Library of Congress Cataloging-in-Publication Data
Ondaatje, Michael, 1943–
The English Patient: a novel / by Michael Ondaatje.
—1st Vintage International ed.
p.   cm.
ISBN 0-679-74520-3
1. World War II, 1939–1945—Italy—Fiction.   2. Italy—Fiction
1.Title.
[PR9199.3.05E54   1993]
813'.54—dc20   93-10492
CIP

Random House Web address: http://www.randomhouse.com/

Book design by Anthea Lingeman

Manufactured in the United States of America
79B8

In memory of
Skip and Mary Dickinson

For Quintin and Griffin

And for Louise Dennys,
with thanks

"Most of you, I am sure, remember the tragic circumstances of the death of Geoffrey Clifton at Gilf Kebir, followed later by the disappearance of his wife, Katharine Clifton, which took place during the 1939 desert expedition in search of Zerzura.

"I cannot begin this meeting tonight without referring very sympathetically to those tragic occurrences.

"The lecture this evening . . ."

From the minutes of the Geographical Society meeting of November 194-, London

Contents

I

The Villa

SHE STANDS UP in the garden where she has been working and looks into the distance. She has sensed a shift in the weather. There is another gust of wind, a buckle of noise in the air, and the tall cypresses sway. She turns and moves uphill towards the house, climbing over a low wall, feeling the first drops of rain on her bare arms. She crosses the loggia and quickly enters the house.

In the kitchen she doesn't pause but goes through it and climbs the stairs which are in darkness and then continues along the long hall, at the end of which is a wedge of light from an open door.

She turns into the room which is another garden—this one made up of trees and bowers painted over its walls and ceiling. The man lies on the bed, his body exposed to the breeze, and he turns his head slowly towards her as she enters.

Every four days she washes his black body, beginning at the destroyed feet. She wets a washcloth and holding it above his ankles squeezes the water onto him, looking up as he murmurs, seeing his smile. Above the shins the burns are worst. Beyond purple. Bone.

She has nursed him for months and she knows the body well, the penis sleeping like a sea horse, the thin tight hips. Hipbones of Christ, she thinks. He is her despairing saint. He lies flat on his back, no pillow, looking up at the foliage painted onto the ceiling, its canopy of branches, and above that, blue sky.

She pours calamine in stripes across his chest where he is less burned, where she can touch him. She loves the hollow below the lowest rib, its cliff of skin. Reaching his shoulders she blows cool air onto his neck, and he mutters.

What? she asks, coming out of her concentration.

He turns his dark face with its grey eyes towards her. She puts her hand into her pocket. She unskins the plum with her teeth, withdraws the stone and passes the flesh of the fruit into his mouth.

He whispers again, dragging the listening heart of the young nurse beside him to wherever his mind is, into that well of memory he kept plunging into during those months before he died.

There are stories the man recites quietly into the room which slip from level to level like a hawk. He wakes in the painted arbour that surrounds him with its spilling flowers, arms of great trees. He remembers picnics, a woman who kissed parts of his body that now are burned into the colour of aubergine.

I have spent weeks in the desert, forgetting to look at the moon, he says, as a married man may spend days never looking into the face of his wife. These are not sins of omission but signs of preoccupation.

His eyes lock onto the young woman's face. If she moves her head, his stare will travel alongside her into the wall. She leans forward. How were you burned?

It is late afternoon. His hands play with a piece of sheet, the back of his fingers caressing it.

I fell burning into the desert.

They found my body and made me a boat of sticks and dragged me across the desert. We were in the Sand Sea, now and then crossing dry riverbeds. Nomads, you see. Bedouin. I flew down and the sand itself caught fire. They saw me stand up naked out of it. The leather helmet on my head in flames. They strapped me onto a cradle, a carcass boat, and feet thudded along as they ran with me. I had broken the spareness of the desert.

The Bedouin knew about fire. They knew about planes that since 1939 had been falling out of the sky. Some of their tools and utensils were made from the metal of crashed planes and tanks. It was the time of the war in heaven. They could recognize the drone of a wounded plane, they knew how to pick their way through such shipwrecks. A small bolt from a cockpit became jewellery. I was perhaps the first one to stand up alive out of a burning machine. A man whose head was on fire. They didn't know my name. I didn't know their tribe.

Who are you?

I don't know. You keep asking me.

You said you were English.

At night he is never tired enough to sleep. She reads to him from whatever book she is able to find in the library downstairs. The candle flickers over the page and over the young nurse's talking face, barely revealing at this hour the trees and vista that decorate the walls. He listens to her, swallowing her words like water.

If it is cold she moves carefully into the bed and lies beside him. She can place no weight upon him without giving him pain, not even her thin wrist.

Sometimes at two a.m. he is not yet asleep, his eyes open in the darkness.

He could smell the oasis before he saw it. The liquid in the air. The rustle of things. Palms and bridles. The banging of tin cans whose deep pitch revealed they were full of water.

They poured oil onto large pieces of soft cloth and placed them on him. He was anointed.

He could sense the one silent man who always remained beside him, the flavour of his breath when he bent down to unwrap him every twenty-four hours at nightfall, to examine his skin in the dark.

Unclothed he was once again the man naked beside the blazing aircraft. They spread the layers of grey felt over him. What great nation had found him, he wondered. What country invented such soft dates to be chewed by the man beside him and then passed from that mouth into his. During this time with these people, he could not remember where he was from. He could have been, for all he knew, the enemy he had been fighting from the air.

Later, at the hospital in Pisa, he thought he saw beside him the face that had come each night and chewed and softened the dates and passed them down into his mouth.

There was no colour during those nights. No speech or song. The Bedouin silenced themselves when he was awake. He was on an altar of hammock and he imagined in his vanity hundreds of them around him and there may have been just two who had found him, plucked the antlered hat of fire from his head. Those two he knew only by the taste of saliva that entered him along with the date or by the sound of their feet running.

She would sit and read, the book under the waver of light. She would glance now and then down the hall of the villa that had been a war hospital, where she had lived with the other nurses before they had all transferred out gradually, the war moving north, the war almost over.

This was the time in her life that she fell upon books as the only door out of her cell. They became half her world. She sat at the night table, hunched over, reading of the young boy in India who learned to memorize diverse jewels and objects on a tray, tossed from teacher to teacher—those who taught him dialect those who taught him memory those who taught him to escape the hypnotic.

The book lay on her lap. She realized that for more than five minutes she had been looking at the porousness of the paper, the crease at the corner of page 17 which someone had folded over as a mark. She brushed her hand over its skin. A scurry in her mind like a mouse in the ceiling, a moth on the night window. She looked down the hall, though there was no one else living there now, no one except the English patient and herself in the Villa San Girolamo. She had enough vegetables planted in the bombed-out orchard above the house for them to survive, a man coming now and then from the town with whom she would trade soap and sheets and whatever there was left in this war hospital for other essentials. Some beans, some meats. The man had left her two bottles of wine, and each night after she had lain with the Englishman and he was asleep, she would ceremoniously pour herself a small beaker and carry it back to the night table just outside the three-quarter-closed door and sip away further into whatever book she was reading.

So the books for the Englishman, as he listened intently or not, had gaps of plot like sections of a road washed out by storms, missing incidents as if locusts had consumed a section of tapestry, as if plaster loosened by the bombing had fallen away from a mural at night.

The villa that she and the Englishman inhabited now was much like that. Some rooms could not be entered because of rubble. One bomb crater allowed moon and rain into the library downstairs—where there was in one corner a permanently soaked armchair.

She was not concerned about the Englishman as far as the gaps in plot were concerned. She gave no summary of the missing chapters. She simply brought out the book and said "page ninety-six" or "page one hundred and eleven." That was the only locator. She lifted both of his hands to her face and smelled them—the odour of sickness still in them.

Your hands are getting rough, he said.

The weeds and thistles and digging.

Be careful. I warned you about the dangers.

I know.

Then she began to read.

Her father had taught her about hands. About a dog's paws. Whenever her father was alone with a dog in a house he would lean over and smell the skin at the base of its paw. This, he would say, as if coming away from a brandy snifter, is the greatest smell in the world! A bouquet! Great rumours of travel! She would pretend disgust, but the dog's paw *was* a wonder: the smell of it never suggested dirt. It's a cathedral! her father had said, so-and-so's garden, that field of grasses, a walk through cyclamen—a concentration of hints of all the paths the animal had taken during the day.

A scurry in the ceiling like a mouse, and she looked up from the book again.

They unwrapped the mask of herbs from his face. The day of the eclipse. They were waiting for it. Where was he? What civilisation was this that understood the predictions of weather and light? El Ahmar or El Abyadd, for they must be one of the northwest desert tribes. Those who could catch a man out of the sky, who covered his face with a mask of oasis reeds knitted together. He had now a bearing of grass. His favourite garden in the world had been the grass garden at Kew, the colours so delicate and various, like levels of ash on a hill.

He gazed onto the landscape under the eclipse. They had taught him by now to raise his arms and drag strength into his body from the universe, the way the desert pulled down planes. He was carried in a palanquin of felt and branch. He saw the moving veins of flamingos across his sight in the half-darkness of the covered sun.

Always there were ointments, or darkness, against his skin. One night he heard what seemed to be wind chimes high in the air, and after a while it stopped and he fell asleep with a hunger for it, that noise like the slowed-down sound from the throat of a bird, perhaps flamingo, or a desert fox, which one of the men kept in a sewn-half-closed pocket in his burnoose.

The next day he heard snatches of the glassy sound as he lay once more covered in cloth. A noise out of the darkness. At twilight the felt was unwrapped and he saw a man's head on a table moving towards him, then realized the man wore a giant yoke from which hung hundreds of small bottles on different lengths of string and wire. Moving as if part of a glass curtain, his body enveloped within that sphere.

The figure resembled most of all those drawings of archangels he had tried to copy as a schoolboy, never solving how one body could have space for the muscles of such wings. The man moved with a long, slow gait, so smoothly there was hardly a tilt in the bottles. A wave of glass, an archangel, all the ointments within the bottles warmed from the sun, so when they were rubbed onto skin they seemed to have been heated especially for a wound. Behind him was translated light

—blues and other colours shivering in the haze and sand. The faint glass noise and the diverse colours and the regal walk and his face like a lean dark gun.

Up close the glass was rough and sandblasted, glass that had lost its civilisation. Each bottle had a minute cork the man plucked out with his teeth and kept in his lips while mixing one bottle's contents with another's, a second cork also in his teeth. He stood over the supine burned body with his wings, sank two sticks deep into the sand and then moved away free of the six-foot yoke, which balanced now within the crutches of the two sticks. He stepped out from under his shop. He sank to his knees and came towards the burned pilot and put his cold hands on his neck and held them there.

He was known to everyone along the camel route from the Sudan north to Giza, the Forty Days Road. He met the caravans, traded spice and liquid, and moved between oases and water camps. He walked through sandstorms with this coat of bottles, his ears plugged with two other small corks so he seemed a vessel to himself, this merchant doctor, this king of oils and perfumes and panaceas, this baptist. He would enter a camp and set up the curtain of bottles in front of whoever was sick.

He crouched by the burned man. He made a skin cup with the soles of his feet and leaned back to pluck, without even looking, certain bottles. With the uncorking of each tiny bottle the perfumes fell out. There was an odour of the sea. The smell of rust. Indigo. Ink. River-mud arrow-wood formaldehyde paraffin ether. The tide of airs chaotic. There were screams of camels in the distance as they picked up the scents. He began to rub green-black paste onto the rib cage. It was ground peacock bone, bartered for in a medina to the west or the south—the most potent healer of skin.

Between the kitchen and the destroyed chapel a door led into an oval-shaped library. The space inside seemed safe except for a large hole at portrait level in the far wall, caused by mortar-shell attack on the villa two months earlier. The rest of the room had adapted itself to this wound, accepting the habits of weather, evening stars, the sound of birds. There was a sofa, a piano covered in a grey sheet, the head of a stuffed bear and high walls of books. The shelves nearest the torn wall bowed with the rain, which had doubled the weight of the books. Lightning came into the room too, again and again, falling across the covered piano and carpet.

At the far end were French doors that were boarded up. If they had been open she could have walked from the library to the loggia, then down thirty-six penitent steps past the chapel towards what had been an ancient meadow, scarred now by phosphorus bombs and explosions. The German army had mined many of the houses they retreated from, so most rooms not needed, like this one, had been sealed for safety, the doors hammered into their frames.

She knew these dangers when she slid into the room, walking into its afternoon darkness. She stood conscious suddenly of her weight on the wooden floor, thinking it was probably enough to trigger whatever mechanism was there. Her feet in dust. The only light poured through the jagged mortar circle that looked onto the sky.

With a crack of separation, as if it were being dismantled from one single unit, she pulled out *The Last of the Mohicans* and even in this half-light was cheered by the aquamarine and lake on the cover illustration, the Indian in the foreground. And then, as if there were someone in the room who was not to be disturbed, she walked backwards, stepping on her own footprints, for safety, but also as part of a private game, so it would seem from the steps that she had entered the room and then the corporeal body had disappeared. She closed the door and replaced the seal of warning.

She sat in the window alcove in the English patient's room, the painted walls on one side of her, the valley on the other. She opened the book. The pages were joined together in a stiff wave. She felt like Crusoe finding a drowned book that had washed up and dried itself on the shore. A *Narrative of 1757.* Illustrated by N. C. Wyeth. As in all of the best books, there was the important page with the list of illustrations, a line of text for each of them.

She entered the story knowing she would emerge from it feeling she had been immersed in the lives of others, in plots that stretched back twenty years, her body full of sentences and moments, as if awaking from sleep with a heaviness caused by unremembered dreams.

Their Italian hill town, sentinel to the northwest route, had been besieged for more than a month, the barrage focusing upon the two villas and the monastery surrounded by apple and plum orchards. There was the Villa Medici, where the generals lived. Just above it the Villa San Girolamo, previously a nunnery, whose castlelike battlements had made it the last stronghold of the German army. It had housed a hundred troops. As the hill town began to be torn apart like a battleship at sea, by fire shells, the troops moved from the barrack tents in the orchard into the now crowded bedrooms of the old nunnery. Sections of the chapel were blown up. Parts of the top storey of the villa crumbled under explosions. When the Allies finally took over the building and made it a hospital, the steps leading to the third level were sealed off, though a section of chimney and roof survived.

She and the Englishman had insisted on remaining behind when the other nurses and patients moved to a safer location in the south. During this time they were very cold, without electricity. Some rooms faced onto the valley with no walls at all. She would open a door and see just a sodden bed huddled against a corner, covered with leaves. Doors opened into land-·
scape. Some rooms had become an open aviary.

The staircase had lost its lower steps during the fire that was set before the soldiers left. She had gone into the library, removed twenty books and nailed them to the floor and then onto each other, in this way rebuilding the two lowest steps. Most of the chairs had been used for fires. The armchair in the library was left there because it was always wet, drenched by evening storms that came in through the mortar hole. Whatever was wet escaped burning during that April of 1945.

There were few beds left. She herself preferred to be no-madic in the house with her pallet or hammock, sleeping sometimes in the English patient's room, sometimes in the hall, depending on temperature or wind or light. In the morn-ing she rolled up her mattress and tied it into a wheel with string. Now it was warmer and she was opening more rooms, airing the dark reaches, letting sunlight dry all the dampness. Some nights she opened doors and slept in rooms that had walls missing. She lay on the pallet on the very edge of the room, facing the drifting landscape of stars, moving clouds, wakened by the growl of thunder and lightning. She was twenty years old and mad and unconcerned with safety dur-ing this time, having no qualms about the dangers of the pos-sibly mined library or the thunder that startled her in the night. She was restless after the cold months, when she had been limited to dark, protected spaces. She entered rooms that had been soiled by soldiers, rooms whose furniture had been burned within them. She cleared out leaves and shit and urine and charred tables. She was living like a vagrant, while elsewhere the English patient reposed in his bed like a king.

From outside, the place seemed devastated. An outdoor staircase disappeared in midair, its railing hanging off. Their life was foraging and tentative safety. They used only essential candlelight at night because of the brigands who annihilated everything they came across. They were protected by the simple fact that the villa seemed a ruin. But she felt safe here, half adult and half child. Coming out of what had happened to her during the war, she drew her own few rules to herself. She would not be ordered again or carry out duties for the greater good. She would care only for the burned patient. She would read to him and bathe him and give him his doses of morphine—her only communication was with him.

She worked in the garden and orchard. She carried the six-foot crucifix from the bombed chapel and used it to build a scarecrow above her seedbed, hanging empty sardine cans from it which clattered and clanked whenever the wind lifted. Within the villa she would step from rubble to a candlelit alcove where there was her neatly packed suitcase, which held little besides some letters, a few rolled-up clothes, a metal box of medical supplies. She had cleared just small sections of the villa, and all this she could burn down if she wished.

She lights a match in the dark hall and moves it onto the wick of the candle. Light lifts itself onto her shoulders. She is on her knees. She puts her hands on her thighs and breathes in the smell of the sulphur. She imagines she also breathes in light.

She moves backwards a few feet and with a piece of white chalk draws a rectangle onto the wood floor. Then continues backwards, drawing more rectangles, so there is a pyramid of them, single then double then single, her left hand braced flat on the floor, her head down, serious. She moves farther and farther away from the light. Till she leans back onto her heels and sits crouching.

She drops the chalk into the pocket of her dress. She stands and pulls up the looseness of her skirt and ties it around her waist. She pulls from another pocket a piece of metal and flings it out in front of her so it falls just beyond the farthest square.

She leaps forward, her legs smashing down, her shadow behind her curling into the depth of the hall. She is very quick, her tennis shoes skidding on the numbers she has drawn into each rectangle, one foot landing, then two feet, then one again, until she reaches the last square.

She bends down and picks up the piece of metal, pauses in that position, motionless, her skirt still tucked up above her thighs, hands hanging down loose, breathing hard. She takes a gulp of air and blows out the candle.

Now she is in darkness. Just a smell of smoke.

She leaps up and in midair turns so she lands facing the other way, then skips forward even wilder now down the black hall, still landing on squares she knows are there, her tennis shoes banging and slamming onto the dark floor—so the sound echoes out into the far reaches of the deserted Italian villa, out towards the moon and the scar of a ravine that half circles the building.

Sometimes at night the burned man hears a faint shudder in the building. He turns up his hearing aid to draw in a banging noise he still cannot interpret or place.

She picks up the notebook that lies on the small table beside his bed. It is the book he brought with him through the fire— a copy of *The Histories* by Herodotus that he has added to, cutting and gluing in pages from other books or writing in his own observations—so they all are cradled within the text of Herodotus.

She begins to read his small gnarled handwriting.

There is a whirlwind in southern Morocco, the *aajej*, against which the fellahin defend themselves with knives. There is the *africo*, which has at times reached into the city of Rome. The *alm*, a fall wind out of Yugoslavia. The *arifi*, also christened *aref* or *rifi*, which scorches with numerous tongues. These are permanent winds that live in the present tense.

There are other, less constant winds that change direction, that can knock down horse and rider and realign themselves anticlockwise. The *bist roz* leaps into Afghanistan for 170 days —burying villages. There is the hot, dry *ghibli* from Tunis, which rolls and rolls and produces a nervous condition. The *haboob*—a Sudan dust storm that dresses in bright yellow walls a thousand metres high and is followed by rain. The *harmattan*, which blows and eventually drowns itself into the Atlantic. *Imbat*, a sea breeze in North Africa. Some winds that just sigh towards the sky. Night dust storms that come with the cold. The *khamsin*, a dust in Egypt from March to May, named after the Arabic word for "fifty," blooming for fifty days—the ninth plague of Egypt. The *datoo* out of Gibraltar, which carries fragrance.

There is also the ———, the secret wind of the desert, whose name was erased by a king after his son died within it.

And the *nafhat*—a blast out of Arabia. The *mezzar-ifoullousen*—a violent and cold southwesterly known to Berbers as "that which plucks the fowls." The *beshabar*, a black and dry north-easterly out of the Caucasus, "black wind." The *Samiel* from Turkey, "poison and wind," used often in battle. As well as the other "poison winds," the *simoom*, of North Africa, and the *solano*, whose dust plucks off rare petals, causing giddiness.

Other, private winds.

Travelling along the ground like a flood. Blasting off paint, throwing down telephone poles, transporting stones and statue heads. The *harmattan* blows across the Sahara filled with red dust, dust as fire, as flour, entering and coagulating in the locks of rifles. Mariners called this red wind the "sea of darkness." Red sand fogs out of the Sahara were deposited as far north as Cornwall and Devon, producing showers of mud so great this was also mistaken for blood. "Blood rains were widely reported in Portugal and Spain in 1901."

There are always millions of tons of dust in the air, just as there are millions of cubes of air in the earth and more living flesh in the soil (worms, beetles, underground creatures) than there is grazing and existing on it. Herodotus records the death of various armies engulfed in the *simoom* who were never seen again. One nation was "so enraged by this evil wind that they declared war on it and marched out in full battle array, only to be rapidly and completely interred."

Dust storms in three shapes. The whirl. The column. The sheet. In the first the horizon is lost. In the second you are surrounded by "waltzing Ginns." The third, the sheet, is "copper-tinted. Nature seems to be on fire."

She looks up from the book and sees his eyes on her. He begins to talk across the darkness.

The Bedouin were keeping me alive for a reason. I was useful, you see. Someone there had assumed I had a skill when my plane crashed in the desert. I am a man who can recognize an unnamed town by its skeletal shape on a map. I have always had information like a sea in me. I am a person who if left alone in someone's home walks to the bookcase, pulls down a volume and inhales it. So history enters us. I knew maps of the sea floor, maps that depict weaknesses in the shield of the earth, charts painted on skin that contain the various routes of the Crusades.

So I knew their place before I crashed among them, knew when Alexander had traversed it in an earlier age, for this cause or that greed. I knew the customs of nomads besotted by silk or wells. One tribe dyed a whole valley floor, blackening it to increase convection and thereby the possibility of rainfall, and built high structures to pierce the belly of a cloud. There were some tribes who held up their open palm against the beginnings of wind. Who believed that if this was done at the right moment they could deflect a storm into an adjacent sphere of the desert, towards another, less loved tribe. There were continual drownings, tribes suddenly made historical with sand across their gasp.

In the desert it is easy to lose a sense of demarcation. When I came out of the air and crashed into the desert, into those troughs of yellow, all I kept thinking was, I must build a raft. . . . I must build a raft.

And here, though I was in the dry sands, I knew I was among water people.

In Tassili I have seen rock engravings from a time when the Sahara people hunted water horses from reed boats. In Wadi Sura I saw caves whose walls were covered with paintings of swimmers. Here there had been a lake. I could draw its shape on a wall for them. I could lead them to its edge, six thousand years ago.

Ask a mariner what is the oldest known sail, and he will describe a trapezoidal one hung from the mast of a reed boat that can be seen in rock drawings in Nubia. Pre-dynastic. Harpoons are still found in the desert. These were water people. Even today caravans look like a river. Still, today it is water who is the stranger here. Water is the exile, carried back in cans and flasks, the ghost between your hands and your mouth.

When I was lost among them, unsure of where I was, all I needed was the name of a small ridge, a local custom, a cell of this historical animal, and the map of the world would slide into place.

What did most of us know of such parts of Africa? The armies of the Nile moved back and forth—a battlefield eight hundred miles deep into the desert. Whippet tanks, Blenheim medium-range bombers. Gladiator biplane fighters. Eight thousand men. But who was the enemy? Who were the allies of this place—the fertile lands of Cyrenaica, the salt marshes of El Agheila? All of Europe were fighting their wars in North Africa, in Sidi Rezegh, in Baguoh.

He travelled on a skid behind the Bedouin for five days in darkness, the hood over his body. He lay within this oil-doused cloth. Then suddenly the temperature fell. They had reached the valley within the red high canyon walls, joining the rest of the desert's water tribe that spilled and slid over sand and stones, their blue robes shifting like a spray of milk or a wing. They lifted the soft cloth off him, off the suck of his body. He was within the larger womb of the canyon. The buzzards high above them slipping down a thousand years into this crack of stone where they camped.

In the morning they took him to the far reach of the *siq*. They were talking loudly around him now. The dialect suddenly clarifying. He was here because of the buried guns.

He was carried towards something, his blindfolded face looking straight ahead, and his hand made to reach out a yard or so. After days of travel, to move this one yard. To lean towards and touch something with a purpose, his arm still held, his palm facing down and open. He touched the Sten barrel and the hand let go of him. A pause among the voices. He was there to translate the guns.

"Twelve-millimetre Breda machine gun. From Italy."

He pulled back the bolt, inserted his finger to find no bullet, pushed it back and pulled the trigger. *Puht.* "Famous gun," he muttered. He was moved forward again.

"French seven-point-five-millimetre Châttelerault. Light machine gun. Nineteen twenty-four."

"German seven-point-nine-millimetre MG-Fifteen air service."

He was brought to each of the guns. The weapons seemed to be from different time periods and from many countries, a museum in the desert. He brushed the contours of the stock and magazine or fingered the sight. He spoke out the gun's name, then was carried to another gun. Eight weapons formally handed to him. He called the names out loud, speaking in French and then the tribe's own language. But what did that matter to them? Perhaps they needed not the name but to know that he knew what the gun was.

He was held by the wrist again and his hand sunk into a box of cartridges. In another box to the right were more shells, seven-millimetre shells this time. Then others.

When he was a child he had grown up with an aunt, and on the grass of her lawn she had scattered a deck of cards face down and taught him the game of Pelmanism. Each player allowed to turn up two cards and, eventually, through memory pairing them off. This had been in another landscape, of trout streams, birdcalls that he could recognize from a halting fragment. A fully named world. Now, with his face blindfolded in a mask of grass fibres, he picked up a shell and moved with his carriers, guiding them towards a gun, inserted the bullet, bolted it, and holding it up in the air fired. The noise cracking crazily down the canyon walls. *"For echo is the soul of the voice exciting itself in hollow places."* A man thought to be sullen and mad had written that sentence down in an English hospital. And he, now in this desert, was sane, with clear thought, picking up the cards, bringing them together with ease, his grin flung out to his aunt, and firing each successful combination into the air, and gradually the unseen men around him replied to each rifle shot with a cheer. He would turn to face one direction, then move back to the Breda this time on his strange human palanquin, followed by a man with a knife who carved a parallel code on shell box and gun stock. He thrived on it—the movement and the cheering after the solitude. This was payment with his skill for the men who had saved him for such a purpose.

There are villages he will travel into with them where there are no women. His knowledge is passed like a counter of usefulness from tribe to tribe. Tribes representing eight thousand individuals. He enters specific customs and specific music. Mostly blindfolded he hears the water-drawing songs of the Mzina tribe with their exultations, *dahhiya* dances, pipe-flutes which are used for carrying messages in times of emergency, the *makruna* double pipe (one pipe constantly sounding a drone). Then into the territory of five-stringed lyres. A village or oasis of preludes and interludes. Hand-clapping. Antiphonal dance.

He is given sight only after dusk, when he can witness his captors and saviours. Now he knows where he is. For some he draws maps that go beyond their own boundaries and for other tribes too he explains the mechanics of guns. The musicians sit across the fire from him. The *simsimiya* lyre notes flung away by a gust of breeze. Or the notes shift towards him over the flames. There is a boy dancing, who in this light is the most desirable thing he has seen. His thin shoulders white as papyrus, light from the fire reflecting sweat on his stomach, nakedness glimpsed through openings in the blue linen he wears as a lure from neck to ankle, revealing himself as a line of brown lightning.

The night desert surrounds them, traversed by a loose order of storms and caravans. There are always secrets and dangers around him, as when blind he moved his hand and cut himself on a double-edged razor in the sand. At times he doesn't know if these are dreams, the cut so clean it leaves no pain, and he must wipe the blood on his skull (his face still untouchable) to signal the wound to his captors. This village of no women he has been brought into in complete silence, or the whole month when he did not see the moon. Was this invented? Dreamed by him while wrapped in oil and felt and darkness?

They had passed wells where water was cursed. In some open spaces there were hidden towns, and he waited while they dug through sand into the buried rooms or waited while they dug into nests of water. And the pure beauty of an innocent dancing boy, like sound from a boy chorister, which he remembered as the purest of sounds, the clearest river water, the most transparent depth of the sea. Here in the desert, which had been an old sea where nothing was strapped down or permanent, everything drifted—like the shift of linen across the boy as if he were embracing or freeing himself from an ocean or his own blue afterbirth. A boy arousing himself, his genitals against the colour of fire.

Then the fire is sanded over, its smoke withering around them. The fall of musical instruments like a pulse or rain. The boy puts his arm across, through the lost fire, to silence the pipe-flutes. There is no boy, there are no footsteps when he leaves. Just the borrowed rags. One of the men crawls forward and collects the semen which has fallen on the sand. He brings it over to the white translator of guns and passes it into his hands. In the desert you celebrate nothing but water.

She stands over the sink, gripping it, looking at the stucco wall. She has removed all mirrors and stacked them away in an empty room. She grips the sink and moves her head from side to side, releasing a movement of shadow. She wets her hands and combs water into her hair till it is completely wet. This cools her and she likes it when she goes outside and the breezes hit her, erasing the thunder.

II

In Near Ruins

THE MAN WITH BANDAGED HANDS had been in the military hospital in Rome for more than four months when by accident he heard about the burned patient and the nurse, heard her name. He turned from the doorway and walked back into the clutch of doctors he had just passed, to discover where she was. He had been recuperating there for a long time, and they knew him as an evasive man. But now he spoke to them, asking about the name, and startled them. During all that time he had never spoken, communicating by signals and grimaces, now and then a grin. He had revealed nothing, not even his name, just wrote out his serial number, which showed he was with the Allies.

His status had been double-checked, and confirmed in messages from London. There was the cluster of known scars on him. So the doctors had come back to him, nodded at the bandages on him. A celebrity, after all, wanting silence. A war hero.

That was how he felt safest. Revealing nothing. Whether they came at him with tenderness or subterfuge or knives. For more than four months he had not said a word. He was a large animal in their presence, in near ruins when he was brought in and given regular doses of morphine for the pain in his hands. He would sit in an armchair in the darkness, watching the tide of movement among patients and nurses in and out of the wards and stockrooms.

But now, walking past the group of doctors in the hall, he heard the woman's name, and he slowed his pace and turned and came up to them and asked specifically which hospital she was working in. They told him that it was in an old nunnery, taken over by the Germans, then converted into a hospital after the Allies had laid siege to it. In the hills north of Florence. Most of it torn apart by bombing. Unsafe. It had been just a temporary field hospital. But the nurse and the patient had refused to leave.

Why didn't you force the two of them down?

She claimed he was too ill to be moved. We could have brought him out safely, of course, but nowadays there is no time to argue. She was in rough shape herself.

Is she injured?

No. Partial shell shock probably. She should have been sent home. The trouble is, the war here is over. You cannot make anyone do anything anymore. Patients are walking out of hospitals. Troops are going AWOL before they get sent back home.

Which villa? he asked.

It's one they say has a ghost in the garden. San Girolamo. Well, she's got her own ghost, a burned patient. There is a face, but it is unrecognizable. The nerves all gone. You can pass a match across his face and there is no expression. The face is asleep.

Who is he? he asked.

We don't know his name.

He won't talk?

The clutch of doctors laughed. No, he talks, he talks all the time, he just doesn't know who he is.

Where did he come from?

The Bedouin brought him into Siwa Oasis. Then he was in Pisa for a while, then . . . One of the Arabs is probably wearing his name tag. He will probably sell it and we'll get it one day, or perhaps they will never sell it. These are great charms. All pilots who fall into the desert—none of them come back with identification. Now he's holed up in a Tuscan villa and the girl won't leave him. Simply refuses. The Allies housed a hundred patients there. Before that the Germans held it with a small army, their last stronghold. Some rooms are painted, each room has a different season. Outside the villa is a gorge. All this is about twenty miles from Florence, in the hills. You will need a pass, of course. We can probably get someone to drive you up. It is still terrible out there. Dead cattle. Horses shot dead, half eaten. People hanging upside down from bridges. The last vices of war. Completely unsafe. The sappers haven't gone in there yet to clear it. The Germans retreated burying and installing mines as they went. A terrible place for a hospital. The smell of the dead is the worst. We need a good snowfall to clean up this country. We need ravens.

Thank you.

He walked out of the hospital into the sun, into open air for the first time in months, out of the green-lit rooms that lay like glass in his mind. He stood there breathing everything in, the hurry of everyone. First, he thought, I need shoes with rubber on the bottom. I need *gelato*.

He found it difficult to fall asleep on the train, shaking from side to side. The others in the compartment smoking. His temple banging against the window frame. Everyone was in dark clothes, and the carriage seemed to be on fire with all the lit cigarettes. He noticed that whenever the train passed a cemetery the travellers around him crossed themselves. *She's in rough shape herself.*

Gelato for tonsils, he remembered. Accompanying a girl and her father to have her tonsils out. She had taken one look at the ward full of other children and simply refused. This, the most adaptable and genial of children, suddenly turned into a stone of refusal, adamant. No one was ripping anything out of *her* throat though the wisdom of the day advised it. She would live with it in, whatever "it" looked like. He still had no idea what a tonsil was.

They never touched my head, he thought, that was strange. The worst times were when he began to imagine what they would have done next, cut next. At those times he always thought of his head.

A scurry in the ceiling like a mouse.

He stood with his valise at the far end of the hall. He put the bag down and waved across the darkness and the intermittent pools of candlelight. There was no clatter of footsteps as he walked towards her, not a sound on the floor, and that surprised her, was somehow familiar and comforting to her, that he could approach this privacy of hers and the English patient's without loudness.

As he passed the lamps in the long hall they flung his shadow forward ahead of him. She turned up the wick on the oil lamp so it enlarged the diameter of light around her. She sat very still, the book on her lap, as he came up to her and then crouched beside her like an uncle.

"Tell me what a tonsil is."

Her eyes staring at him.

"I keep remembering how you stormed out of the hospital followed by two grown men."

She nodded.

"Is your patient in there? Can I go in?"

She shook her head, kept shaking it until he spoke again.

"I'll see him tomorrow, then. Just tell me where to go. I don't need sheets. Is there a kitchen? Such a strange journey I took in order to find you."

When he had gone along the hall she came back to the table and sat down, trembling. Needing this table, this half-finished book in order to collect herself. A man she knew had come all the way by train and walked the four miles uphill from the village and along the hall to this table just to see her. After a few minutes she walked into the Englishman's room and stood there looking down on him. Moonlight across the foliage on the walls. This was the only light that made the trompe l'oeil seem convincing. She could pluck that flower and pin it onto her dress.

The man named Caravaggio pushes open all the windows in the room so he can hear the noises of the night. He undresses, rubs his palms gently over his neck and for a while lies down on the unmade bed. The noise of the trees, the breaking of moon into silver fish bouncing off the leaves of asters outside.

The moon is on him like skin, a sheaf of water. An hour later he is on the roof of the villa. Up on the peak he is aware of the shelled sections along the slope of roofs, the two acres of destroyed gardens and orchards that neighbour the villa. He looks over where they are in Italy.

In the morning by the fountain they talk tentatively.

"Now you are in Italy you should find out more about Verdi."

"What?" She looks up from the bedding that she is washing out in the fountain.

He reminds her. "You told me once you were in love with him."

Hana bows her head, embarrassed.

Caravaggio walks around, looking at the building for the first time, peering down from the loggia into the garden.

"Yes, you used to love him. You used to drive us all *mad* with your new information about Giuseppe. What a man! The best in every way, you'd say. We all had to agree with you, the cocky sixteen-year-old."

"I wonder what happened to her." She spreads the washed sheet over the rim of the fountain.

"You were someone with a dangerous will."

She walks over the paved stones, grass in the cracks. He watches her black-stockinged feet, the thin brown dress. She leans over the balustrade.

"I think I did come here, I have to admit, something at the back of my mind made me, for Verdi. And then of course you had left and my dad had left for the war. . . . Look at the hawks. They are here every morning. Everything else is damaged and in pieces here. The only running water in this whole villa is in this fountain. The Allies dismantled water pipes when they left. They thought that would make me leave."

"You should have. They still have to clear this region. There are unexploded bombs all over the place."

She comes up to him and puts her fingers on his mouth.

"I'm glad to see you, Caravaggio. No one else. Don't say you have come here to try and persuade me to leave."

"I want to find a small bar with a Wurlitzer and drink without a fucking bomb going off. Listen to Frank Sinatra singing. We have to get some music," he says. "Good for your patient."

"He's still in Africa."

He is watching her, waiting for her to say more, but there is nothing more about the English patient to be said. He mutters. "Some of the English love Africa. A part of their brain reflects the desert precisely. So they're not foreigners there."

He sees her head nod slightly. A lean face with hair cut short, without the mask and mystery of her long hair. If anything, she seems calm in this universe of hers. The fountain gurgling in the background, the hawks, the ruined garden of the villa.

Maybe this is the way to come out of a war, he thinks. A burned man to care for, some sheets to wash in a fountain, a room painted like a garden. As if all that remains is a capsule from the past, long before Verdi, the Medicis considering a balustrade or window, holding up a candle at night in the presence of an invited architect—the best architect in the fifteenth century—and requesting something more satisfying to frame that vista.

"If you are staying," she says, "we are going to need more food. I have planted vegetables, we have a sack of beans, but we need some chickens." She is looking at Caravaggio, knowing his skills from the past, not quite saying it.

"I lost my nerve," he says.

"I'll come with you, then," Hana offers. "We'll do it together. You can teach me to steal, show me what to do."

"You don't understand. I lost my nerve."

"Why?"

"I was caught. They nearly chopped off my fucking hands."

At night sometimes, when the English patient is asleep or even after she has read alone outside his door for a while, she goes looking for Caravaggio. He will be in the garden lying along the stone rim of the fountain looking up at stars, or she will come across him on a lower terrace. In this early-summer weather he finds it difficult to stay indoors at night. Most of the time he is on the roof beside the broken chimney, but he slips down silently when he sees her figure cross the terrace looking for him. She will find him near the headless statue of a count, upon whose stub of neck one of the local cats likes to sit, solemn and drooling when humans appear. She is always made to feel that she is the one who has found him, this man who knows darkness, who when drunk used to claim he was brought up by a family of owls.

Two of them on a promontory, Florence and her lights in the distance. Sometimes he seems frantic to her, or he will be too calm. In daylight she notices better how he moves, notices the stiffened arms above the bandaged hands, how his whole body turns instead of just the neck when she points to something farther up the hill. But she has said nothing about these things to him.

"My patient thinks peacock bone ground up is a great healer."

He looks up into the night sky. "Yes."

"Were you a spy then?"

"Not quite."

He feels more comfortable, more disguised from her in the

dark garden, a flicker of the lamp from the patient's room looking down. "At times we were sent in to steal. Here I was, an Italian and a thief. They couldn't believe their luck, they were falling over themselves to use me. There were about four or five of us. I did well for some time. Then I was accidentally photographed. Can you imagine that?

"I was in a tuxedo, a monkey suit, in order to get into this gathering, a party, to steal some papers. Really I was still a thief. No great patriot. No great hero. They had just made my skills official. But one of the women had brought a camera and was snapping at the German officers, and I was caught in mid-step, walking across the ballroom. In mid-step, the beginning of the shutter's noise making me jerk my head towards it. So suddenly everything in the future was dangerous. Some general's girlfriend.

"All photographs taken during the war were processed officially in government labs, checked by the Gestapo, and so there I would be, obviously not part of any list, to be filed away by an official when the film went to the Milan laboratory. So it meant having to try and steal that film back somehow."

She looks in on the English patient, whose sleeping body is probably miles away in the desert, being healed by a man who continues to dip his fingers into the bowl made with the joined soles of his feet, leaning forward, pressing the dark paste against the burned face. She imagines the weight of the hand on her own cheek.

She walks down the hall and climbs into her hammock, giving it a swing as she leaves the ground.

Moments before sleep are when she feels most alive, leaping across fragments of the day, bringing each moment into the bed with her like a child with schoolbooks and pencils. The day seems to have no order until these times, which are like a ledger for her, her body full of stories and situations. Caravaggio has for instance given her something. His motive, a drama, and a stolen image.

He leaves the party in a car. It crunches over the slowly curving gravel path leading out of the grounds, the automobile purring, serene as ink within the summer night. For the rest of the evening during the Villa Cosima gathering he had been looking at the photographer, spinning his body away whenever she lifted the camera to photograph in his direction. Now that he knows of its existence he can avoid it. He moves into the range of her dialogue, her name is Anna, mistress to an officer, who will be staying here in the villa for the night and then in the morning will travel north through Tuscany. The death of the woman or the woman's sudden disappearance will only arouse suspicion. Nowadays anything out of the ordinary is investigated.

Four hours later, he runs over the grass in his socks, his shadow curled under him, painted by the moon. He stops at the gravel path and moves slowly over the grit. He looks up at the Villa Cosima, at the square moons of window. A palace of war-women.

A car beam—like something sprayed out of a hose—lights up the room he is in, and he pauses once again in mid-step, seeing that same woman's eyes on him, a man moving on top of her, his fingers in her blonde hair. And she has seen, he knows, even though now he is naked, the same man she photographed earlier in the crowded party, for by accident he stands the same way now, half turned in surprise at the light that reveals his body in the darkness. The car lights sweep up into a corner of the room and disappear.

Then there is blackness. He doesn't know whether to move, whether she will whisper to the man fucking her about the other person in the room. A naked thief. A naked assassin. Should he move—his hands out to break a neck—towards the couple on the bed?

He hears the man's lovemaking continue, hears the silence of the woman—no whisper—hears her thinking, her eyes aimed towards him in the darkness. The word should be *thinkering*. Caravaggio's mind slips into this consideration, another syllable to suggest collecting a thought as one tinkers with a half-completed bicycle. Words are tricky things, a friend of his has told him, they're much more tricky than violins. His mind recalls the woman's blonde hair, the black ribbon in it.

He hears the car turning and waits for another moment of light. The face that emerges out of the dark is still an arrow upon him. The light moves from her face down onto the body of the general, over the carpet, and then touches and slides over Caravaggio once more. He can no longer see her. He shakes his head, then mimes the cutting of his throat. The camera is in his hands for her to understand. Then he is in darkness again. He hears a moan of pleasure now from her towards her lover, and he is aware it is her agreement with him. No words, no hint of irony, just a contract with him, the morse of understanding, so he knows he can now move safely to the verandah and drop out into the night.

Finding her room had been more difficult. He had entered the villa and silently passed the half-lit seventeenth-century murals along the corridors. Somewhere there were bedrooms like dark pockets in a gold suit. The only way he could get past guards was to be revealed as an innocent. He had stripped completely and left his clothes in a flower bed.

He ambles naked up the stairs to the second floor, where the guards are, bending down to laugh at some privacy, so his face is almost at his hip, nudging the guards about his evening's invitation, *al fresco,* was that it? Or seduction *a cappella*?

One long hall on the third floor. A guard by the stair and one at the far end twenty yards away, too many yards away. So a long theatrical walk, and Caravaggio now having to perform it, watched with quiet suspicion and scornfully by the two bookended sentries, the ass-and-cock walk, pausing at a section of mural to peer at a painted donkey in a grove. He leans his head on the wall, almost falling asleep, then walks again, stumbles and immediately pulls himself together into a military gait. His stray left hand waves to the ceiling of cherubs bum-naked as he is, a salute from a thief, a brief waltz while the mural scene drifts haphazardly past him, castles, black-and-white duomos, uplifted saints on this Tuesday during the war, in order to save his disguise and his life. Caravaggio is out on the tiles looking for a photograph of himself.

He pats his bare chest as if looking for his pass, grabs his penis and pretends to use it as a key to let him into the room that is being guarded. Laughing, he staggers back, peeved at his woeful failure, and slips into the next room humming.

He opens the window and steps out onto the verandah. A dark, beautiful night. Then he climbs off it and swings onto the verandah one level below. Only now can he enter the room of Anna and her general. Nothing more than a perfume in their midst. Printless foot. Shadowless. The story he told someone's child years ago about the person who searched for his shadow—as he is now looking for this image of himself on a piece of film.

In the room he is immediately aware of the beginnings of sexual movement. His hands within her clothing thrown onto chair backs, dropped upon the floor. He lies down and rolls across the carpet in order to feel anything hard like a camera, touching the skin of the room. He rolls in silence in the shape of fans, finding nothing. There is not even a grain of light.

He gets to his feet and sways his arms out slowly, touches a breast of marble. His hand moves along a stone hand—he understands the way the woman thinks now—off which the camera hangs with its sling. Then he hears the vehicle and simultaneously as he turns is seen by the woman in the sudden spray of car light.

Caravaggio watches Hana, who sits across from him looking into his eyes, trying to read him, trying to figure the flow of thought the way his wife used to do. He watches her sniffing him out, searching for the trace. He buries it and looks back at her, knowing his eyes are faultless, clear as any river, un-impeachable as a landscape. People, he knows, get lost in them, and he is able to hide well. But the girl watches him quizzically, tilting her head in a question as a dog would when spoken to in a tone or pitch that is not human. She sits across from him in front of the dark, blood-red walls, whose colour he doesn't like, and in her black hair and with that look, slim, tanned olive from all the light in this country, she reminds him of his wife.

Nowadays he doesn't think of his wife, though he knows he can turn around and evoke every move of her, describe any aspect of her, the weight of her wrist on his heart during the night.

He sits with his hands below the table, watching the girl eat. He still prefers to eat alone, though he always sits with Hana during meals. Vanity, he thinks. Mortal vanity. She has seen him from a window eating with his hands as he sits on one of the thirty-six steps by the chapel, not a fork or a knife in sight, as if he were learning to eat like someone from the East. In his greying stubble-beard, in his dark jacket, she sees the Italian finally in him. She notices this more and more.

He watches her darkness against the brown-and-red walls, her skin, her cropped dark hair. He had known her and her father in Toronto before the war. Then he had been a thief, a married man, slipped through his chosen world with a lazy confidence, brilliant in deceit against the rich, or charm towards his wife Giannetta or with this young daughter of his friend.

But now there is hardly a world around them and they are forced back on themselves. During these days in the hill town near Florence, indoors during the days of rain, daydreaming in the one soft chair in the kitchen or on the bed or on the roof, he has no plots to set in motion, is interested only in Hana. And it seems she has chained herself to the dying man upstairs.

During meals he sits opposite this girl and watches her eat.

Half a year earlier, from a window at the end of the long hall in Santa Chiara Hospital in Pisa, Hana had been able to see a white lion. It stood alone on top of the battlements, linked by colour to the white marble of the Duomo and the Camposanto, though its roughness and naive form seemed part of another era. Like some gift from the past that had to be accepted. Yet she accepted it most of all among the things surrounding this hospital. At midnight she would look through the window and know it stood within the curfew blackout and that it would emerge like her into the dawn shift. She would look up at five or five-thirty and then at six to see its silhouette and growing detail. Every night it was her sentinel while she moved among patients. Even through the shelling the army had left it there, much more concerned about the rest of the fabulous compound—with its mad logic of a tower leaning like a person in shell shock.

Their hospital buildings lay in old monastery grounds. The topiary carved for thousands of years by too careful monks was no longer bound within recognizable animal forms, and during the day nurses wheeled patients among the lost shapes. It seemed that only white stone remained permanent.

Nurses too became shell-shocked from the dying around them. Or from something as small as a letter. They would carry a severed arm down a hall, or swab at blood that never stopped, as if the wound were a well, and they began to believe in nothing, trusted nothing. They broke the way a man dismantling a mine broke the second his geography exploded. The way Hana broke in Santa Chiara Hospital when an official walked down the space between a hundred beds and gave her a letter that told her of the death of her father.

A white lion.

It was sometime after this that she had come across the English patient—someone who looked like a burned animal, taut and dark, a pool for her. And now, months later, he is her last patient in the Villa San Girolamo, their war over, both of them refusing to return with the others to the safety of the Pisa hospitals. All the coastal ports, such as Sorrento and Marina di Pisa, are now filled with North American and British troops waiting to be sent home. But she washed her uniform, folded it and returned it to the departing nurses. The war is not over everywhere, she was told. The war is over. This war is over. The war here. She was told it would be like desertion. This is not desertion. I will stay here. She was warned of the uncleared mines, lack of water and food. She came upstairs to the burned man, the English patient, and told him she would stay as well.

He said nothing, unable even to turn his head towards her, but his fingers slipped into her white hand, and when she bent forward to him he put his dark fingers into her hair and felt it cool within the valley of his fingers.

How old are you?

Twenty.

There was a duke, he said, who when he was dying wanted to be carried halfway up the tower in Pisa so he could die looking out into the middle distance.

A friend of my father's wanted to die while Shanghai-dancing. I don't know what it is. He had just heard of it himself.

What does your father do?

He is . . . he is in the war.

You're in the war too.

She does not know anything about him. Even after a month or so of caring for him and allotting him the needles of morphine. There was shyness at first within both of them, made more evident by the fact that they were now alone. Then it was suddenly overcome. The patients and doctors and nurses and equipment and sheets and towels—all went back down the hill into Florence and then to Pisa. She had salted away codeine tablets, as well as the morphine. She watched the departures, the line of trucks. Good-bye, then. She waved from his window, bringing the shutters to a close.

Behind the villa a rock wall rose higher than the house. To the west of the building was a long enclosed garden, and twenty miles away was the carpet of the city of Florence, which often disappeared under the mist of the valley. Rumour had it one of the generals living in the old Medici villa next door had eaten a nightingale.

The Villa San Girolamo, built to protect inhabitants from the flesh of the devil, had the look of a besieged fortress, the limbs of most of the statues blown off during the first days of shelling. There seemed little demarcation between house and landscape, between damaged building and the burned and shelled remnants of the earth. To Hana the wild gardens were like further rooms. She worked along the edges of them aware always of unexploded mines. In one soil-rich area beside the house she began to garden with a furious passion that could come only to someone who had grown up in a city. In spite of the burned earth, in spite of the lack of water. Someday there would be a bower of limes, rooms of green light.

Caravaggio came into the kitchen to find Hana sitting hunched over the table. He could not see her face or her arms tucked in under her body, only the naked back, the bare shoulders.

She was not still or asleep. With each shudder her head shook over the table.

Caravaggio stood there. Those who weep lose more energy than they lose during any other act. It was not yet dawn. Her face against the darkness of the table wood.

"Hana," he said, and she stilled herself as if she could be camouflaged by stillness.

"Hana."

She began to moan so the sound would be a barrier between them, a river across which she could not be reached.

He was uncertain at first about touching her in her nakedness, said "Hana," and then lay his bandaged hand on her shoulder. She did not stop shaking. The deepest sorrow, he thought. Where the only way to survive is to excavate everything.

She raised herself, her head down still, then stood up against him as if dragging herself away from the magnet of the table.

"Don't touch me if you're going to try and fuck me."

The skin pale above her skirt, which was all she wore in this kitchen, as if she had risen from the bed, dressed partially and come out here, the cool air from the hills entering the kitchen doorway and cloaking her.

Her face was red and wet.

"Hana."

"Do you understand?"

"Why do you adore him so much?"

"I love him."

"You don't love him, you adore him."

"Go away, Caravaggio. Please."

"You've tied yourself to a corpse for some reason."

"He is a saint. I think. A despairing saint. Are there such things? Our desire is to protect them."

"He doesn't even care!"

"I can love him."

"A twenty-year-old who throws herself out of the world to love a ghost!"

Caravaggio paused. "You have to protect yourself from sadness. Sadness is very close to hate. Let me tell you this. This is the thing I learned. If you take in someone else's poison—thinking you can cure them by sharing it—you will instead store it within you. Those men in the desert were smarter than you. They assumed he could be useful. So they saved him, but when he was no longer useful they left him."

"Leave me alone."

When she is solitary she will sit, aware of the nerve at her ankle, damp from the long grasses of the orchard. She peels a plum from the orchard that she has found and carried in the dark cotton pocket of her dress. When she is solitary she tries to imagine who might come along the old road under the green hood of the eighteen cypress trees.

As the Englishman wakes she bends over his body and places a third of the plum into his mouth. His open mouth holds it, like water, the jaw not moving. He looks as if he will cry from this pleasure. She can sense the plum being swallowed.

He brings his hand up and wipes from his lip the last dribble, which his tongue cannot reach, and puts his finger in his
mouth to suck it. Let me tell you about plums, he says. When
I was a boy . . .

After the first nights, after most of the beds had been burned for fuel against the cold, she had taken a dead man's hammock and begun to use it. She would bang spikes into whatever walls she desired, whichever room she wanted to wake in, floating above all the filth and cordite and water on the floors, the rats that had started to appear coming down from the third storey. Each night she climbed into the khaki ghostline of hammock she had taken from a dead soldier, someone who had died under her care.

A pair of tennis shoes and a hammock. What she had taken from others in this war. She would wake under the slide of moonlight on the ceiling, wrapped in an old shirt she always slept in, her dress hanging on a nail by the door. There was more heat now, and she could sleep this way. Before, when it had been cold, they had had to burn things.

Her hammock and her shoes and her frock. She was secure in the miniature world she had built; the two other men seemed distant planets, each in his own sphere of memory and solitude. Caravaggio, who had been her father's gregarious friend in Canada, in those days was capable of standing still and causing havoc within the caravan of women he seemed to give himself over to. He now lay in his darkness. He had been a thief who refused to work with men, because he did not trust them, who talked with men but who preferred talking to women and when he began talking to women was soon caught in the nets of relationship. When she would sneak home in the early hours of the morning she would find him asleep on her father's armchair, exhausted from professional or personal robberies.

She thought about Caravaggio—some people you just had to embrace, in some way or another, had to bite into the muscle, to remain sane in their company. You needed to grab their hair and clutch it like a drowner so they would pull you into their midst. Otherwise they, walking casually down the street towards you, almost about to wave, would leap over a wall and be gone for months. As an uncle he had been a disappearer.

Caravaggio would disturb you by simply enfolding you in his arms, his wings. With him you were embraced by character. But now he lay in darkness, like her, in some outpost of the large house. So there was Caravaggio. And there was the desert Englishman.

Throughout the war, with all of her worst patients, she survived by keeping a coldness hidden in her role as nurse. I will survive this. I won't fall apart at this. These were buried sentences all through her war, all through the towns they crept towards and through, Urbino, Anghiari, Monterchi, until they entered Florence and then went farther and finally reached the other sea near Pisa.

In the Pisa hospital she had seen the English patient for the first time. A man with no face. An ebony pool. All identification consumed in a fire. Parts of his burned body and face had been sprayed with tannic acid, that hardened into a protective shell over his raw skin. The area around his eyes was coated with a thick layer of gentian violet. There was nothing to recognize in him.

Sometimes she collects several blankets and lies under them, enjoying them more for their weight than for the warmth they bring. And when moonlight slides onto the ceiling it wakes her, and she lies in the hammock, her mind skating. She finds rest as opposed to sleep the truly pleasurable state. If she were a writer she would collect her pencils and notebooks and favourite cat and write in bed. Strangers and lovers would never get past the locked door.

To rest was to receive all aspects of the world without judgement. A bath in the sea, a fuck with a soldier who never knew your name. Tenderness towards the unknown and anonymous, which was a tenderness to the self.

Her legs move under the burden of military blankets. She swims in their wool as the English patient moved in his cloth placenta.

What she misses here is slow twilight, the sound of familiar trees. All through her youth in Toronto she learned to read the summer night. It was where she could be herself, lying in a bed, stepping onto a fire escape half asleep with a cat in her arms.

In her childhood her classroom had been Caravaggio. He had taught her the somersault. Now, with his hands always in his pockets, he just gestures with his shoulders. Who knew what country the war had made him live in. She herself had been trained at Women's College Hospital and then sent overseas during the Sicilian invasion. That was in 1943. The First Canadian Infantry Division worked its way up Italy, and the destroyed bodies were fed back to the field hospitals like mud passed back by tunnellers in the dark. After the battle of Arezzo, when the first barrage of troops recoiled, she was surrounded day and night by their wounds. After three full days without rest, she finally lay down on the floor beside a mattress where someone lay dead, and slept for twelve hours, closing her eyes against the world around her.

When she woke, she picked up a pair of scissors out of the porcelain bowl, leaned over and began to cut her hair, not concerned with shape or length, just cutting it away—the irritation of its presence during the previous days still in her mind—when she had bent forward and her hair had touched blood in a wound. She would have nothing to link her, to lock her, to death. She gripped what was left to make sure there were no more strands and turned again to face the rooms full of the wounded.

She never looked at herself in mirrors again. As the war got darker she received reports about how certain people she had known had died. She feared the day she would remove blood from a patient's face and discover her father or someone who had served her food across a counter on Danforth Avenue. She grew harsh with herself and the patients. Reason was the only thing that might save them, and there was no reason. The thermometer of blood moved up the country. Where was and what was Toronto anymore in her mind? This was treacherous opera. People hardened against those around them—soldiers, doctors, nurses, civilians. Hana bent closer to the wounds she cared for, her mouth whispering to soldiers.

She called everyone "Buddy," and laughed at the song that had the lines

Each time I chanced to see Franklin D.
He always said "Hi, Buddy" to me.

She swabbed arms that kept bleeding. She removed so many pieces of shrapnel she felt she'd transported a ton of metal out of the huge body of the human that she was caring for while the army travelled north. One night when one of the patients died she ignored all rules and took the pair of tennis shoes he had with him in his pack and put them on. They were slightly too big for her but she was comfortable.

Her face became tougher and leaner, the face Caravaggio would meet later. She was thin, mostly from tiredness. She was always hungry and found it a furious exhaustion to feed a patient who couldn't eat or didn't want to, watching the bread crumble away, the soup cool, which she desired to swallow fast. She wanted nothing exotic, just bread, meat. One of the towns had a bread-making section attached to the hospital and in her free time she moved among the bakers, inhaling the dust and the promise of food. Later, when they were east of Rome, someone gave her a gift of a Jerusalem artichoke.

It was strange sleeping in the basilicas, or monasteries, or wherever the wounded were billeted, always moving north. She broke the small cardboard flag off the foot of the bed when someone died, so that orderlies would know glancing from a distance. Then she would leave the thick-stoned building and walk outside into spring or winter or summer, seasons that seemed archaic, that sat like old gentlemen throughout the war. She would step outside whatever the weather. She wanted air that smelled of nothing human, wanted moonlight even if it came with a rainstorm.

Hello Buddy, good-bye Buddy. Caring was brief. There was a contract only until death. Nothing in her spirit or past had taught her to be a nurse. But cutting her hair was a contract, and it lasted until they were bivouacked in the Villa San Girolamo north of Florence. Here there were four other nurses, two doctors, one hundred patients. The war in Italy moved farther north and they were what had been left behind.

Then, during the celebrations of some local victory, somewhat plaintive in this hill town, she had said she was not going back to Florence or Rome or any other hospital, her war was over. She would remain with the one burned man they called "the English patient," who, it was now clear to her, should never be moved because of the fragility of his limbs. She would lay belladonna over his eyes, give him saline baths for the keloided skin and extensive burns. She was told the hospital was unsafe—the nunnery that had been for months a German defence, barraged with shells and flares by the Allies. Nothing would be left for her, there would be no safety from brigands.

She still refused to leave, got out of her nurse's uniform, unbundled the brown print frock she had carried for months, and wore that with her tennis shoes. She stepped away from the war. She had moved back and forth at their desire. Till the nuns reclaimed it she would sit in this villa with the Englishman. There was something about him she wanted to learn, grow into, and hide in, where she could turn away from being an adult. There was some little waltz in the way he spoke to her and the way he thought. She wanted to save him, this nameless, almost faceless man who had been one of the two hundred or so placed in her care during the invasion north.

In her print dress she walked away from the celebration. She went into the room she shared with the other nurses and sat down. Something flickered in her eye as she sat, and she caught the eye of a small round mirror. She got up slowly and went towards it. It was very small but even so seemed a luxury. She had refused to look at herself for more than a year, now and then just her shadow on walls. The mirror revealed only her cheek, she had to move it back to arm's length, her hand wavering. She watched the little portrait of herself as if within a clasped brooch. She. Through the window there was the sound of the patients being brought out into the sunlight in their chairs, laughing and cheering with the staff. Only those who were seriously ill were still indoors. She smiled at that. Hi Buddy, she said. She peered into her look, trying to recognize herself.

Darkness between Hana and Caravaggio as they walk in the garden. Now he begins to talk in his familiar slow drawl.

"It was someone's birthday party late at night on Danforth Avenue. The Night Crawler restaurant. Do you remember, Hana? Everyone had to stand and sing a song. Your father, me, Giannetta, friends, and you said you wanted to as well—for the first time. You were still at school then, and you had learned the song in a French class.

"You did it formally, stood on the bench and then one more step up onto the wooden table between the plates and the candles burning.

" 'Alonson fon!'

"You sang out, your left hand to your heart. *Alonson fon!* Half the people there didn't know what the hell you were singing, and maybe you didn't know what the exact words meant, but you knew what the song was about.

"The breeze from the window was swaying your skirt over so it almost touched a candle, and your ankles seemed fire-white in the bar. Your father's eyes looking up at you, miraculous with this new language, the cause pouring out so distinct, flawless, no hesitations, and the candles swerving away, not touching your dress but almost touching. We stood up at the end and you walked off the table into his arms."

"I would remove those bandages on your hands. I *am* a nurse, you know."

"They're comfortable. Like gloves."

"How did this happen."

"I was caught jumping from a woman's window. That woman I told you about, who took the photograph. Not her fault."

She grips his arm, kneading the muscle. "Let me do it." She pulls the bandaged hands out of his coat pockets. She has seen them grey in daylight, but in this light they are almost luminous.

As she loosens the bandages he steps backwards, the white coming out of his arms as if he were a magician, till he is free of them. She walks towards the uncle from childhood, sees his eyes hoping to catch hers to postpone this, so she looks at nothing but his eyes.

His hands held together like a human bowl. She reaches for them while her face goes up to his cheek, then nestles in his neck. What she holds seems firm, healed.

"I tell you I had to negotiate for what they left me."

"How did you do that?"

"All those skills I used to have."

"Oh, I remember. No, don't move. Don't drift away from me."

"It is a strange time, the end of a war."

"Yes. A period of adjustment."

"Yes."

He raises his hands up as if to cup the quarter-moon.

"They removed both thumbs, Hana. See."

He holds his hands in front of her. Showing her directly what she has glimpsed. He turns one hand over as if to reveal that it is no trick, that what looks like a gill is where the thumb has been cut away. He moves the hand towards her blouse.

She feels the cloth lift in the area below her shoulder as he holds it with two fingers and tugs it softly towards him.

"I touch cotton like this."

"When I was a child I thought of you always as the Scarlet Pimpernel, and in my dreams I stepped onto the night roofs with you. You came home with cold meals in your pockets, pencil cases, sheet music off some Forest Hill piano for me."

She speaks into the darkness of his face, a shadow of leaves washing over his mouth like a rich woman's lace. "You like women, don't you? You liked them."

"I like them. Why the past tense?"

"It seems unimportant now, with the war and such things."

He nods and the pattern of leaves rolls off him.

"You used to be like those artists who painted only at night, a single light on in their street. Like the worm-pickers with their old coffee cans strapped to their ankles and the helmet of light shooting down into the grass. All over the city parks. You took me to that place, that café where they sold them. It was like the stock exchange, you said, where the price of worms kept dropping and rising, five cents, ten cents. People were ruined or made fortunes. Do you remember?"

"Yes."

"Walk back with me, it's getting cold."

"The great pickpockets are born with the second and third fingers almost the same length. They do not need to go as deep into a pocket. The great distance of half an inch!"

They move towards the house, under the trees.

"Who did that to you?"

"They found a woman to do it. They thought it was more trenchant. They brought in one of their nurses. My wrists handcuffed to the table legs. When they cut off my thumbs my hands slipped out of them without any power. Like a wish in a dream. But the man who called her in, he was really in charge—he was the one. Ranuccio Tommasoni. She was an innocent, knew nothing about me, my name or nationality or what I may have done."

When they came into the house the English patient was shouting. Hana let go of Caravaggio and he watched her run up the stairs, her tennis shoes flashing as she ascended and wheeled around with the banister.

The voice filled the halls. Caravaggio walked into the kitchen, tore off a section of bread and followed Hana up the stairs. As he walked towards the room the shouts became more frantic. When he stepped into the bedroom the Englishman was staring at a dog—the dog's head angled back as if stunned by the screaming. Hana looked over to Caravaggio and grinned.

"I haven't seen a dog for *years*. All through the war I saw no dog."

She crouched and hugged the animal, smelling its hair and the odour of hill grasses within it. She steered the dog towards Caravaggio, who was offering it the heel of bread. The Englishman saw Caravaggio then and his jaw dropped. It must have seemed to him that the dog—now blocked by Hana's back —had turned into a man. Caravaggio collected the dog in his arms and left the room.

I have been thinking, the English patient said, that this must be Poliziano's room. This must have been his villa we are in. It is the water coming out of that wall, that ancient fountain. It is a famous room. They all met here.

It was a hospital, she said quietly. Before that, long before that a nunnery. Then armies took it over.

I think this was the Villa Bruscoli. Poliziano—the great protégé of Lorenzo. I'm talking about 1483. In Florence, in Santa Trinità Church, you can see the painting of the Medicis with Poliziano in the foreground, wearing a red cloak. Brilliant, awful man. A genius who worked his way up into society.

It was long past midnight and he was wide awake again.

Okay, tell me, she thought, take me somewhere. Her mind still upon Caravaggio's hands. Caravaggio, who was by now probably feeding the stray dog something from the kitchen of the Villa Bruscoli, if that was what its name was.

It was a bloody life. Daggers and politics and three-decker hats and colonial padded stockings and wigs. Wigs of silk! Of course Savonarola came later, not much later, and there was his Bonfire of the Vanities. Poliziano translated Homer. He wrote a great poem on Simonetta Vespucci, you know her?

No, said Hana, laughing.

Paintings of her all over Florence. Died of consumption at twenty-three. He made her famous with *Le Stanze per la Giostra* and then Botticelli painted scenes from it. Leonardo painted scenes from it. Poliziano would lecture every day for two hours in Latin in the morning, two hours in Greek in the afternoon. He had a friend called Pico della Mirandola, a wild socialite who suddenly converted and joined Savonarola.

That was my nickname when I was a kid. *Pico*.

Yes, I think a lot happened here. This fountain in the wall. Pico and Lorenzo and Poliziano and the young Michelangelo. They held in each hand the new world and the old world. The library hunted down the last four books of Cicero. They imported a giraffe, a rhinoceros, a dodo. Toscanelli drew maps of the world based on correspondence with merchants. They sat in this room with a bust of Plato and argued all night.

And then came Savonarola's cry out of the streets: *"Repentance! The deluge is coming!"* And everything was swept away —free will, the desire to be elegant, fame, the right to worship Plato as well as Christ. Now came the bonfires—the burning of wigs, books, animal hides, maps. More than four hundred years later they opened up the graves. Pico's bones were preserved. Poliziano's had crumbled into dust.

Hana listened as the Englishman turned the pages of his commonplace book and read the information glued in from other books—about great maps lost in the bonfires and the burning of Plato's statue, whose marble exfoliated in the heat, the cracks across wisdom like precise reports across the valley as Poliziano stood on the grass hills smelling the future. Pico down there somewhere as well, in his grey cell, watching everything with the third eye of salvation.

He poured some water into a bowl for the dog. An old mongrel, older than the war.

He sat down with the carafe of wine the monks from the monastery had given Hana. It was Hana's house and he moved carefully, rearranging nothing. He noticed her civilisation in the small wildflowers, the small gifts to herself. Even in the overgrown garden he would come across a square foot of grass snipped down with her nurse's scissors. If he had been a younger man he would have fallen in love with this.

He was no longer young. How did she see him? With his wounds, his unbalance, the grey curls at the back of his neck. He had never imagined himself to be a man with a sense of age and wisdom. They had all grown older, but he still did not feel he had wisdom to go with his aging.

He crouched down to watch the dog drinking and he rebalanced himself too late, grabbing the table, upsetting the carafe of wine.

Your name is David Caravaggio, right?

They had handcuffed him to the thick legs of an oak table. At one point he rose with it in his embrace, blood pouring away from his left hand, and tried to run with it through the thin door and falling. The woman stopped, dropping the knife, refusing to do more. The drawer of the table slid out and fell against his chest, and all its contents, and he thought perhaps there was a gun that he could use. Then Ranuccio Tommasoni picked up the razor and came over to him. *Caravaggio, right?* He still wasn't sure.

As he lay under the table, the blood from his hands fell into his face, and he suddenly thought clearly and slipped the handcuff off the table leg, flinging the chair away to drown out the pain and then leaning to the left to step out of the other cuff. Blood everywhere now. His hands already useless. For months afterwards he found himself looking at only the thumbs of people, as if the incident had changed him just by producing envy. But the event had produced age, as if during the one night when he was locked to that table they had poured a solution into him that slowed him.

He stood up dizzy above the dog, above the red wine–soaked table. Two guards, the woman, Tommasoni, the telephones ringing, ringing, interrupting Tommasoni, who would put down the razor, caustically whisper *Excuse me* and pick up the phone with his bloody hand and listen. He had, he thought, said nothing of worth to them. But they let him go, so perhaps he was wrong.

Then he had walked along the Via di Santo Spirito to the one geographical location he had hidden away in his brain. Walked past Brunelleschi's church towards the library of the German Institute, where he knew a certain person would look after him. Suddenly he realized this was why they had let him go. Letting him walk freely would fool him into revealing this contact. He arced into a side street, not looking back, never looking back. He wanted a street fire so he could stanch his wounds, hang them over the smoke from a tar cauldron so black smoke would envelop his hands. He was on the Santa

Trinità Bridge. There was nothing around, no traffic, which surprised him. He sat on the smooth balustrade of the bridge, then lay back. No sounds. Earlier, when he had walked, his hands in his wet pockets, there had been the manic movement of tanks and jeeps.

As he lay there the mined bridge exploded and he was flung upwards and then down as part of the end of the world. He opened his eyes and there was a giant head beside him. He breathed in and his chest filled with water. He was underwater. There was a bearded head beside him in the shallow water of the Arno. He reached towards it but couldn't even nudge it. Light was pouring into the river. He swam up to the surface, parts of which were on fire.

When he told Hana the story later that evening she said, "They stopped torturing you because the Allies were coming. The Germans were getting out of the city, blowing up bridges as they left."

"I don't know. Maybe I told them everything. Whose head was it? There were constant phone calls into that room. There would be a hush, and the man would pull back from me, and all of them would watch him on the phone listening to the silence of the *other* voice, which we could not hear. Whose voice? Whose head?"

"*They were leaving,* David."

She opens *The Last of the Mohicans* to the blank page at the back and begins to write in it.

> *There is a man named Caravaggio, a friend of my father's. I have always loved him. He is older than I am, about forty-five, I think. He is in a time of darkness, has no confidence. For some reason I am cared for by this friend of my father.*

She closes the book and then walks down into the library and conceals it in one of the high shelves.

 The Englishman was asleep, breathing through his mouth as he always did, awake or asleep. She got up from her chair and gently pulled free the lit candle held in his hands. She walked to the window and blew it out there, so the smoke went out of the room. She disliked his lying there with a candle in his hands, mocking a deathlike posture, wax falling unnoticed onto his wrist. As if he was preparing himself, as if he wanted to slip into his own death by imitating its climate and light.

She stood by the window and her fingers clutched the hair on her head with a tough grip, pulling it. In darkness, in any light after dusk, you can slit a vein and the blood is black.

She needed to move from the room. Suddenly she was claustrophobic, untired. She strode down the hall and leapt down the stairs and went out onto the terrace of the villa, then looked up, as if trying to discern the figure of the girl she had stepped away from. She walked back into the building. She pushed at the stiff swollen door and came into the library and then removed the boards from the French doors at the far end of the room, opening them, letting in the night air. Where Caravaggio was, she didn't know. He was out most evenings now, usually returning a few hours before dawn. In any case there was no sign of him.

She grabbed the grey sheet that covered the piano and walked away to a corner of the room hauling it in after her, a winding-cloth, a net of fish.

No light. She heard a far grumble of thunder.

She was standing in front of the piano. Without looking

down she lowered her hands and started to play, just chording sound, reducing melody to a skeleton. She paused after each set of notes as if bringing her hands out of water to see what she had caught, then continued, placing down the main bones of the tune. She slowed the movements of her fingers even more. She was looking down as two men slipped through the French doors and placed their guns on the end of the piano and stood in front of her. The noise of chords still in the air of the changed room.

Her arms down her sides, one bare foot on the bass pedal, continuing with the song her mother had taught her, that she practised on any surface, a kitchen table, a wall while she walked upstairs, her own bed before she fell asleep. They had had no piano. She used to go to the community centre on Saturday mornings and play there, but all week she practised wherever she was, learning the chalked notes that her mother had drawn onto the kitchen table and then wiped off later. This was the first time she had played on the villa's piano, even though she had been here for three months, her eye catching its shape on her first day there through the French doors. In Canada pianos needed water. You opened up the back and left a full glass of water, and a month later the glass would be empty. Her father had told her about the dwarfs who drank only at pianos, never in bars. She had never believed that but had at first thought it was perhaps mice.

A lightning flash across the valley, the storm had been coming all night, and she saw one of the men was a Sikh. Now she paused and smiled, somewhat amazed, relieved anyway, the cyclorama of light behind them so brief that it was just a quick glimpse of his turban and the bright wet guns. The high flap of the piano had been removed and used as a hospital table several months earlier, so their guns lay on the far side of the ditch of keys. The English patient could have identified the weapons. Hell. She was surrounded by foreign men. Not one pure Italian. A villa romance. What would Poliziano have thought of this 1945 tableau, two men and a woman across a piano and the war almost over and the guns in their wet brightness whenever the lightning slipped itself into the room filling everything with colour and shadow as it was doing now every half-minute thunder crackling all over the valley and the music antiphonal, the press of chords, *When I take my sugar to tea* . . .

Do you know the words?

There was no movement from them. She broke free of the chords and released her fingers into intricacy, tumbling into what she had held back, the jazz detail that split open notes and angles from the chestnut of melody.

> *When I take my sugar to tea*
> *All the boys are jealous of me,*
> *So I never take her where the gang goes*
> *When I take my sugar to tea.*

Their clothes wet while they watched her whenever the lightning was in the room among them, her hands playing now against and within the lightning and thunder, counter to it, filling up the darkness between light. Her face so concentrated they knew they were invisible to her, to her brain struggling to remember her mother's hand ripping newspaper and wetting it under a kitchen tap and using it to wipe the table free of the shaded notes, the hopscotch of keys. After which she went for her weekly lesson at the community hall, where she would play, her feet still unable to reach the pedals if she sat, so she preferred to stand, her summer sandal on the left pedal and the metronome ticking.

She did not want to end this. To give up these words from an old song. She saw the places they went, where the gang

never went, crowded with aspidistra. She looked up and nodded towards them, an acknowledgement that she would stop
now.

Caravaggio did not see all this. When he returned he found
Hana and the two soldiers from a sapper unit in the kitchen
making up sandwiches.

III

Sometime a Fire

THE LAST MEDIAEVAL WAR was fought in Italy in 1943 and 1944. Fortress towns on great promontories which had been battled over since the eighth century had the armies of new kings flung carelessly against them. Around the outcrops of rocks were the traffic of stretchers, butchered vineyards, where, if you dug deep beneath the tank ruts, you found blood-axe and spear. Monterchi, Cortona, Urbino, Arezzo, Sansepolcro, Anghiari. And then the coast.

Cats slept in the gun turrets looking south. English and Americans and Indians and Australians and Canadians advanced north, and the shell traces exploded and dissolved in the air. When the armies assembled at Sansepolcro, a town whose symbol is the crossbow, some soldiers acquired them and fired them silently at night over the walls of the untaken city. Field Marshal Kesselring of the retreating German army seriously considered the pouring of hot oil from battlements.

Mediaeval scholars were pulled out of Oxford colleges and flown into Umbria. Their average age was sixty. They were billeted with the troops, and in meetings with strategic command they kept forgetting the invention of the airplane. They spoke of towns in terms of the art in them. At Monterchi there was the *Madonna del Parto* by Piero della Francesca, located in the chapel next to the town graveyard. When the thirteenth-century castle was finally taken during the spring rains, troops were billeted under the high dome of the church and slept by the stone pulpit where Hercules slays the Hydra. There was only bad water. Many died of typhoid and other fevers. Looking up with service binoculars in the Gothic church at Arezzo soldiers would come upon their contemporary faces in the Piero della Francesca frescoes. The Queen of Sheba conversing with King Solomon. Nearby a twig from the Tree of Good and Evil inserted into the mouth of the dead Adam. Years later this queen would realize that the bridge over the Siloam was made from the wood of this sacred tree.

It was always raining and cold, and there was no order but for the great maps of art that showed judgement, piety and sacrifice. The Eighth Army came upon river after river of destroyed bridges, and their sapper units clambered down banks on ladders of rope within enemy gunfire and swam or waded across. Food and tents were washed away. Men who were tied to equipment disappeared. Once across the river they tried to ascend out of the water. They sank their hands and wrists into the mud wall of the cliff face and hung there. They wanted the mud to harden and hold them.

The young Sikh sapper put his cheek against the mud and thought of the Queen of Sheba's face, the texture of her skin. There was no comfort in this river except for his desire for her, which somehow kept him warm. He would pull the veil off her hair. He would put his right hand between her neck and olive blouse. He too was tired and sad, as the wise king and guilty queen he had seen in Arezzo two weeks earlier.

He hung over the water, his hands locked into the mudbank. Character, that subtle art, disappeared among them during those days and nights, existed only in a book or on a painted wall. Who was sadder in that dome's mural? He leaned forward to rest on the skin of her frail neck. He fell in love with her downcast eye. This woman who would someday know the sacredness of bridges.

At night in the camp bed, his arms stretched out into distance like two armies. There was no promise of solution or victory except for the temporary pact between him and that painted fresco's royalty who would forget him, never acknowledge his existence or be aware of him, a Sikh, halfway up a sapper's ladder in the rain, erecting a Bailey bridge for the army behind him. But he remembered the painting of their story. And when a month later the battalions reached the sea, after they had survived everything and entered the coastal town of Cattolica and the engineers had cleared the beach of mines in a twenty-yard stretch so the men could go down naked into the sea, he approached one of the mediaevalists who had befriended him—who had once simply talked with him and shared some Spam—and promised to show him something in return for his kindness.

The sapper signed out a Triumph motorbike, strapped a crimson emergency light onto his arm, and they rode back the way they had come—back into and through the now innocent towns like Urbino and Anghiari, along the winding crest of the mountain ridge that was a spine down Italy, the old man bundled up behind him hugging him, and down the western slope towards Arezzo. The piazza at night was empty of troops, and the sapper parked in front of the church. He helped the mediaevalist off, collected his equipment and walked into the church. A colder darkness. A greater emptiness, the sound of his boots filling the area. Once more he smelled the old stone and wood. He lit three flares. He slung block and tackle across the columns above the nave, then fired a rivet already threaded with rope into a high wooden beam. The professor was watching him bemused, now and then peering up into the high darkness. The young sapper circled him and knotted a sling across his waist and shoulders, taped a small lit flare to the old man's chest.

He left him there by the communion rail and noisily climbed

the stairs to the upper level, where the other end of the rope was. Holding onto it, he stepped off the balcony into the darkness, and the old man was simultaneously swung up, hoisted up fast until, when the sapper touched ground, he swung idly in midair within three feet of the frescoed walls, the flare brightening a halo around him. Still holding the rope the sapper walked forward until the man swung to the right to hover in front of *The Flight of Emperor Maxentius.*

Five minutes later he let the man down. He lit a flare for himself and hoisted his body up into the dome within the deep blue of the artificial sky. He remembered its gold stars from the time he had gazed on it with binoculars. Looking down he saw the mediaevalist sitting on a bench, exhausted. He was now aware of the depth of this church, not its height. The liquid sense of it. The hollowness and darkness of a well. The flare sprayed out of his hand like a wand. He pulleyed himself across to her face, his Queen of Sadness, and his brown hand reached out small against the giant neck.

The Sikh sets up a tent in the far reaches of the garden, where Hana thinks lavender was once grown. She has found dry leaves in that area which she has rolled in her fingers and identified. Now and then after a rain she recognizes the perfume of it.

At first he will not come into the house at all. He walks past on some duty or other to do with the dismantling of mines. Always courteous. A little nod of his head. Hana sees him wash at a basin of collected rainwater, placed formally on top of a sundial. The garden tap, used in previous times for the seedbeds, is now dry. She sees his shirtless brown body as he tosses water over himself like a bird using its wing. During the day she notices mostly his arms in the short-sleeved army shirt and the rifle which is always with him, even though battles seem now to be over for them.

He has various postures with the gun—half-staff, half a crook for his elbows when it is over his shoulders. He will turn, suddenly realizing she is watching him. He is a survivor of his fears, will step around anything suspicious, acknowledging her look in this panorama as if claiming he can deal with it all.

He is a relief to her in his self-sufficiency, to all of them in the house, though Caravaggio grumbles at the sapper's continuous humming of Western songs he has learned for himself in the last three years of the war. The other sapper, who had arrived with him in the rainstorm, Hardy he was called, is billeted elsewhere, nearer the town, though she has seen them working together, entering a garden with their wands of gadgetry to clear mines.

The dog has stuck by Caravaggio. The young soldier, who will run and leap with the dog along the path, refuses to give it food of any kind, feeling it should survive on its own. If he finds food he eats it himself. His courtesy goes only so far. Some nights he sleeps on the parapet that overlooks the valley, crawling into his tent only if it rains.

He, for his part, witnesses Caravaggio's wanderings at night. On two occasions the sapper trails Caravaggio at a distance. But two days later Caravaggio stops him and says, Don't follow me again. He begins to deny it, but the older man puts his hand across his lying face and quiets him. So the soldier knows Caravaggio was aware of him two nights before. In any case, the trailing was simply a remnant of a habit he had been taught during the war. Just as even now he desires to aim his rifle and fire and hit some target precisely. Again and again he aims at a nose on a statue or one of the brown hawks veering across the sky of the valley.

He is still very much a youth. He wolfs down food, jumps up to clear away his plate, allowing himself half an hour for lunch.

She has watched him at work, careful and timeless as a cat, in the orchard and within the overgrown garden that rises behind the house. She notices the darker brown skin of his wrist, which slides freely within the bangle that clinks sometimes when he drinks a cup of tea in front of her.

He never speaks about the danger that comes with his kind of searching. Now and then an explosion brings her and Caravaggio quickly out of the house, her heart taut from the muffled blast. She runs out or runs to a window seeing Caravaggio too in the corner of her vision, and they will see the sapper waving lazily towards the house, not even turning around from the herb terrace.

Once Caravaggio entered the library and saw the sapper up by the ceiling, against the trompe l'oeil—only Caravaggio would walk into a room and look up into the high corners to see if he was alone—and the young soldier, his eyes not leaving their focus, put out his palm and snapped his fingers, halting Caravaggio in his entrance, a warning to leave the room for safety as he unthreaded and cut a fuze wire he had traced to that corner, hidden above the valance.

He is always humming or whistling. "Who is whistling?" asks the English patient one night, having not met or even seen the newcomer. Always singing to himself as he lies upon the parapet looking up at a shift of clouds.

When he steps into the seemingly empty villa he is noisy. He is the only one of them who has remained in uniform. Immaculate, buckles shined, the sapper appears out of his tent, his turban symmetrically layered, the boots clean and banging into the wood or stone floors of the house. On a dime he turns from a problem he is working on and breaks into laughter. He seems unconsciously in love with his body, with his physicalness, bending over to pick up a slice of bread, his knuckles brushing the grass, even twirling the rifle absent-mindedly like a huge mace as he walks along the path of cypresses to meet the other sappers in the village.

He seems casually content with this small group in the villa, some kind of loose star on the edge of their system. This is like a holiday for him after the war of mud and rivers and bridges. He enters the house only when invited in, just a tentative visitor, the way he had done that first night when he had followed the faltering sound of Hana's piano and come up the cypress-lined path and stepped into the library.

He had approached the villa on that night of the storm not out of curiosity about the music but because of a danger to the piano player. The retreating army often left pencil mines within musical instruments. Returning owners opened up pianos and lost their hands. People would revive the swing on a grandfather clock, and a glass bomb would blow out half a wall and whoever was nearby.

He followed the noise of the piano, rushing up the hill with Hardy, climbed over the stone wall and entered the villa. As long as there was no pause it meant the player would not lean forward and pull out the thin metal band to set the metronome going. Most pencil bombs were hidden in these—the easiest place to solder the thin layer of wire upright. Bombs were attached to taps, to the spines of books, they were drilled into fruit trees so an apple falling onto a lower branch would detonate the tree, just as a hand gripping that branch would. He was unable to look at a room or field without seeing the possibilities of weapons there.

He had paused by the French doors, leaned his head against the frame, then slid into the room and except for moments of lightning remained within the darkness. There was a girl standing, as if waiting for him, looking down at the keys she was playing. His eyes took in the room before they took her in, swept across it like a spray of radar. The metronome was ticking already, swaying innocently back and forth. There was no danger, no tiny wire. He stood there in his wet uniform, the young woman at first unaware of his entrance.

Beside his tent the antenna of a crystal set is strung up into the trees. She can see the phosphorus green from the radio dial if she looks over there at night with Caravaggio's field glasses, the sapper's shifting body covering it up suddenly if he moves across the path of vision. He wears the portable contraption during the day, just one earphone attached to his head, the other loose under his chin, so he can hear sounds from the rest of the world that might be important to him. He will come into the house to pass on whatever information he has picked up that he thinks might be interesting to them. One afternoon he announces that the bandleader Glenn Miller has died, his plane having crashed somewhere between England and France.

So he moves among them. She sees him in the distance of a defunct garden with the diviner or, if he has found something, unravelling that knot of wires and fuzes someone has left him like a terrible letter.

He is always washing his hands. Caravaggio at first thinks he is too fussy. "How did you get through a war?" Caravaggio laughs.

"I grew up in India, Uncle. You wash your hands all the time. Before all meals. A habit. I was born in the Punjab."

"I'm from Upper America," she says.

He sleeps half in and half out of the tent. She sees his hands remove the earphone and drop it onto his lap.

Then Hana puts down the glasses and turns away.

They were under the huge vault. The sergeant lit a flare, and the sapper lay on the floor and looked up through the rifle's telescope, looked at the ochre faces as if he were searching for a brother in the crowd. The cross hairs shook along the biblical figures, the light dousing the coloured vestments and flesh darkened by hundreds of years of oil and candle smoke. And now this yellow gas smoke, which they knew was outrageous in this sanctuary, so the soldiers would be thrown out, would be remembered for abusing the permission they received to see the Great Hall, which they had come to, wading up beachheads and the one thousand skirmishes of small wars and the bombing of Monte Cassino and then walking in hushed politeness through the Raphael Stanze till they were here, finally, seventeen men who had landed in Sicily and fought their way up the ankle of the country to be here— where they were offered just a mostly dark hall. As if being in the presence of the place was enough.

And one of them had said, "Damn. Maybe more light, Sergeant Shand?" And the sergeant released the catch of the flare and held it up in his outstretched arm, the niagara of its light pouring off his fist, and stood there for the length of its burn like that. The rest of them stood looking up at the figures and faces crowded onto the ceiling that emerged in the light. But the young sapper was already on his back, the rifle aimed, his eye almost brushing the beards of Noah and Abraham and the variety of demons until he reached the great face and was stilled by it, the face like a spear, wise, unforgiving.

The guards were yelling at the entrance and he could hear the running steps, just another thirty seconds left on the flare. He rolled over and handed the rifle to the padre. "That one. Who is he? At three o'clock northwest, who is he? Quick, the flare is almost out."

The padre cradled the rifle and swept it over to the corner, and the flare died.

He returned the rifle to the young Sikh.

"You know we shall all be in serious trouble over this lighting of weapons in the Sistine Chapel. I should not have come here. But I also must thank Sergeant Shand, he was heroic to do it. No real damage has been done, I suppose."

"Did you see it? The face. Who was it?"

"Ah yes, it *is* a great face."

"You saw it."

"Yes. Isaiah."

When the Eighth Army got to Gabicce on the east coast, the sapper was head of night patrol. On the second night he received a signal over the shortwave that there was enemy movement in the water. The patrol sent out a shell and the water erupted, a rough warning shot. They did not hit anything, but in the white spray of the explosion he picked up a darker outline of movement. He raised the rifle and held the drifting shadow in his sights for a full minute, deciding not to shoot in order to see if there would be other movement nearby. The enemy was still camped up north, in Rimini, on the edge of the city. He had the shadow in his sights when the halo was suddenly illuminated around the head of the Virgin Mary. She was coming out of the sea.

She was standing in a boat. Two men rowed. Two other men held her upright, and as they touched the beach the people of the town began to applaud from their dark and opened windows.

The sapper could see the cream-coloured face and the halo of small battery lights. He was lying on the concrete pillbox, between the town and the sea, watching her as the four men climbed out of the boat and lifted the five-foot-tall plaster statue into their arms. They walked up the beach, without pausing, no hesitation for the mines. Perhaps they had watched them being buried and charted them when the Germans had been there. Their feet sank into the sand. This was Gabicce Mare on May 29, 1944. Marine Festival of the Virgin Mary.

Adults and children were on the streets. Men in band uniforms had also emerged. The band would not play and break the rules of curfew, but the instruments were still part of the ceremony, immaculately polished.

He slid from the darkness, the mortar tube strapped to his back, carrying the rifle in his hands. In his turban and with the weapons he was a shock to them. They had not expected him to emerge too out of the no-man's-land of the beach.

He raised his rifle and picked up her face in the gun sight —ageless, without sexuality, the foreground of the men's dark hands reaching into her light, the gracious nod of the twenty small light bulbs. The figure wore a pale blue cloak, her left knee raised slightly to suggest drapery.

They were not romantic people. They had survived the Fascists, the English, Gauls, Goths and Germans. They had been owned so often it meant nothing. But this blue and cream plaster figure had come out of the sea, was placed in a grape truck full of flowers, while the band marched ahead of her in silence. Whatever protection he was supposed to provide for this town was meaningless. He couldn't walk among their children in white dresses with these guns.

He moved one street south of them and walked at the speed of the statue's movement, so they reached the joining streets at the same time. He raised his rifle to pick up her face once again in his sights. It all ended on a promontory overlooking the sea, where they left her and returned to their homes. None of them was aware of his continued presence on the periphery.

Her face was still lit. The four men who had brought her by boat sat in a square around her like sentries. The battery attached to her back began to fade; it died at about four-thirty in the morning. He glanced at his watch then. He picked up the men with the rifle telescope. Two were asleep. He swung the sights up to her face and studied her again. A different look in the fading light around her. A face which in the darkness looked more like someone he knew. A sister. Someday a daughter. If he could have parted with it, the sapper would have left something there as his gesture. But he had his own faith after all.

Caravaggio enters the library. He has been spending most afternoons there. As always, books are mystical creatures to him. He plucks one out and opens it to the title page. He is in the room about five minutes before he hears a slight groan.

He turns and sees Hana asleep on the sofa. He closes the book and leans back against the thigh-high ledge under the shelves. She is curled up, her left cheek on the dusty brocade and her right arm up towards her face, a fist against her jaw. Her eyebrows shift, the face concentrating within sleep.

When he had first seen her after all this time she had looked taut, boiled down to just body enough to get her through this efficiently. Her body had been in a war and, as in love, it had used every part of itself.

He sneezed out loud, and when he looked up from the movement of his tossed-down head she was awake, the eyes open staring ahead at him.

"Guess what time it is."

"About four-oh-five. No, four-oh-seven," she said.

It was an old game between a man and a child. He slipped out of the room to look for the clock, and by his movement and assuredness she could tell he had recently taken morphine, was refreshed and precise, with his familiar confidence. She sat up and smiled when he came back shaking his head with wonder at her accuracy.

"I was born with a sundial in my head, right?"

"And at night?"

"Do they have moondials? Has anyone invented one? Perhaps every architect preparing a villa hides a moondial for thieves, like a necessary tithe."

"A good worry for the rich."

"Meet me at the moondial, David. A place where the weak can enter the strong."

"Like the English patient and you?"

"I was almost going to have a baby a year ago."

Now that his mind is light and exact with the drug, she can whip around and he will be with her, thinking alongside her. And she is being open, not quite realizing she is awake and conversing, as if still speaking in a dream, as if his sneeze had been the sneeze in a dream.

Caravaggio is familiar with this state. He has often met people at the moondial. Disturbing them at two a.m. as a whole bedroom cupboard came crashing down by mistake. Such shocks, he discovered, kept them away from fear and violence. Disturbed by owners of houses he was robbing, he would clap his hands and converse frantically, flinging an expensive clock into the air and catching it in his hands, quickly asking them questions, about where things were.

"I lost the child. I mean, I had to lose it. The father was already dead. There was a war."

"Were you in Italy?"

"In Sicily, about the time this happened. All through the time we came up the Adriatic behind the troops I thought of it. I had continued conversations with the child. I worked very hard in the hospitals and retreated from everybody around me. Except the child, who I shared everything with. In my head. I was talking to him while I bathed and nursed patients. I was a little crazy."

"And then your father died."

"Yes. Then Patrick died. I was in Pisa when I heard."

She was awake. Sitting up.

"You knew, huh?"

"I got a letter from home."

"Is that why you came here, because you knew?"

"No."

"Good. I don't think that he believed in wakes and such things. Patrick used to say he wanted a duet by two women on musical instruments when he died. Squeeze-box and violin. That's all. He was so damn sentimental."

"Yes. You could really make him do anything. Find him a woman in distress and he was lost."

The wind rose up out of the valley to their hill so the cypress trees that lined the thirty-six steps outside the chapel wrestled with it. Drops of earlier rain nudged off, falling with a ticking sound upon the two of them sitting on the balustrade by the steps. It was long after midnight. She was lying on the concrete ledge, and he paced or leaned out looking down into the valley. Only the sound of the dislodged rain.

"When did you stop talking to the baby?"

"It all got too busy, suddenly. Troops were going into battles at the Moro Bridge and then into Urbino. Maybe in Urbino I stopped. You felt you could be shot anytime there, not just if you were a soldier, but a priest or nurse. It was a rabbit warren, those narrow tilted streets. Soldiers were coming in with just bits of their bodies, falling in love with me for an hour and then dying. It was important to remember their names. But I kept seeing the child whenever they died. Being washed away. Some would sit up and rip all their dressings off trying to breathe better. Some would be worried about tiny scratches on their arms when they died. Then the bubble in the mouth. That little pop. I leaned forward to close a dead soldier's eyes, and he opened them and sneered, "Can't wait to have me dead? You *bitch!*" He sat up and swept everything on my tray to the floor. So furious. Who would want to die like that? To die with that kind of anger. You *bitch*! After that I always waited for the bubble in their mouths. I know death now, David. I know all the smells, I know how to divert them from agony. When to give the quick jolt of morphine in a major vein. The saline solution. To make them empty their bowels before they die. Every damn general should have had my job. Every damn general. It should have been a prerequisite for any river crossing. Who the hell were we to be given this responsibility, expected to be wise as old priests, to know how to lead people towards something no one wanted and somehow make them feel comfortable. I could never believe in all those services they gave for the dead. Their vulgar rhetoric. How dare they! How dare they talk like that about a human being dying."

There was no light, all lamps out, the sky mostly cloud-hidden. It was safer not to draw attention to the civilisation of existing homes. They were used to walking the grounds of the house in darkness.

"You know why the army didn't want you to stay here, with the English patient? Do you?"

"An embarrassing marriage? My father complex?" She was smiling at him.

"How's the old guy?"

"He still hasn't calmed down about that dog."

"Tell him he came with me."

"He's not really sure you are staying here either. Thinks you might walk off with the china."

"Do you think he would like some wine? I managed to scrounge a bottle today."

"From?"

"Do you want it or not?"

"Let's just have it now. Let's forget him."

"Ah, the breakthrough!"

"*Not* the breakthrough. I badly need a serious drink."

"Twenty years old. By the time I was twenty . . ."

"Yes, yes, why don't you scrounge a gramophone someday. By the way, I think this is called looting."

"My country taught me all this. It's what I did for them during the war."

He went through the bombed chapel into the house.

Hana sat up, slightly dizzy, off balance. "And look what they did to you," she said to herself.

Even among those she worked closely with she hardly talked during the war. She needed an uncle, a member of the family. She needed the father of the child, while she waited in this hill town to get drunk for the first time in years, while a burned man upstairs had fallen into his four hours of sleep and an old friend of her father's was now rifling through her medicine chest, breaking the glass tab, tightening a bootlace round his arm and injecting the morphine quickly into himself, in the time it took for him to turn around.

At night, in the mountains around them, even by ten o'clock, only the earth is dark. Clear grey sky and the green hills.

"I was sick of the hunger. Of just being lusted at. So I stepped away, from the dates, the jeep rides, the courtship. The last dances before they died—I was considered a snob. I worked harder than others. Double shifts, under fire, did anything for them, emptied every bedpan. I became a snob because I wouldn't go out and spend their money. I wanted to go home and there was no one at home. And I was sick of Europe. Sick of being treated like gold because I was female. I courted one man and he died and the child died. I mean, the child didn't just die, I was the one who destroyed it. After that I stepped so far back no one could get near me. Not with talk of snobs. Not with anyone's death. Then I met him, the man burned black. Who turned out to be, up close, an Englishman.

"It has been a long time, David, since I thought of anything to do with a man."

After a week of the Sikh sapper's presence around the villa they adapted to his habits of eating. Wherever he was—on the hill or in the village—he would return around twelve-thirty and join Hana and Caravaggio, pull out the small bundle of blue handkerchief from his shoulder bag and spread it onto the table alongside their meal. His onions and his herbs—which Caravaggio suspected he was taking from the Franciscans' garden during the time he spent there sweeping the place for mines. He peeled the onions with the same knife he used to strip rubber from a fuze wire. This was followed by fruit. Caravaggio suspected he had gone through the whole invasion never eating from a mess canteen.

In fact he had always been dutifully in line at the crack of dawn, holding out his cup for the English tea he loved, adding to it his own supply of condensed milk. He would drink slowly, standing in sunlight to watch the slow movement of troops who, if they were stationary that day, would already be playing canasta by nine a.m.

Now, at dawn, under the scarred trees in the half-bombed gardens of the Villa San Girolamo, he takes a mouthful of water from his canteen. He pours tooth powder onto the brush and begins a ten-minute session of lackadaisical brushing as he wanders around looking down into the valley still buried in the mist, his mind curious rather than awestruck at the vista he happens now to be living above. The brushing of teeth, since he was a child, has always been for him an outdoor activity.

The landscape around him is just a temporary thing, there

is no permanence to it. He simply acknowledges the possibility of rain, a certain odour from a shrub. As if his mind, even when unused, is radar, his eyes locating the choreography of inanimate objects for the quarter-mile around him, which is the killing radius of small arms. He studies the two onions he has pulled out of the earth with care, aware that gardens too have been mined by retreating armies.

At lunch there is Caravaggio's avuncular glance at the objects on the blue handkerchief. There is probably some rare animal, Caravaggio thinks, who eats the same foods that this young soldier eats with his right hand, his fingers carrying it to his mouth. He uses the knife only to peel the skin from the onion, to slice fruit.

The two men take a trip by cart down into the valley to pick up a sack of flour. Also, the soldier has to deliver maps of the cleared areas to headquarters at San Domenico. Finding it difficult to ask questions about each other, they speak about Hana. There are many questions before the older man admits having known her before the war.

"In Canada?"

"Yes, I knew her there."

They pass numerous bonfires on the sides of the road and Caravaggio diverts the young soldier's attention to them. The sapper's nickname is Kip. "Get Kip." "Here comes Kip." The name had attached itself to him curiously. In his first bomb disposal report in England some butter had marked his paper, and the officer had exclaimed, "What's this? Kipper grease?" and laughter surrounded him. He had no idea what a kipper was, but the young Sikh had been thereby translated into a salty English fish. Within a week his real name, Kirpal Singh, had been forgotten. He hadn't minded this. Lord Suffolk and his demolition team took to calling him by his nickname,

which he preferred to the English habit of calling people by
their surname.

That summer the English patient wore his hearing aid so he
was alive to everything in the house. The amber shell hung
within his ear with its translations of casual noises—the chair
in the hall scraping against the floor, the click of the dog's
claws outside his room so he would turn up the volume and
even hear its damn breathing, or the shout on the terrace from
the sapper. The English patient within a few days of the young
soldier's arrival had thus become aware of his presence around
the house, though Hana kept them separate, knowing they
would probably not like each other.

But she entered the Englishman's room one day to find the
sapper there. He was standing at the foot of the bed, his arms
hung over the rifle that rested across his shoulders. She disliked this casual handling of the gun, his lazy spin towards her
entrance as if his body were the axle of a wheel, as if the
weapon had been sewn along his shoulders and arms and into
his small brown wrists.

The Englishman turned to her and said, "We're getting
along famously!"

She was put out that the sapper had strolled casually into
this domain, seemed able to surround her, be everywhere.
Kip, hearing from Caravaggio that the patient knew about
guns, had begun to discuss the search for bombs with the
Englishman. He had come up to the room and found him a
reservoir of information about Allied and enemy weaponry.
The Englishman not only knew about the absurd Italian fuzes
but also knew the detailed topography of this region of Tus-

cany. Soon they were drawing outlines of bombs for each other and talking out the theory of each specific circuit.

"The Italian fuzes seem to be put in vertically. And not always at the tail."

"Well, that depends. The ones made in Naples are that way, but the factories in Rome follow the German system. Of course, Naples, going back to the fifteenth century . . ."

It meant having to listen to the patient talk in his circuitous way, and the young soldier was not used to remaining still and silent. He would get restless and kept interrupting the pauses and silences the Englishman always allowed himself, trying to energize the train of thought. The soldier rolled his head back and looked at the ceiling.

"What we should do is make a sling," the sapper mused, turning to Hana as she entered, "and carry him around the house." She looked at both of them, shrugged and walked out of the room.

When Caravaggio passed her in the hall she was smiling. They stood in the hall and listened to the conversation inside the room.

Did I tell you my concept of Virgilian man, Kip? Let me . . .

Is your hearing aid on?

What?

Turn it—

"I think he's found a friend," she said to Caravaggio.

She walks out into the sunlight and the courtyard. At noon the taps deliver water into the villa's fountain and for twenty minutes it bursts forth. She removes her shoes, climbs into the dry bowl of the fountain and waits.

At this hour the smell of hay grass is everywhere. Bluebottles stumble in the air and bang into humans as if slamming into a wall, then retreat unconcerned. She notices where water spiders have nested beneath the upper bowl of the fountain, her face in the shade of its overhang. She likes to sit in this cradle of stone, the smell of cool and dark hidden air emerging from the still empty spout near her, like air from a basement opened for the first time in late spring so the heat outside hangs in contrast. She brushes her arms and toes free of dust, of the crimp of shoes, and stretches.

Too many men in the house. Her mouth leans against the bare arm of her shoulder. She smells her skin, the familiarity of it. One's own taste and flavour. She remembers when she had first grown aware of it, somewhere in her teens—it seemed a place rather than a time—kissing her forearm to practise kissing, smelling her wrist or bending down to her thigh. Breathing into her own cupped hands so breath would bounce back towards her nose. She rubs her bare white feet now against the brindle colour of the fountain. The sapper has told her about statues he came across during the fighting, how he had slept beside one who was a grieving angel, half male, half female, that he had found beautiful. He had lain back, looking at the body, and for the first time during the war felt at peace.

She sniffs the stone, the cool moth smell of it.

Did her father struggle into his death or die calm? Did he lie the way the English patient reposes grandly on his cot? Was he nursed by a stranger? A man not of your own blood can break upon your emotions more than someone of your own blood. As if falling into the arms of a stranger you discover the mirror of your choice. Unlike the sapper, her father was never fully comfortable in the world. His conversations lost some of their syllables out of shyness. In any of Patrick's sentences, her mother had complained, you lost two or three crucial words. But Hana liked that about him, there seemed to be no feudal spirit around him. He had a vagueness, an uncertainty that allowed him tentative charm. He was unlike most men. Even the wounded English patient had the familiar purpose of the feudal. But her father was a hungry ghost, liking those around him to be confident, even raucous.

Did he move towards his death with the same casual sense of being there at an accident? Or in fury? He was the least furious man she knew, hating argument, just walking out of a room if someone spoke badly of Roosevelt or Tim Buck or praised certain Toronto mayors. He had never attempted to convert anyone in his life, just bandaging or celebrating events that occurred near him. That was all. A novel is a mirror walking down a road. She had read that in one of the books the English patient recommended, and that was the way she remembered her father—whenever she collected the moments of him—stopping his car under one specific bridge in Toronto north of Pottery Road at midnight and telling her that this was where the starlings and pigeons uncomfortably and not too happily shared the rafters during the night. So they had paused there on a summer night and leaned their heads out into the racket of noise and sleepy chirpings.

I was told Patrick died in a dove-cot, Caravaggio said.

Her father loved a city of his own invention, whose streets and walls and borders he and his friends had painted. He never truly stepped out of that world. She realizes everything she knew about the real world she learned on her own or from Caravaggio or, during the time they lived together, from her stepmother, Clara. Clara, who had once been an actress, the articulate one, who had articulated fury when they all left for the war. All through the last year in Italy she has carried the letters from Clara. Letters she knows were written on a pink rock on an island in Georgian Bay, written with the wind coming over the water and curling the paper of her notebook before she finally tore the pages out and put them in an envelope for Hana. She carried them in her suitcase, each containing a flake of pink rock and that wind. But she has never answered them. She has missed Clara with a woe but is unable to write to her, now, after all that has happened to her. She cannot bear to talk of or even acknowledge the death of Patrick.

And now, on this continent, the war having travelled elsewhere, the nunneries and churches that were turned briefly into hospitals are solitary, cut off in the hills of Tuscany and Umbria. They hold the remnants of war societies, small moraines left by a vast glacier. All around them now is the holy forest.

She tucks her feet under her thin frock and rests her arms along her thighs. Everything is still. She hears the familiar hollow churn, restless in the pipe that is buried in the central column of the fountain. Then silence. Then suddenly there is a crash as the water arrives bursting around her.

The tales Hana had read to the English patient, travelling with the old wanderer in *Kim* or with Fabrizio in *The Charterhouse of Parma*, had intoxicated them in a swirl of armies and horses and wagons—those running away from or running towards a war. Stacked in one corner of his bedroom were other books she had read to him whose landscapes they have already walked through.

Many books open with an author's assurance of order. One slipped into their waters with a silent paddle.

I begin my work at the time when Servius Galba was Consul. . . . The histories of Tiberius, Caligula, Claudius and Nero, while they were a power, were falsified through terror and after their death were written under a fresh hatred.

So Tacitus began his *Annals*.

But novels commenced with hesitation or chaos. Readers were never fully in balance. A door a lock a weir opened and they rushed through, one hand holding a gunnel, the other a hat.

When she begins a book she enters through stilted doorways into large courtyards. Parma and Paris and India spread their carpets.

He sat, in defiance of municipal orders, astride the gun Zam-Zammah on her brick platform opposite the old Ajaib-Gher— the Wonder House, as the natives called the Lahore Museum. Who hold Zam-Zammah, that "fire-breathing dragon," hold the Punjab; for the great green-bronze piece is always first of the conqueror's loot.

"Read him slowly, dear girl, you must read Kipling slowly. Watch carefully where the commas fall so you can discover the natural pauses. He is a writer who used pen and ink. He looked up from the page a lot, I believe, stared through his window and listened to birds, as most writers who are alone do. Some do not know the names of birds, though he did. Your eye is too quick and North American. Think about the speed of his pen. What an appalling, barnacled old first paragraph it is otherwise."

That was the English patient's first lesson about reading. He did not interrupt again. If he happened to fall asleep she would continue, never looking up until she herself was fatigued. If he had missed the last half-hour of plot, just one room would be dark in a story he probably already knew. He was familiar with the map of the story. There was Benares to the east and Chilianwallah in the north of the Punjab. (All this occurred before the sapper entered their lives, as if out of this fiction. As if the pages of Kipling had been rubbed in the night like a magic lamp. A drug of wonders.)

She had turned from the ending of *Kim*, with its delicate and holy sentences—and now clean diction—and picked up the patient's notebook, the book he had somehow managed to carry with him out of the fire. The book splayed open, almost twice its original thickness.

There was thin paper from a Bible, torn out and glued into the text.

King David was old and stricken in years and they covered him with clothes but he received no heat.

Whereupon his servants said, Let there be sought for the King a young virgin: and let her cherish him, and let her lie in this bosom, that our King may have heat.

So they sought for a fair damsel throughout all the coasts of Israel, and found Abishag a Shunammite. And the damsel cherished the King, and ministered to him: but the King knew her not.

The ———— tribe that had saved the burned pilot brought him into the British base at Siwa in 1944. He was moved in the midnight ambulance train from the Western Desert to Tunis, then shipped to Italy. At that time of the war there were hundreds of soldiers lost from themselves, more innocent than devious. Those who claimed to be uncertain of their nationalities were housed in compounds in Tirrenia, where the sea hospital was. The burned pilot was one more enigma, with no identification, unrecognizable. In the criminal compound nearby they kept the American poet Ezra Pound in a cage, where he hid on his body and pockets, moving it daily for his own image of security, the propeller of eucalyptus he had bent down and plucked from his traitor's garden when he was arrested. *"Eucalyptus that is for memory."*

"You should be trying to trick me," the burned pilot told his interrogators, "make me speak German, which I can, by the way, ask me about Don Bradman. Ask me about Marmite, the great Gertrude Jekyll." He knew where every Giotto was in Europe, and most of the places where a person could find convincing trompe l'oeil.

The sea hospital was created out of bathing cabins along the beach that tourists had rented at the turn of the century. During the heat the old Campari umbrellas were placed once more into their table sockets, and the bandaged and the wounded and the comatose would sit under them in the sea air and talk slowly or stare or talk all the time. The burned man noticed the young nurse, separate from the others. He was familiar with such dead glances, knew she was more patient than nurse. He spoke only to her when he needed something.

He was interrogated again. Everything about him was very English except for the fact that his skin was tarred black, a bogman from history among the interrogating officers.

They asked him where the Allies stood in Italy, and he said he assumed they had taken Florence but were held up by the hill towns north of them. The Gothic Line. "Your division is stuck in Florence and cannot get past bases like Prato and Fiesole for instance because the Germans have barracked themselves into villas and convents and they are brilliantly defended. It's an old story—the Crusaders made the same mistake against the Saracens. And like them you now need the fortress towns. They have never been abandoned except during times of cholera."

He had rambled on, driving them mad, traitor or ally, leaving them never quite sure who he was.

Now, months later in the Villa San Girolamo, in the hill town north of Florence, in the arbour room that is his bedroom, he reposes like the sculpture of the dead knight in Ravenna. He speaks in fragments about oasis towns, the later Medicis, the prose style of Kipling, the woman who bit into his flesh. And in his commonplace book, his 1890 edition of Herodotus' *Histories,* are other fragments—maps, diary entries, writings in many languages, paragraphs cut out of other books. All that is missing is his own name. There is still no clue to who he actually is, nameless, without rank or battalion or squadron. The references in his book are all pre-war, the deserts of Egypt and Libya in the 1930s, interspersed with references to cave art or gallery art or journal notes in his own small handwriting. "There are no brunettes," the English patient says to Hana as she bends over him, "among Florentine Madonnas."

The book is in his hands. She carries it away from his

sleeping body and puts it on the side table. Leaving it open she stands there, looking down, and reads. She promises herself she will not turn the page.

May 1936.
I will read you a poem, Clifton's wife said, in her formal voice, which is how she always seems unless you are very close to her. We were all at the southern campsite, within the firelight.

> *I walked in a desert.*
> *And I cried:*
> *"Ah, God, take me from this place!"*
> *A voice said: "It is no desert."*
> *I cried: "Well, but—*
> *The sand, the heat, the vacant horizon."*
> *A voice said: "It is no desert."*

No one said anything.
She said, That was by Stephen Crane, he never came to the desert.
He came to the desert, Madox said.

July 1936.
There are betrayals in war that are childlike compared with our human betrayals during peace. The new lover enters the habits of the other. Things are smashed, revealed in new light. This is done with nervous or tender sentences, although the heart is an organ of fire.

A love story is not about those who lose their heart but about those who find that sullen inhabitant who, when it is stumbled upon, means the body can fool no one, can fool nothing—not the wisdom of sleep or the habit of social graces. It is a consuming of oneself and the past.

It is almost dark in the green room. Hana turns and realizes her neck is stiff from stillness. She has been focused and submerged within the crabbed handwriting in his thick-leaved

sea-book of maps and texts. There is even a small fern glued
into it. *The Histories.* She doesn't close the book, hasn't
touched it since she laid it on the side table. She walks away
from it.

Kip was in a field north of the villa when he found the large
mine, his foot—almost on the green wire as he crossed the
orchard—twisting away, so he lost his balance and was on his
knees. He lifted the wire until it was taut, then followed it,
zigzagging among the trees.

He sat down at the source with the canvas bag on his lap.
The mine shocked him. They had covered it with concrete.
They had laid the explosive there and then plastered wet concrete over it to disguise its mechanism and what its strength
was. There was a bare tree about four yards away. Another
tree about ten yards away. Two months' grass had grown over
the concrete ball.

He opened his bag and with scissors clipped the grass away.
He laced a small hammock of rope around it and after attach-
ing a rope and pulley to the tree branch slowly lifted the
concrete into the air. Two wires led from the concrete towards
the earth. He sat down, leaned against the tree and looked at
it. Speed did not matter now. He pulled the crystal set out of
the bag and placed the earphones to his head. Soon the radio
was filling him with American music from the AIF station.
Two and a half minutes average for each song or dance number. He could work his way back along "A String of Pearls,"
"C-Jam Blues" and other tunes to discover how long he had
been there, receiving the background music subconsciously.

Noise did not matter. There would be no faint tickings

or clickings to signal danger on this kind of bomb. The distraction of music helped him towards clear thought, to the possible forms of structure in the mine, to the personality that had laid the city of threads and then poured wet concrete over it.

The tightening of the concrete ball in midair, braced with a second rope, meant the two wires would not pull away, no matter how hard he attacked it. He stood up and began to chisel the disguised mine gently, blowing away loose grain with his mouth, using the feather stick, chipping more concrete off. He stopped his focus only when the music slipped off the wavelength and he had to realign the station, bringing clarity back to the swing tunes. Very slowly he unearthed the series of wires. There were six wires jumbled up, tied together, all painted black.

He brushed the dust off the mapboard the wires lay on.

Six black wires. When he was a child his father had bunched up his fingers and, disguising all but the tips of them, made him guess which was the long one. His own small finger would touch his choice, and his father's hand would unfold, blossoming, to reveal the boy's mistake. One could of course make a red wire negative. But this opponent had not just concreted the thing but painted all the characters black. Kip was being pulled into a psychological vortex. With the knife he began to scrape the paint free, revealing a red, a blue, a green. Would his opponent have also switched them? He'd have to set up a detour with black wire of his own like an oxbow river and then test the loop for positive or negative power. Then he would check it for fading power and know where the danger lay.

Hana was carrying a long mirror in front of her down the hall. She would pause because of the weight of it and then move forward, the mirror reflecting the old dark pink of the passageway.

The Englishman had wanted to see himself. Before she stepped into the room she carefully turned the reflection upon herself, not wanting the light to bounce indirectly from the window onto his face.

He lay there in his dark skin, the only paleness the hearing aid in his ear and the seeming blaze of light from his pillow. He pushed the sheets down with his hands. Here, do this, pushing as far as he could, and Hana flicked the sheet to the base of the bed.

She stood on a chair at the foot of the bed and slowly tilted the mirror down at him. She was in this position, her hands braced out in front of her, when she heard the faint shouts.

She ignored them at first. The house often picked up noise from the valley. The use of megaphones by the clearance military had constantly unnerved her when she was living alone with the English patient.

"Keep the mirror still, my dear," he said.

"I think there is someone shouting. Do you hear it?"

His left hand turned up the hearing aid.

"It's the boy. You'd better go and find out."

She leaned the mirror against the wall and rushed down the corridor. She paused outside waiting for the next yell. When it came she took off through the garden and into the fields above the house.

He stood, his hands raised above him as if he were holding a giant cobweb. He was shaking his head to get free of the earphones. As she ran towards him he yelled at her to circle to the left, there were mine wires all over the place. She stopped. It was a walk she had taken numerous times with no sense of danger. She raised her skirt and moved forward, watching her feet as they entered the long grass.

His hands were still up in the air as she came alongside him. He had been tricked, ending up holding two live wires he could not put down without the safety of a descant chord. He needed a third hand to negate one of them and he needed to go back once more to the fuze head. He passed the wires carefully to her and dropped his arms, getting blood back into them.

"I'll take them back in a minute."

"It's okay."

"Keep very still."

He opened up his satchel for the Geiger counter and magnet. He ran the dial up and along the wires she was holding. No swerve to negative. No clue. Nothing. He stepped backwards, wondering where the trick could be.

"Let me tape those to the tree, and you leave."

"No. I'll hold it. They won't reach the tree."

"No."

"Kip—I can hold them."

"We have an impasse. There's a joke. I don't know where to go from here. I don't know how complete the trick is."

Leaving her, he ran back to where he had first sighted the wire. He raised it and followed it all the way this time, the Geiger counter alongside it. Then he was crouched about ten yards from her, thinking, now and then looking up, looking right through her, watching only the two tributaries of wire she held in her hands. I don't know, he said out loud, slowly, *I don't know.* I think I have to cut the wire in your left hand, you must leave. He was pulling the radio earphones on over his head, so the sound came back into him fully, filling him with clarity. He schemed along the different paths of the wire and swerved into the convolutions of their knots, the sudden corners, the buried switches that translated them from positive to negative. The tinderbox. He remembered the dog, whose eyes were as big as saucers. He raced with the music along the wires, and all the while he was staring at the girl's hands, which were very still holding onto them.

"You'd better go."

"You need another hand to cut it, don't you?"

"I can attach it to the tree."

"I'll hold it."

He picked the wire like a thin adder from her left hand. Then the other. She didn't move away. He said nothing more, he now had to think as clearly as he could, as if he were alone. She came up to him and took back one of the wires. He was not conscious of this at all, her presence erased. He travelled the path of the bomb fuze again, alongside the mind that had choreographed this, touching all the key points, seeing the X ray of it, the band music filling everything else.

Stepping up to her, he cut the wire below her left fist before the theorem faded, the sound like something bitten through with a tooth. He saw the dark print of her dress along her shoulder, against her neck. The bomb was dead. He dropped the cutters and put his hand on her shoulder, needing to touch something human. She was saying something he couldn't hear, and she reached forward and pulled the earphones off so silence invaded. Breeze and a rustle. He realized the click of the wire being cut had not been heard at all, just felt, the snap of it, the break of a small rabbit bone. Not letting go of her, he moved his hand down her arm and pulled the seven inches of wire out of her still tight grip.

She was looking at him, quizzical, waiting for his answer to what she had said, but he hadn't heard her. She shook her head and sat down. He started collecting various objects around himself, putting them into his satchel. She looked up into the tree and then only by chance looked back down and saw his hands shaking, tense and hard like an epileptic's, his breathing deep and fast, over in a moment. He was crouched over.

"Did you hear what I said?"

"No. What was it?"

"I thought I was going to die. I wanted to die. And I thought if I was going to die I would die with you. Someone like you, young as I am, I saw so many dying near me in the last year. I didn't feel scared. I certainly wasn't brave just now. I thought to myself, We have this villa this grass, we should have lain down together, you in my arms, before we died. I wanted to touch that bone at your neck, collarbone, it's like a small hard wing under your skin. I wanted to place my fingers against it. I've always liked flesh the colour of rivers and rocks or like the brown eye of a Susan, do you know what that flower is? Have you seen them? I am so tired, Kip, I want to sleep. I want to sleep under this tree, put my eye against your collarbone I just want to close my eyes without thinking of others, want to find the crook of a tree and climb into it and sleep. What a careful mind! To know which wire to cut. How did you know? You kept saying I don't know I don't know, but you did. Right? Don't shake, you have to be a still bed for me, let me curl up as if you were a good grandfather I could hug, I love the word 'curl,' such a slow word, you can't rush it. . . ."

Her mouth was against his shirt. He lay with her on the ground as still as he had to, his eyes clear, looking up into a branch. He could hear her deep breath. When he had put his arm around her shoulder she was already asleep but had gripped it against herself. Glancing down he noticed she still had the wire, she must have picked it up again.

It was her breath that was most alive. Her weight seemed so light she must have balanced most of it away from him. How long could he lie like this, unable to move or turn to busyness. It was essential to remain still, the way he had

relied on statues during those months when they moved up
the coast fighting into and beyond each fortress town until
there was no difference in them, the same narrow streets
everywhere that became sewers of blood so he would dream
that if he lost balance he would slip down those slopes on the
red liquid and be flung off the cliff into the valley. Every night
he had walked into the coldness of a captured church and
found a statue for the night to be his sentinel. He had given
his trust only to this race of stones, moving as close as possible
against them in the darkness, a grieving angel whose thigh
was a woman's perfect thigh, whose line and shadow appeared
so soft. He would place his head on the lap of such creatures
and release himself into sleep.

She suddenly let more weight onto him. And now her
breathing stretched deeper, like the voice of a cello. He
watched her sleeping face. He was still annoyed the girl had
stayed with him when he defused the bomb, as if by that she
had made him owe her something. Making him feel in retro-
spect responsible for her, though there was no thought of that
at the time. As if *that* could usefully influence what he chose
to do with a mine.

But he felt he was now within something, perhaps a painting he had seen somewhere in the last year. Some secure
couple in a field. How many he had seen with their laziness of
sleep, with no thought of work or the dangers of the world.
Beside him there were the mouselike movements within
Hana's breath; her eyebrows rode upon argument, a small fury
in her dreaming. He turned his eyes away, up towards the tree
and the sky of white cloud. Her hand gripped him as mud had
clung along the bank of the Moro River, his fist plunging into
the wet earth to stop himself slipping back into the already
crossed torrent.

If he were a hero in a painting, he could claim a just sleep.

But as even she had said, he was the brownness of a rock, the brownness of a muddy storm-fed river. And something in him made him step back from even the naive innocence of such a remark. The successful defusing of a bomb ended novels. Wise white fatherly men shook hands, were acknowledged, and limped away, having been coaxed out of solitude for this special occasion. But he was a professional. And he remained the foreigner, the Sikh. His only human and personal contact was this enemy who had made the bomb and departed brushing his tracks with a branch behind him.

Why couldn't he sleep? Why couldn't he turn towards the girl, stop thinking everything was still half lit, hanging fire? In a painting of his imagining the field surrounding this embrace would have been in flames. He had once followed a sapper's entrance into a mined house with binoculars. He had seen him brush a box of matches off the edge of a table and be enveloped by light for the half-second before the crumpling sound of the bomb reached him. What lightning was like in 1944. How could he trust even this circle of elastic on the sleeve of the girl's frock that gripped her arm? Or the rattle in her intimate breath as deep as stones within a river.

She woke when the caterpillar moved from the collar of her dress onto her cheek, and she opened her eyes, saw him crouched over her. He plucked it from her face, not touching her skin, and placed it in the grass. She noticed he had already packed up his equipment. He moved back and sat against the tree, watching her as she rolled slowly onto her back and then stretched, holding that moment for as long as she could. It must have been afternoon, the sun over there. She leaned her head back and looked at him.

"You were supposed to hold onto me!"

"I did. Till you moved away."

"How long did you hold me?"

"Until you moved. Until you needed to move."

"I wasn't taken advantage of, was I?" Adding, "Just joking," as she saw him beginning to blush.

"Do you want to go down to the house?"

"Yes, I'm hungry."

She could hardly stand up, the dazzle of sun, her tired legs. How long they had been there she still didn't know. She could not forget the depth of her sleep, the lightness of the plummet.

Aparty began in the English patient's room when Caravaggio revealed the gramophone he had found somewhere.

"I will use it to teach you to dance, Hana. Not what your young friend there knows. I have seen and turned my back on certain dances. But this tune, 'How Long Has This Been Going On,' is one of the great songs because the introduction's melody is purer than the song it introduces. And only great jazzmen have acknowledged that. Now, we can have this party on the terrace, which would allow us to invite the dog, or we can invade the Englishman and have it in the bedroom up-stairs. Your young friend who doesn't drink managed to find bottles of wine yesterday in San Domenico. We have not just music. Give me your arm. No. First we must chalk the floor and practise. Three main steps—one-two-three—now give me your arm. What happened to you today?"

"He dismantled a large bomb, a difficult one. Let him tell you about it."

The sapper shrugged, not modestly, but as if it was too complicated to explain. Night fell fast, night filled up the valley and then the mountains and they were left once more with lanterns.

They were shuffling together in the corridors towards the English patient's bedroom, Caravaggio carrying the gramo-phone, one hand holding its arm and needle.

"Now, before you begin on your histories," he said to the static figure in the bed, "I will present you with 'My Romance.' "

"Written in 1935 by Mr. Lorenz Hart, I believe," muttered the Englishman. Kip was sitting at the window, and she said she wanted to dance with the sapper.

"Not until I've taught you, dear worm."

She looked up at Caravaggio strangely; that was her father's term of endearment for her. He pulled her into his thick grizzled embrace and said "dear worm" again, and began the dancing lesson.

She had put on a clean but unironed dress. Each time they spun she saw the sapper singing to himself, following the lyrics. If they had had electricity they could have had a radio, they could have had news of the war somewhere. All they had was the crystal set belonging to Kip, but he had courteously left it in his tent. The English patient was discussing the unfortunate life of Lorenz Hart. Some of his best lyrics to "Manhattan," he claimed, had been changed and he now broke into those verses

> *"We'll bathe at Brighton;*
> *The fish we'll frighten*
> *When we're in.*
> *Your bathing suit so thin*
> *Will make the shellfish grin*
> *Fin to fin.*

"Splendid lines, and erotic, but Richard Rodgers, one suspects, wanted more dignity."

"You must guess my moves, you see."

"Why don't you guess mine?"

"I will when you know what to do. At present I'm the only one who does."

"I bet Kip knows."

"He may know but he won't do it."

"I shall have some wine," the English patient said, and the

sapper picked up a glass of water, flung the contents through the window and poured wine for the Englishman.

"This is my first drink in a year."

There was a muffled noise, and the sapper turned quickly and looked out of the window, into the darkness. The others froze. It could have been a mine. He turned back to the party and said, "It's all right, it wasn't a mine. That seemed to come from a cleared area."

"Turn the record over, Kip. Now I will introduce you to 'How Long Has This Been Going On,' written by—" He left an opening for the English patient, who was stymied, shaking his head, grinning with the wine in his mouth.

"This alcohol will probably kill me."

"Nothing will kill you, my friend. You are pure carbon."

"Caravaggio!"

"George and Ira Gershwin. Listen."

He and Hana were gliding to that sadness of the saxophone. He was right. The phrasing so slow, so drawn out, she could sense the musician did not wish to leave the small parlour of the introduction and enter the song, kept wanting to remain there, where the story had not yet begun, as if enamoured by a maid in the prologue. The Englishman murmured that the introductions to such songs were called "burdens."

Her cheek rested against the muscles of Caravaggio's shoulder. She could feel those terrible paws on her back against the clean frock, and they moved in the limited space between the bed and the wall, between bed and door, between the bed and the window alcove that Kip sat within. Every now and then as they turned she would see his face. His knees up and his arms resting on them. Or he would be looking out of the window into darkness.

"Do any of you know a dance called the Bosphorus hug?" the Englishman asked.

"No such thing."

Kip watched the large shadows slide over the ceiling, over the painted wall. He struggled up and walked to the English patient to fill his empty glass, and touched the rim of his glass with the bottle in a toast. West wind coming into the room. And he turned suddenly, angry. A frail scent of cordite reaching him, a percentage of it in the air, and then he slipped out of the room, gesturing weariness, leaving Hana in the arms of Caravaggio.

There was no light with him as he ran along the dark hall. He scooped up the satchel, was out of the house and racing down the thirty-six chapel steps to the road, just running, cancelling the thought of exhaustion from his body.

Was it a sapper or was it a civilian? The smell of flower and herb along the road wall, the beginning stitch at his side. An accident or wrong choice. The sappers kept to themselves for the most part. They were an odd group as far as character went, somewhat like people who worked with jewels or stone, they had a hardness and clarity within them, their decisions frightening even to others in the same trade. Kip had recognized that quality among gem-cutters but never in himself, though he knew others saw it there. The sappers never became familiar with each other. When they talked they passed only information along, new devices, habits of the enemy. He would step into the town hall, where they were billeted, and his eyes would take in the three faces and be aware of the absence of the fourth. Or there would be four of them and in a field somewhere would be the body of an old man or a girl.

He had learned diagrams of order when he joined the army, blueprints that became more and more complicated, like great knots or musical scores. He found out he had the skill of the three-dimensional gaze, the rogue gaze that could look at an object or page of information and realign it, see all the false descants. He was by nature conservative but able also to imagine the worst devices, the capacity for accident in a room—a plum on a table, a child approaching and eating the pit of poison, a man walking into a dark room and before joining his wife in bed brushing loose a paraffin lamp from its bracket. Any room was full of such choreography. The rogue gaze could see the buried line under the surface, how a knot might weave when out of sight. He turned away from mystery books with irritation, able to pinpoint villains with too much ease. He was most comfortable with men who had the abstract madness of autodidacts, like his mentor, Lord Suffolk, like the English patient.

He did not yet have a faith in books. In recent days, Hana had watched him sitting beside the English patient, and it seemed to her a reversal of *Kim*. The young student was now Indian, the wise old teacher was English. But it was Hana in the night who stayed with the old man, who guided him over the mountains to the sacred river. They had even read that book together, Hana's voice slow when wind flattened the candle flame beside her, the page dark for a moment.

He squatted in a corner of the clanging waiting-room, rapt from all other thoughts; hands folded in lap, and pupils contracted to pin-points. In a minute—in another half second— he felt he would arrive at the solution of the tremendous puzzle . . .

And in some way on those long nights of reading and listening, she supposed, they had prepared themselves for the young soldier, the boy grown up, who would join them. But it was Hana who was the young boy in the story. And if Kip was anyone, he was the officer Creighton.

A book, a map of knots, a fuze board, a room of four people

in an abandoned villa lit only by candlelight and now and then light from a storm, now and then the possible light from an explosion. The mountains and hills and Florence blinded without electricity. Candlelight travels less than fifty yards. From a greater distance there was nothing here that belonged to the outside world. They had celebrated in this evening's brief dance in the English patient's room their own simple adventures—Hana her sleep, Caravaggio his "finding" of the gramophone, and Kip a difficult defusing, though he had almost forgotten such a moment already. He was someone who felt uncomfortable in celebrations, in victories.

Just fifty yards away, there had been no representation of them in the world, no sound or sight of them from the valley's eye as Hana's and Caravaggio's shadows glided across the walls and Kip sat comfortably encased in the alcove and the English patient sipped his wine and felt its spirit percolate through his unused body so it was quickly drunk, his voice bringing forth the whistle of a desert fox bringing forth a flutter of the English wood thrush he said was found only in Essex, for it thrived in the vicinity of lavender and wormwood. All of the burned man's desire was in the brain, the sapper had been thinking to himself, sitting in the stone alcove. Then he turned his head suddenly, knowing everything as he heard the sound, certain of it. He had looked back at them and for the first time in his life lied—"It's all right, it wasn't a mine. That seemed to come from a cleared area"—prepared to wait till the smell of the cordite reached him.

Now, hours later, Kip sits once again in the window alcove. If he could walk the seven yards across the Englishman's room and touch her he would be sane. There was so little light in the room, just the candle at the table where she sat, not reading tonight; he thought perhaps she was slightly drunk.

He had returned from the source of the mine explosion to find Caravaggio asleep on the library sofa with the dog in his arms. The hound watched him as he paused at the open door, moving as little of its body as it had to, to acknowledge it was awake and guarding the place. Its quiet growl rising above Caravaggio's snore.

He took off his boots, tied the laces together and slung them over his shoulder as he went upstairs. It had started to rain and he needed a tarpaulin for his tent. From the hall he saw the light still on in the English patient's room.

She sat in the chair, one elbow on the table where the low candle sprayed its light, her head leaning back. He lowered his boots to the floor and came silently into the room, where the party had been going on three hours earlier. He could smell alcohol in the air. She put her fingers to her lips as he entered and then pointed to the patient. He wouldn't hear Kip's silent walk. The sapper sat in the well of the window again. If he could walk across the room and touch her he would be sane. But between them lay a treacherous and complex journey. It was a very wide world. And the Englishman woke at any sound, the hearing aid turned to full level when he slept, so he could be secure in his own awareness. The girl's eyes darted around and then were still when she faced Kip in the rectangle of window.

He had found the location of the death and what was left there and they had buried his second-in-command, Hardy. And afterwards he kept thinking of the girl that afternoon, suddenly terrified for her, angry at her for involving herself. She had tried to damage her life so casually. She stared. Her last communication had been the finger to her lips. He leaned over and wiped the side of his cheek against the lanyard on his shoulder.

He had walked back through the village, rain falling into

pollarded trees of the town square untrimmed since the start of the war, past the strange statue of two men shaking hands on horseback. And now he was here, the candlelight swaying, altering her look so he could not tell what she thought. Wisdom or sadness or curiosity.

If she had been reading or if she had been bending over the Englishman, he would have nodded to her and probably left, but he is now watching Hana as someone young and alone. Tonight, gazing at the scene of the mine blast, he had begun to fear her presence during the afternoon dismantling. He had to remove it, or she would be with him each time he approached a fuze. He would be pregnant with her. When he worked, clarity and music filled him, the human world extinguished. Now she was within him or on his shoulder, the way he had once seen a live goat being carried by an officer out of a tunnel they were attempting to flood.

No.

That wasn't true. He wanted Hana's shoulder, wanted to place his palm over it as he had done in the sunlight when she slept and he had lain there as if in someone's rifle sights, awkward with her. Within the imaginary painter's landscape. He did not want comfort but he wanted to surround the girl with it, to guide her from this room. He refused to believe in his own weaknesses, and with her he had not found a weakness to fit himself against. Neither of them was willing to reveal such a possibility to the other. Hana sat so still. She looked at him, and the candle wavered and altered her look. He was unaware that for her he was just a silhouette, his slight body and his skin part of the darkness.

Earlier, when she saw that he had left the window alcove, she had been enraged. Knowing that he was protecting them like children from the mine. She had clung closer to Caravaggio. It had been an insult. And tonight the growing exhilaration of the evening didn't permit her to read after Caravaggio had gone to bed, stopping to rifle through her medicine box first, and after the English patient had plucked at the air with his bony finger and, when she had bent over, kissed her cheek.

She had blown out the other candles, lit just the night stub at the bedside table and sat there, the Englishman's body facing her in silence after the wildness of his drunken speeches. *"Sometime a horse I'll be, sometime a hound. A hog, a headless bear, sometime a fire."* She could hear the spill of the wax into the metal tray beside her. The sapper had gone through town to some reach of the hill where the explosion had taken place, and his unnecessary silence still angered her.

She could not read. She sat in the room with her eternally dying man, the small of her back still feeling bruised from an accidental slam against the wall during her dance with Caravaggio.

Now if he moves towards her she will stare him out, will treat him to a similar silence. Let him guess, make a move. She has been approached before by soldiers.

But what he does is this. He is halfway across the room, his hand sunk to the wrist in his open satchel which still hangs off his shoulder. His walk silent. He turns and pauses beside the bed. As the English patient completes one of his long exhalations he snips the wire of his hearing aid with the cutters and drops them back into the satchel. He turns and grins towards her.

"I'll rewire him in the morning."

He puts his left hand on her shoulder.

Davidd Caravaggio—an absurd name for you, of course . . ."

"At least I have a name."

"Yes."

Caravaggio sits in Hana's chair. Afternoon sun fills the room, revealing the swimming motes. The Englishman's dark lean face with its angular nose has the appearance of a still hawk swaddled in sheets. The coffin of a hawk, Caravaggio thinks.

The Englishman turns to him.

"There's a painting by Caravaggio, done late in his life. *David with the Head of Goliath.* In it, the young warrior holds at the end of his outstretched arm the head of Goliath, ravaged and old. But that is not the true sadness in the picture. It is assumed that the face of David is a portrait of the youthful Caravaggio and the head of Goliath is a portrait of him as an older man, how he looked when he did the painting. Youth judging age at the end of its outstretched hand. The judging of one's own mortality. I think when I see him at the foot of my bed that Kip is my David."

Caravaggio sits there in silence, thoughts lost among the floating motes. War has unbalanced him and he can return to no other world as he is, wearing these false limbs that morphine promises. He is a man in middle age who has never become accustomed to families. All his life he has avoided permanent intimacy. Till this war he has been a better lover than husband. He has been a man who slips away, in the way lovers leave chaos, the way thieves leave reduced houses.

He watches the man in the bed. He needs to know who this Englishman from the desert is, and reveal him for Hana's sake. Or perhaps invent a skin for him, the way tannic acid camouflages a burned man's rawness.

Working in Cairo during the early days of the war, he had been trained to invent double agents or phantoms who would take on flesh. He had been in charge of a mythical agent named "Cheese," and he spent weeks clothing him with facts, giving him qualities of character—such as greed and a weakness for drink when he would spill false rumours to the enemy. Just as some in Cairo he worked for invented whole platoons in the desert. He had lived through a time of war when everything offered up to those around him was a lie. He had felt like a man in the darkness of a room imitating the calls of a bird.

But here they were shedding skins. They could imitate nothing but what they were. There was no defence but to look for the truth in others.

She pulls down the copy of *Kim* from the library shelf and, standing against the piano, begins to write into the flyleaf in its last pages.

> *He says the gun—the Zam-Zammah cannon—is still there outside the museum in Lahore. There were two guns, made up of metal cups and bowls taken from every Hindu household in the city—as* jizya, or tax. *These were melted down and made into the guns. They were used in many battles in the eighteenth and nineteenth centuries against Sikhs. The other gun was lost during a battle crossing in the Chenab River—*

She closes the book, climbs onto a chair and nestles the book into the high, invisible shelf.

She enters the painted bedroom with a new book and announces the title.

"No books now, Hana."

She looks at him. He has, even now, she thinks, beautiful eyes. Everything occurs there, in that grey stare out of his darkness. There is a sense of numerous gazes that flicker onto her for a moment, then shift away like a lighthouse.

"No more books. Just give me the Herodotus."

She puts the thick, soiled book into his hands.

"I have seen editions of *The Histories* with a sculpted portrait on the cover. Some statue found in a French museum. But I never imagine Herodotus this way. I see him more as one of those spare men of the desert who travel from oasis to oasis, trading legends as if it is the exchange of seeds, consuming everything without suspicion, piecing together a mirage. 'This history of mine,' Herodotus says, 'has from the beginning sought out the supplementary to the main argument.' What you find in him are cul-de-sacs within the sweep of history—how people betray each other for the sake of nations, how people fall in love. . . . How old did you say you were?"

"Twenty."

"I was much older when I fell in love."

Hana pauses. "Who was she?"

But his eyes are away from her now.

Birds prefer trees with dead branches," said Caravaggio. "They have complete vistas from where they perch. They can take off in any direction."

"If you are talking about me," Hana said, "I'm not a bird. The real bird is the man upstairs."

Kip tried to imagine her as a bird.

"Tell me, is it possible to love someone who is not as smart as you are?" Caravaggio, in a belligerent morphine rush, wanted the mood of argument. "This is something that has concerned me most of my sexual life—which began late, I must announce to this select company. In the same way the sexual pleasure of conversation came to me only after I was married. I had never thought words erotic. Sometimes I really do like to talk more than fuck. Sentences. Buckets of this buckets of that and then buckets of this again. The trouble with words is that you can really talk yourself into a corner. Whereas you can't fuck yourself into a corner."

"That's a man talking," muttered Hana.

"Well, I haven't," Caravaggio continued, "maybe you have, Kip, when you came down to Bombay from the hills, when you came to England for military training. Has anyone, I wonder, fucked themselves into a corner. How old are you, Kip?"

"Twenty-six."

"Older than I am."

"Older than Hana. Could you fall in love with her if she wasn't smarter than you? I mean, she may not be smarter than you. But isn't it important for you to *think* she is smarter than you in order to fall in love? Think now. She can be obsessed by the Englishman because he knows more. We're in a huge field when we talk to that guy. We don't even know if he's English. He's probably not. You see, I think it is easier to fall in love with *him* than with *you*. Why is that? Because we want to *know* things, how the pieces fit. Talkers seduce, words direct us into corners. We want more than anything to grow and change. Brave new world."

"I don't think so," said Hana.

"Neither do I. Let me tell you about people my age. The worst thing is others assume you have developed your character by now. The trouble with middle age is they think you are fully formed. *Here.*"

Here Caravaggio lifted up his hands, so they faced Hana and Kip. She got up and went behind him and put her arm around his neck.

"Don't do this, okay, David?"

She wrapped her hands softly around his.

"We've already got one crazy talker upstairs."

"Look at us—we sit here like the filthy rich in their filthy villas up in the filthy hills when the city gets too hot. It's nine in the morning—the old guy upstairs is asleep. Hana's obsessed with him. I am obsessed with the sanity of Hana, I'm obsessed with my 'balance,' and Kip will probably get blown up one of these days. Why? For whose sake? He's twenty-six years old. The British army teaches him the skills and the Americans teach him further skills and the team of sappers are given lectures, are decorated and sent off into the rich hills. You are being used, boyo, as the Welsh say. I'm not staying here much longer. I want to take you home. Get the hell out of Dodge City."

"Stop it, David. He'll survive."

"The sapper who got blown up the other night, what was his name?"

Nothing from Kip.

"What was his name?"

"Sam Hardy." Kip went to the window and looked out, leaving their conversation.

"The trouble with all of us is we are where we shouldn't be. What are we doing in Africa, in Italy? What is Kip doing dismantling bombs in orchards, for God's sake? What is he doing fighting English wars? A farmer on the western front cannot prune a tree without ruining his saw. Why? Because of the amount of shrapnel shot into it during the *last* war. Even the trees are thick with diseases we brought. The armies indoctrinate you and leave you here and they fuck off somewhere else to cause trouble, inky-dinky parlez-vous. We should all move out together."

"We can't leave the Englishman."

"The Englishman left months ago, Hana, he's with the Bedouin or in some English garden with its phlox and shit. He probably can't even remember the woman he's circling around, trying to talk about. He doesn't know where the fuck he is.

"You think I'm angry at you, don't you? Because you have fallen in love. Don't you? A jealous uncle. I'm terrified for you. I want to kill the Englishman, because that is the only thing that will save you, get you out of here. And I am beginning to like him. Desert your post. How can Kip love you if you are not smart enough to make him stop risking his life?"

"Because. Because he believes in a civilised world. He's a civilised man."

"First mistake. The correct move is to get on a train, go and have babies together. Shall we go and ask the Englishman, the bird, what he thinks?

"Why are you not smarter? It's only the rich who can't afford to be smart. They're compromised. They got locked years ago into privilege. They have to protect their belongings.

No one is meaner than the rich. Trust me. But they have to follow the rules of their shitty civilised world. They declare war, they have honour, and they can't leave. But you two. We three. We're free. How many sappers die? Why aren't you dead yet? Be irresponsible. Luck runs out."

Hana was pouring milk into her cup. As she finished she moved the lip of the jug over Kip's hand and continued pouring the milk over his brown hand and up his arm to his elbow and then stopped. He didn't move it away.

There are two levels of long, narrow garden to the west of the house. A formal terrace and, higher up, the darker garden, where stone steps and concrete statues almost disappear under the green mildew of the rains. The sapper has his tent pitched here. Rain falls and mist rises out of the valley, and the other rain from the branches of cypress and fir falls upon this half-cleared pocket on the side of the hill.

Only bonfires can dry the permanently wet and shadowed upper garden. The refuse of planks, rafters from prior shellings, dragged branches, weeds pulled up by Hana during the afternoons, scythed grass and nettles—all are brought here and burned by them during the late afternoon's pivot into dusk. The damp fires steam and burn, and the plant-odoured smoke sidles into the bushes, up into the trees, then withers on the terrace in front of the house. It reaches the window of the English patient, who can hear the drift of voices, now and then a laugh from the smoky garden. He translates the smell, evolving it backwards to what had been burned. Rosemary, he thinks, milkweed, wormwood, something else is also there, scentless, perhaps the dog violet, or the false sunflower, which loves the slightly acidic soil of this hill.

The English patient advises Hana on what to grow. "Get your Italian friend to find seeds for you, he seems capable in that category. What you want are plum leaves. Also fire pink and Indian pink—if you want the Latin name for your Latin friend, it is *Silene virginica*. Red savory is good. If you want finches get hazel and chokecherries."

She writes everything down. Then puts the fountain pen

into the drawer of the small table where she keeps the book she is reading to him, along with two candles, Vesta matches. There are no medical supplies in this room. She hides them in other rooms. If Caravaggio is to hunt them out, she doesn't want him disturbing the Englishman. She puts the slip of paper with the names of plants into the pocket of her dress to give to Caravaggio. Now that physical attraction has raised its head, she has begun to feel awkward in the company of the three men.

If it is physical attraction. If all this has to do with love of Kip. She likes to lay her face against the upper reaches of his arm, that dark brown river, and to wake submerged within it, against the pulse of an unseen vein in his flesh beside her. The vein she would have to locate and insert a saline solution into if he were dying.

At two or three in the morning, after leaving the Englishman, she walks through the garden towards the sapper's hurricane lamp, which hangs off the arm of St. Christopher. Absolute darkness between her and the light, but she knows every shrub and bush in her path, the location of the bonfire she passes, low and pink in its near completion. Sometimes she cups a hand over the glass funnel and blows out the flame, and sometimes she leaves it burning and ducks under it and enters through the open flaps, to crawl in against his body, the arm she wants, her tongue instead of a swab, her tooth instead of a needle, her mouth instead of the mask with the codeine drops to make him sleep, to make his immortal ticking brain slow into sleepiness. She folds her paisley dress and places it on top of her tennis shoes. She knows that for him the world burns around them with only a few crucial rules. You replace TNT with steam, you drain it, you—all this she knows is in his head as she sleeps beside him virtuous as a sister.

The tent and the dark wood surround them.

They are only a step past the comfort she has given others in the temporary hospitals in Ortona or Monterchi. Her body for last warmth, her whisper for comfort, her needle for sleep. But the sapper's body allows nothing to enter him that comes from another world. A boy in love who will not eat the food she gathers, who does not need or want the drug in a needle she could slide into his arm, as Caravaggio does, or those ointments of desert invention the Englishman craves, ointments and pollen to reassemble himself the way the Bedouin had done for him. Just for the comfort of sleep.

There are ornaments he places around himself. Certain leaves she has given him, a stub of candle, and in his tent the crystal set and the shoulder bag full of the objects of discipline. He has emerged from the fighting with a calm which, even if false, means order for him. He continues his strictness, following the hawk in its float along the valley within the V of his rifle sight, opening up a bomb and never taking his eyes off what he is searching for as he pulls a Thermos towards him and unscrews the top and drinks, never even looking at the metal cup.

The rest of us are just periphery, she thinks, his eyes are only on what is dangerous, his listening ear on whatever is happening in Helsinki or Berlin that comes over the short-wave. Even when he is a tender lover, and her left hand holds him above the *kara,* where the muscles of his forearm tense, she feels invisible to that lost look till his groan when his head falls against her neck. Everything else, apart from danger, is periphery. She has taught him to make a noise, desired it of him, and if he is relaxed at all since the fighting it is only in this, as if finally willing to admit his whereabouts in the darkness, to signal out his pleasure with a human sound.

How much she is in love with him or he with her we don't know. Or how much it is a game of secrets. As they grow intimate the space between them during the day grows larger. She likes the distance he leaves her, the space he assumes is their right. It gives each of them a private energy, a code of air between them when he passes below her window without a word, walking the half-mile to assemble with the other sappers in the town. He passes a plate or some food into her hands. She places a leaf across his brown wrist. Or they work with Caravaggio between them mortaring up a collapsing wall. The sapper sings his Western songs, which Caravaggio enjoys but pretends not to.

"Pennsylvania six-five-oh-oh-oh," the young soldier gasps.

She learns all the varieties of his darkness. The colour of his forearm against the colour of his neck. The colour of his palms, his cheek, the skin under the turban. The darkness of fingers separating red and black wires, or against bread he picks off the gunmetal plate he still uses for food. Then he stands up. His self-sufficiency seems rude to them, though no doubt he feels it is excessive politeness.

She loves most the wet colours of his neck when he bathes. And his chest with its sweat which her fingers grip when he is over her, and the dark, tough arms in the darkness of his tent, or one time in her room when light from the valley's city, finally free of curfew, rose among them like twilight and lit the colour of his body.

Later she will realize he never allowed himself to be beholden to her, or her to him. She will stare at the word in a novel, lift it off the book and carry it to a dictionary. *Beholden. To be under obligation.* And he, she knows, never allowed that. If she crosses the two hundred yards of dark garden to him it is her choice, and she might find him asleep, not from a lack of love but from necessity, to be clear-minded towards the next day's treacherous objects.

He thinks her remarkable. He wakes and sees her in the spray of the lamp. He loves most her face's smart look. Or in the evenings he loves her voice as she argues Caravaggio out of a foolishness. And the way she crawls in against his body like a saint.

They talk, the slight singsong of his voice within the canvas smell of their tent, which has been his all through the Italian campaign, which he reaches up to touch with his slight fingers as if it too belonged to his body, a khaki wing he folds over himself during the night. It is his world. She feels displaced out of Canada during these nights. He asks her why she cannot sleep. She lies there irritated at his self-sufficiency, his ability to turn so easily away from the world. She wants a tin roof for the rain, two poplar trees to shiver outside her window, a noise she can sleep against, sleeping trees and sleeping roofs that she grew up with in the east end of Toronto and then for a couple of years with Patrick and Clara along the Skootamatta River and later Georgian Bay. She has not found a sleeping tree, even in the density of this garden.

"Kiss me. It's your mouth I'm most purely in love with. Your teeth." And later, when his head has fallen to one side, towards the air by the tent's opening, she has whispered aloud, heard only by herself, "Perhaps we should ask Caravaggio. My father told me once that Caravaggio was a man always in love. Not just *in* love but always sinking within it. Always confused. Always happy. Kip? Do you hear me? I'm so happy with you. To be with you like this."

Most of all she wished for a river they could swim in. There was a formality in swimming which she assumed was like being in a ballroom. But he had a different sense of rivers, had entered the Moro in silence and pulled the harness of cables attached to the folding Bailey bridge, the bolted steel panels of it slipping into the water behind him like a creature, and the sky then had lit up with shell fire and someone was sinking beside him in mid-river. Again and again the sappers dove for the lost pulleys, grappling hooks in the water among them, mud and surface and faces lit up by phosphorus flares in the sky around them.

All through the night, weeping and shouting, they had to stop each other going crazy. Their clothes full of winter river, the bridge slowly eased into a road above their heads. And two days later another river. Every river they came to was bridgeless, as if its name had been erased, as if the sky were starless, homes doorless. The sapper units slid in with ropes, carried cables over their shoulders and spannered the bolts, oil-covered to silence the metals, and then the army marched over. Drove over the prefabricated bridge with the sappers still in the water below.

So often they were caught in midstream when the shells came, flaring into mudbanks breaking apart the steel and iron into stones. Nothing would protect them then, the brown river thin as silk against metals that ripped through it.

He turned from that. He knew the trick of quick sleep

against this one who had her own rivers and was lost from them.

Yes, Caravaggio would explain to her how she could sink into love. Even how to sink into cautious love. "I want to take you to the Skootamatta River, Kip," she said. "I want to show you Smoke Lake. The woman my father loved lives out on the lakes, slips into canoes more easily than into a car. I miss thunder that blinks out electricity. I want you to meet Clara of the canoes, the last one in my family. There are no others now. My father forsook her for a war."

She walks towards his night tent without a false step or any hesitation. The trees make a sieve of moonlight, as if she is caught within the light of a dance hall's globe. She enters his tent and puts an ear to his sleeping chest and listens to his beating heart, the way he will listen to a clock on a mine. Two a.m. Everyone is asleep but her.

IV

South Cairo 1930–1938

THERE IS, after Herodotus, little interest by the Western world towards the desert for hundreds of years. From 425 B.C. to the beginning of the twentieth century there is an averting of eyes. Silence. The nineteenth century was an age of river seekers. And then in the 1920s there is a sweet postscript history on this pocket of earth, made mostly by privately funded expeditions and followed by modest lectures given at the Geographical Society in London at Kensington Gore. These lectures are given by sunburned, exhausted men who, like Conrad's sailors, are not too comfortable with the etiquette of taxis, the quick, flat wit of bus conductors.

When they travel by local trains from the suburbs towards Knightsbridge on their way to Society meetings, they are often lost, tickets misplaced, clinging only to their old maps and carrying their lecture notes—which were slowly and painfully written—in their ever present knapsacks which will always be a part of their bodies. These men of all nations travel at that early evening hour, six o'clock, when there is the light of the solitary. It is an anonymous time, most of the city is going home. The explorers arrive too early at Kensington Gore, eat at the Lyons Corner House and then enter the Geographical Society, where they sit in the upstairs hall next to the large Maori canoe, going over their notes. At eight o'clock the talks begin.

Every other week there is a lecture. Someone will introduce the talk and someone will give thanks. The concluding speaker usually argues or tests the lecture for hard currency, is pertinently critical but never impertinent. The main speakers, everyone assumes, stay close to the facts, and even obsessive assumptions are presented modestly.

> *My journey through the Libyan Desert from Sokum on the Mediterranean to El Obeid in the Sudan was made over one of the few tracks of the earth's surface which present a number and variety of interesting geographical problems. . . .*

The years of preparation and research and fund-raising are never mentioned in these oak rooms. The previous week's lecturer recorded the loss of thirty people in ice in Antarctica. Similar losses in extreme heat or windstorm are announced with minimal eulogy. All human and financial behaviour lies on the far side of the issue being discussed—which is the earth's surface and its "interesting geographical problems."

> *Can other depressions in this region, besides the much-discussed Wadi Rayan, be considered possible of utilization in connection with irrigation or drainage of the Nile Delta? Are the artesian water supplies of the oases gradually diminishing? Where shall we look for the mysterious "Zerzura"? Are there any other "lost" oases remaining to be discovered? Where are the tortoise marshes of Ptolemy?*

John Bell, director of Desert Surveys in Egypt, asked these questions in 1927. By the 1930s the papers grew even more modest. *"I should like to add a few remarks on some of the points raised in the interesting discussion on the 'Prehistoric Geography of Kharga Oasis.'"* By the mid-1930s the lost oasis of Zerzura was found by Ladislaus de Almásy and his companions.

In 1939 the great decade of Libyan Desert expeditions came to an end, and this vast and silent pocket of the earth became one of the theatres of war.

In the arboured bedroom the burned patient views great distances. The way that dead knight in Ravenna, whose marble body seems alive, almost liquid, has his head raised upon a stone pillow, so it can gaze beyond his feet into vista. Farther than the desired rain of Africa. Towards all their lives in Cairo. Their works and days.

Hana sits by his bed, and she travels like a squire beside him during these journeys.

In 1930 we had begun mapping the greater part of the Gilf Kebir Plateau, looking for the lost oasis that was called Zerzura. The City of Acacias.

We were desert Europeans. John Bell had sighted the Gilf in 1917. Then Kemal el Din. Then Bagnold, who found his way south into the Sand Sea. Madox, Walpole of Desert Surveys, His Excellency Wasfi Bey, Casparius the photographer, Dr. Kadar the geologist and Bermann. And the Gilf Kebir—that large plateau resting in the Libyan Desert, the size of Switzerland, as Madox liked to say—was our heart, its escarpments precipitous to the east and west, the plateau sloping gradually to the north. It rose out of the desert four hundred miles west of the Nile.

For the early Egyptians there was supposedly no water west of the oasis towns. The world ended out there. The interior was waterless. But in the emptiness of deserts you are always surrounded by lost history. Tebu and Senussi tribes had roamed there possessing wells that they guarded with great secrecy. There were rumours of fertile lands that nestled within the desert's interior. Arab writers in the thirteenth century spoke of Zerzura. "The Oasis of Little Birds." "The City of Acacias." In *The Book of Hidden Treasures*, the *Kitab al Kanuz*, Zerzura is depicted as a white city, "white as a dove."

Look at a map of the Libyan Desert and you will see names. Kemal el Din in 1925, who, almost solitary, carried out the first great modern expedition. Bagnold 1930–1932. Almásy–Madox 1931–1937. Just north of the Tropic of Cancer.

We were a small clutch of a nation between the wars, mapping and re-exploring. We gathered at Dakhla and Kufra as if they were bars or cafés. An oasis society, Bagnold called it. We knew each other's intimacies, each other's skills and weaknesses. We forgave Bagnold everything for the way he wrote about dunes. *"The grooves and the corrugated sand resemble the hollow of the roof of a dog's mouth."* That was the real Bagnold, a man who would put his inquiring hand into the jaws of a dog.

1930. Our first journey, moving south from Jaghbub into the desert among the preserve of Zwaya and Majabra's tribes. A seven-day journey to El Taj. Madox and Bermann, four others. Some camels a horse and a dog. As we left they told us the old joke. "To start a journey in a sandstorm is good luck."

We camped the first night twenty miles south. The next morning we woke and came out of our tents at five. Too cold to sleep. We stepped towards the fires and sat in their light in the larger darkness. Above us were the last stars. There would be no sunrise for another two hours. We passed around hot glasses of tea. The camels were being fed, half asleep, chewing the dates along with the date stones. We ate breakfast and then drank three more glasses of tea.

Hours later we were in the sandstorm that hit us out of clear morning, coming from nowhere. The breeze that had been refreshing had gradually strengthened. Eventually we

looked down, and the surface of the desert was changed. Pass
me the book . . . here. This is Hassanein Bey's wonderful
account of such storms—

*"It is as though the surface were underlaid with steam-pipes,
with thousands of orifices through which tiny jets of steam are
puffing out. The sand leaps in little spurts and whirls. Inch by inch
the disturbance rises as the wind increases its force. It seems as
though the whole surface of the desert were rising in obedience to
some upthrusting force beneath. Larger pebbles strike against the
shins, the knees, the thighs. The sand-grains climb the body till it
strikes the face and goes over the head. The sky is shut out, all but
the nearest objects fade from view, the universe is filled."*

We had to keep moving. If you pause sand builds up as it
would around anything stationary, and locks you in. You are
lost forever. A sandstorm can last five hours. Even when we
were in trucks in later years we would have to keep driving
with no vision. The worst terrors came at night. Once, north
of Kufra, we were hit by a storm in the darkness. Three a.m.
The gale swept the tents from their moorings and we rolled
with them, taking in sand like a sinking boat takes in water,
weighed down, suffocating, till we were cut free by a camel
driver.

We travelled through three storms during nine days. We
missed small desert towns where we expected to locate more
supplies. The horse vanished. Three of the camels died. For
the last two days there was no food, only tea. The last link
with any other world was the clink of the fire-black tea urn
and the long spoon and the glass which came towards us in
the darkness of the mornings. After the third night we gave
up talking. All that mattered was the fire and the minimal
brown liquid.

Only by luck did we stumble on the desert town of El Taj.
I walked through the souk, the alley of clocks chiming, into

the street of barometers, past the rifle-cartridge stalls, stands of Italian tomato sauce and other tinned food from Benghazi, calico from Egypt, ostrich-tail decorations, street dentists, book merchants. We were still mute, each of us dispersing along our own paths. We received this new world slowly, as if coming out of a drowning. In the central square of El Taj we sat and ate lamb, rice, *badawi* cakes, and drank milk with almond pulp beaten into it. All this after the long wait for three ceremonial glasses of tea flavoured with amber and mint.

Sometime in 1931 I joined a Bedouin caravan and was told there was another one of us there. Fenelon-Barnes, it turned out. I went to his tent. He was out for the day on some small expedition, cataloguing fossil trees. I looked around his tent, the sheaf of maps, the photos he always carried of his family, et cetera. As I was leaving I saw a mirror tacked up high against the skin wall, and looking at it I saw the reflection of the bed. There seemed to be a small lump, a dog possibly, under the covers. I pulled back the *djellaba* and there was a small Arab girl tied up, sleeping there.

By 1932, Bagnold was finished and Madox and the rest of us were everywhere. Looking for the lost army of Cambyses. Looking for Zerzura. 1932 and 1933 and 1934. Not seeing each other for months. Just the Bedouin and us, crisscrossing the Forty Days Road. There were rivers of desert tribes, the most beautiful humans I've met in my life. We were German, English, Hungarian, African—all of us insignificant to them. Gradually we became nationless. I came to hate nations. We are deformed by nation-states. Madox died because of nations.

The desert could not be claimed or owned—it was a piece of cloth carried by winds, never held down by stones, and given a hundred shifting names long before Canterbury existed, long before battles and treaties quilted Europe and the East. Its caravans, those strange rambling feasts and cultures, left nothing behind, not an ember. All of us, even those with European homes and children in the distance, wished to remove the clothing of our countries. It was a place of faith. We disappeared into landscape. Fire and sand. We left the harbours of oasis. The places water came to and touched . . . *Ain, Bir, Wadi, Foggara, Khottara, Shaduf.* I didn't want my name against such beautiful names. Erase the family name! Erase nations! I was taught such things by the desert.

Still, some wanted their mark there. On that dry watercourse, on this shingled knoll. Small vanities in this plot of land northwest of the Sudan, south of Cyrenaica. Fenelon-Barnes wanted the fossil trees he discovered to bear his name. He even wanted a tribe to take his name, and spent a year on the negotiations. Then Bauchan outdid him, having a type of sand dune named after him. But I wanted to erase my name and the place I had come from. By the time war arrived, after ten years in the desert, it was easy for me to slip across borders, not to belong to anyone, to any nation.

1933 or 1934. I forget the year. Madox, Casparius, Bermann, myself, two Sudanese drivers and a cook. By now we travel in A-type Ford cars with box bodies and are using for the first time large balloon tires known as air wheels. They ride better on sand, but the gamble is whether they will stand up to stone fields and splinter rocks.

We leave Kharga on March 22. Bermann and I have theorized that three wadis written about by Williamson in 1838 make up Zerzura.

Southwest of the Gilf Kebir are three isolated granite massifs rising out of the plain—Gebel Arkanu, Gebel Uweinat, and Gebel Kissu. The three are fifteen miles apart from each other. Good water in several of the ravines, though the wells at Gebel Arkanu are bitter, not drinkable except in an emergency. Williamson said three wadis formed Zerzura, but he never located them and this is considered fable. Yet even one rain oasis in these crater-shaped hills would solve the riddle of how Cambyses and his army could attempt to cross such a desert, of the Senussi raids during the Great War, when the black giant raiders crossed a desert which supposedly has no water or pasture. This was a world that had been civilised for centuries, had a thousand paths and roads.

We find jars at Abu Ballas with the classic Greek amphora shape. Herodotus speaks of such jars.

Bermann and I talk to a snakelike mysterious old man in the fortress of El Jof—in the stone hall that once had been the library of the great Senussi sheik. An old Tebu, a caravan guide by profession, speaking accented Arabic. Later Bermann says "like the screeching of bats," quoting Herodotus. We talk to him all day, all night, and he gives nothing away. The Senussi creed, their foremost doctrine, is still not to reveal the secrets of the desert to strangers.

At Wadi el Melik we see birds of an unknown species.

On May 5, I climb a stone cliff and approach the Uweinat plateau from a new direction. I find myself in a broad wadi full of acacia trees.

There was a time when mapmakers named the places they travelled through with the names of lovers rather than their own. Someone seen bathing in a desert caravan, holding up muslin with one arm in front of her. Some old Arab poet's woman, whose white-dove shoulders made him describe an oasis with her name. The skin bucket spreads water over her, she wraps herself in the cloth, and the old scribe turns from her to describe Zerzura.

So a man in the desert can slip into a name as if within a discovered well, and in its shadowed coolness be tempted never to leave such containment. My great desire was to remain there, among those acacias. I was walking not in a place where no one had walked before but in a place where there were sudden, brief populations over the centuries—a fourteenth-century army, a Tebu caravan, the Senussi raiders of 1915. And in between these times—nothing was there. When no rain fell the acacias withered, the wadis dried out . . . until water suddenly reappeared fifty or a hundred years later. Sporadic appearances and disappearances, like legends and rumours through history.

In the desert the most loved waters, like a lover's name, are carried blue in your hands, enter your throat. One swallows absence. A woman in Cairo curves the white length of her body up from the bed and leans out of the window into a rainstorm to allow her nakedness to receive it.

Hana leans forward, sensing his drifting, watching him, not saying a word. Who is she, this woman?

The ends of the earth are never the points on a map that colonists push against, enlarging their sphere of influence. On one side servants and slaves and tides of power and correspondence with the Geographical Society. On the other the first step by a white man across a great river, the first sight (by a white eye) of a mountain that has been there forever.

When we are young we do not look into mirrors. It is when we are old, concerned with our name, our legend, what our lives will mean to the future. We become vain with the names we own, our claims to have been the first eyes, the strongest army, the cleverest merchant. It is when he is old that Narcissus wants a graven image of himself.

But we were interested in how our lives could mean something to the past. We sailed into the past. We were young. We knew power and great finance were temporary things. We all slept with Herodotus. *"For those cities that were great in earlier times must have now become small, and those that were great in my time were small in the time before. . . . Man's good fortune never abides in the same place."*

In 1936 a young man named Geoffrey Clifton had met a friend at Oxford who mentioned what we were doing. He contacted me, got married the next day, and two weeks later flew with his wife to Cairo.

The couple entered our world—the four of us, Prince Kemal el Din, Bell, Almásy and Madox. The name that still filled our mouths was Gilf Kebir. Somewhere in the Gilf nestled Zerzura, whose name occurs in Arab writings as far back as the thirteenth century. When you travel that far in time you need a plane, and young Clifton was rich and he could fly and he had a plane.

Clifton met us in El Jof, north of Uweinat. He sat in his two-seater plane and we walked towards him from the base camp. He stood up in the cockpit and poured a drink out of his flask. His new wife sat beside him.

"I name this site the Bir Messaha Country Club," he announced.

I watched the friendly uncertainty scattered across his wife's face, her lionlike hair when she pulled off the leather helmet.

They were youth, felt like our children. They climbed out of the plane and shook hands with us.

That was 1936, the beginning of our story. . . .

They jumped off the wing of the Moth. Clifton walked towards us holding out the flask, and we all sipped the warm alcohol. He was one for ceremonies. He had named his plane *Rupert Bear*. I don't think he loved the desert, but he had an affection for it that grew out of awe at our stark order, into which he wanted to fit himself—like a joyous undergraduate who respects silent behaviour in a library. We had not expected him to bring his wife, but we were I suppose courteous about it. She stood there while the sand collected in her mane of hair.

What were we to this young couple? Some of us had written books about dune formation, the disappearance and reappearance of oases, the lost culture of deserts. We seemed to be interested only in things that could not be bought or sold, of no interest to the outside world. We argued about latitudes, or about an event that had happened seven hundred years earlier. The theorems of exploration. That Abd el Melik Ibrahim el Zwaya who lived in Zuck oasis pasturing camels was the first man among those tribes who could understand the concept of photographs.

The Cliftons were on the last days of their honeymoon. I left them with the others and went to join a man in Kufra and spent many days with him, trying out theories I had kept secret from the rest of the expedition. I returned to the base camp at El Jof three nights later.

The desert fire was between us. The Cliftons, Madox, Bell and myself. If a man leaned back a few inches he would disappear into darkness. Katharine Clifton began to recite something, and my head was no longer in the halo of the camp's twig fire.

There was classical blood in her face. Her parents were famous, apparently, in the world of legal history. I am a man who did not enjoy poetry until I heard a woman recite it to us.

And in that desert she dragged her university days into our midst to describe the stars—the way Adam tenderly taught a woman with gracious metaphors.

> *These then, though unbeheld in deep of night,*
> *Shine not in vain, nor think, though men were none,*
> *That Heav'n would want spectators, God want praise;*
> *Millions of spiritual Creatures walk the Earth*
> *Unseen, both when we wake, and when we sleep:*
> *All these with ceaseless praise his works behold*
> *Both day and night: how often from the steep*
> *Of echoing Hill or Thicket have we heard*
> *Celestial voices to the midnight air,*
> *Sole, or responsive each to other's note*
> *Singing their great Creator . . .*

That night I fell in love with a voice. Only a voice. I wanted to hear nothing more. I got up and walked away.

She was a willow. What would she be like in winter, at my age? I see her still, always, with the eye of Adam. She had been these awkward limbs climbing out of a plane, bending down in our midst to prod at a fire, her elbow up and pointed towards me as she drank from a canteen.

A few months later, she waltzed with me, as we danced as a group in Cairo. Though slightly drunk she wore an unconquerable face. Even now the face I believe that most revealed her was the one she had that time when we were both half drunk, not lovers.

All these years I have been trying to unearth what she was handing me with that look. It seemed to be contempt. So it appeared to me. Now I think she was studying me. She was an innocent, surprised at something in me. I was behaving the way I usually behave in bars, but this time with the wrong company. I am a man who kept the codes of my behaviour separate. I was forgetting she was younger than I.

She was *studying* me. Such a simple thing. And I was watching for one wrong move in her statue-like gaze, something that would give her away.

Give me a map and I'll build you a city. Give me a pencil and I will draw you a room in South Cairo, desert charts on the wall. Always the desert was among us. I could wake and raise my eyes to the map of old settlements along the Mediterranean coast—Gazala, Tobruk, Mersa Matruh—and south of that the hand-painted wadis, and surrounding those the shades of yellowness that we invaded, tried to lose ourselves in. *"My task is to describe briefly the several expeditions which have attacked the Gilf Kebir. Dr. Bermann will later take us back to the desert as it existed thousands of years ago. . . ."*

That is the way Madox spoke to other geographers at Kensington Gore. But you do not find adultery in the minutes of the Geographical Society. Our room never appears in the detailed reports which chartered every knoll and every incident of history.

In the street of imported parrots in Cairo one is hectored by almost articulate birds. The birds bark and whistle in rows, like a plumed avenue. I knew which tribe had travelled which silk or camel road carrying them in their petite palanquins across the deserts. Forty-day journeys, after the birds were caught by slaves or picked like flowers in equatorial gardens and then placed in bamboo cages to enter the river that is trade. They appeared like brides in a mediaeval courtship.

We stood among them. I was showing her a city that was new to her.

Her hand touched me at the wrist.

"If I gave you my life, you would drop it. Wouldn't you?"

I didn't say anything.

V

Katharine

THE FIRST TIME she dreamed of him she woke up beside her husband screaming.

In their bedroom she stared down onto the sheet, mouth open. Her husband put his hand on her back.

"Nightmare. Don't worry."

"Yes."

"Shall I get you some water?"

"Yes."

She wouldn't move. Wouldn't lie back into that zone they had been in.

The dream had taken place in this room—his hand on her neck (she touched it now), his anger towards her that she had sensed the first few times she had met him. No, not anger, a lack of interest, irritation at a married woman being among them. They had been bent over like animals, and he had yoked her neck back so she had been unable to breathe within her arousal.

Her husband brought her the glass on a saucer but she could not lift her arms, they were shaking, loose. He put the glass awkwardly against her mouth so she could gulp the chlorinated water, some coming down her chin, falling to her stomach. When she lay back she hardly had time to think of what she had witnessed, she fell into a quick deep sleep.

That had been the first recognition. She remembered it sometime during the next day, but she was busy then and she refused to nestle with its significance for long, dismissed it; it was an accidental collision on a crowded night, nothing more.

A year later the other, more dangerous, peaceful dreams came. And even within the first one of these she recalled the hands at her neck and waited for the mood of calmness between them to swerve to violence.

Who lays the crumbs of food that tempt you? Towards a person you never considered. A dream. Then later another series of dreams.

He said later it was propinquity. Propinquity in the desert. It does that here, he said. He loved the word—the propinquity of water, the propinquity of two or three bodies in a car driving the Sand Sea for six hours. Her sweating knee beside the gearbox of the truck, the knee swerving, rising with the bumps. In the desert you have time to look everywhere, to theorize on the choreography of all things around you.

When he talked like that she hated him, her eyes remaining polite, her mind wanting to slap him. She always had the desire to slap him, and she realized even that was sexual. For him all relationships fell into patterns. You fell into propinquity or distance. Just as, for him, the histories in Herodotus clarified all societies. He assumed he was experienced in the ways of the world he had essentially left years earlier, struggling ever since to explore a half-invented world of the desert.

At Cairo aerodrome they loaded the equipment into the vehicles, her husband staying on to check the petrol lines of the Moth before the three men left the next morning. Madox went off to one of the embassies to send a wire. And *he* was going into town to get drunk, the usual final evening in

Cairo, first at Madame Badin's Opera Casino, and later to disappear into the streets behind the Pasha Hotel. He would pack before the evening began, which would allow him to just climb into the truck the next morning, hung over.

So he drove her into town, the air humid, the traffic bad and slow because of the hour.

"It's so hot. I need a beer. Do you want one?"

"No, I have to arrange for a lot of things in the next couple of hours. You'll have to excuse me."

"That's all right," she said. "I don't want to interfere."

"I'll have one with you when I come back."

"In three weeks, right?"

"About that."

"I wish I were going too."

He said nothing in answer to that. They crossed the Bulaq Bridge and the traffic got worse. Too many carts, too many pedestrians who owned the streets. He cut south along the Nile towards the Semiramis Hotel, where she was staying, just beyond the barracks.

"You're going to find Zerzura this time, aren't you."

"I'm going to find it this time."

He was like his old self. He hardly looked at her on the drive, even when they were stalled for more than five minutes in one spot.

At the hotel he was excessively polite. When he behaved this way she liked him even less; they all had to pretend this pose was courtesy, graciousness. It reminded her of a dog in clothes. To hell with him. If her husband didn't have to work with him she would prefer not to see him again.

He pulled her pack out of the rear and was about to carry it into the lobby.

"Here, I can take that." Her shirt was damp at the back when she got out of the passenger seat.

The doorman offered to take the pack, but he said, "No, she wants to carry it," and she was angry again at his assumption. The doorman left them. She turned to him and he passed her the bag so she was facing him, both hands awkwardly carrying the heavy case in front of her.

"So. Good-bye. Good luck."

"Yes. I'll look after them all. They'll be safe."

She nodded. She was in shadow, and he, as if unaware of the harsh sunlight, stood in it.

Then he came up to her, closer, and she thought for a moment he was going to embrace her. Instead he put his right arm forward and drew it in a gesture across her bare neck so her skin was touched by the whole length of his damp forearm.

"Good-bye."

He walked back to the truck. She could feel his sweat now, like blood left by a blade which the gesture of his arm seemed to have imitated.

She picks up a cushion and places it onto her lap as a shield against him. "If you make love to me I won't lie about it. If I make love to you I won't lie about it."

She moves the cushion against her heart, as if she would suffocate that part of herself which has broken free.

"What do you hate most?" he asks.

"A lie. And you?"

"Ownership," he says. "When you leave me, forget me."

Her fist swings towards him and hits hard into the bone just below his eye. She dresses and leaves.

Each day he would return home and look at the black bruise in the mirror. He became curious, not so much about the bruise, but about the shape of his face. The long eyebrows he had never really noticed before, the beginning of grey in his sandy hair. He had not looked at himself like this in a mirror for years. That was a long eyebrow.

Nothing can keep him from her.

When he is not in the desert with Madox or with Bermann in the Arab libraries, he meets her in Groppi Park—beside the heavily watered plum gardens. She is happiest here. She is a woman who misses moisture, who has always loved low green hedges and ferns. While for him this much greenery feels like a carnival.

From Groppi Park they arc out into the old city, South Cairo, markets where few Europeans go. In his rooms maps cover the walls. And in spite of his attempts at furnishing there is still a sense of base camp to his quarters.

They lie in each other's arms, the pulse and shadow of the fan on them. All morning he and Bermann have worked in the archaeological museum placing Arabic texts and European histories beside each other in an attempt to recognize echo, coincidence, name changes—back past Herodotus to the *Kitab al Kanuz*, where Zerzura is named after the bathing woman in a desert caravan. And there too the slow blink of a fan's shadow. And here too the intimate exchange and echo of childhood history, of scar, of manner of kiss.

"I don't know what to do. I don't know what to do! How can I be your lover? He will go mad."

A list of wounds.

The various colours of the bruise—bright russet leading to brown. The plate she walked across the room with, flinging its contents aside, and broke across his head, the blood rising up into the straw hair. The fork that entered the back of his shoulder, leaving its bite marks the doctor suspected were caused by a fox.

He would step into an embrace with her, glancing first to see what moveable objects were around. He would meet her with others in public with bruises or a bandaged head and explain about the taxi jerking to a halt so that he had hit the open side window. Or with iodine on his forearm that covered a welt. Madox worried about his becoming suddenly accident-prone. She sneered quietly at the weakness of his explanation. Maybe it's his age, maybe he needs glasses, said her husband, nudging Madox. Maybe it's a woman he met, she said. Look, isn't that a woman's scratch or bite?

It was a scorpion, he said. *Androctonus australis*.

A postcard. Neat handwriting fills the rectangle.

> *Half my days I cannot bear not to touch you.*
> *The rest of the time I feel it doesn't matter*
> *if I ever see you again. It isn't the morality,*
> *it is how much you can bear.*

No date, no name attached.

Sometimes when she is able to spend the night with him they are wakened by the three minarets of the city beginning their prayers before dawn. He walks with her through the indigo markets that lie between South Cairo and her home. The beautiful songs of faith enter the air like arrows, one minaret answering another, as if passing on a rumour of the two of them as they walk through the cold morning air, the smell of charcoal and hemp already making the air profound. Sinners in a holy city.

He sweeps his arm across plates and glasses on a restaurant table so she might look up somewhere else in the city hearing this cause of noise. When he is without her. He, who has never felt alone in the miles of longitude between desert towns. A man in a desert can hold absence in his cupped hands knowing it is something that feeds him more than water. There is a plant he knows of near El Taj, whose heart, if one cuts it out, is replaced with a fluid containing herbal goodness. Every morning one can drink the liquid the amount of a missing heart. The plant continues to flourish for a year before it dies from some lack or other.

He lies in his room surrounded by the pale maps. He is without Katharine. His hunger wishes to burn down all social rules, all courtesy.

Her life with others no longer interests him. He wants only her stalking beauty, her theatre of expressions. He wants the minute and secret reflection between them, the depth of field minimal, their foreignness intimate like two pages of a closed book.

He has been disassembled by her.

And if she has brought him to this, what has he brought her to?

When she is within the wall of her class and he is beside her in larger groups he tells jokes he doesn't laugh at himself. Uncharacteristically manic, he attacks the history of exploration. When he is unhappy he does this. Only Madox recognizes the habit. But she will not even catch his eye. She smiles to everyone, to the objects in the room, praises a flower arrangement, worthless impersonal things. She misinterprets his behaviour, assuming this is what he wants, and doubles the size of the wall to protect herself.

But now he cannot bear this wall in her. You built your walls too, she tells him, so I have my wall. She says it glittering in a beauty he cannot stand. She with her beautiful clothes, with her pale face that laughs at everyone who smiles at her, with the uncertain grin for his angry jokes. He continues his appalling statements about this and that in some expedition they are all familiar with.

The minute she turns away from him in the lobby of Groppi's bar after he greets her, he is insane. He knows the only way he can accept losing her is if he can continue to hold her or be held by her. If they can somehow nurse each other out of this. Not with a wall.

Sunlight pours into his Cairo room. His hand flabby over the Herodotus journal, all the tension in the rest of his body, so he writes words down wrong, the pen sprawling as if without spine. He can hardly write down the word *sunlight*. The words *in love*.

In the apartment there is light only from the river and the desert beyond it. It falls upon her neck her feet the vaccination scar he loves on her right arm. She sits on the bed hugging nakedness. He slides his open palm along the sweat of her shoulder. This is my shoulder, he thinks, not her husband's, this is my shoulder. As lovers they have offered parts of their bodies to each other, like this. In this room on the periphery of the river.

In the few hours they have, the room has darkened to this pitch of light. Just river and desert light. Only when there is the rare shock of rain do they go towards the window and put their arms out, stretching, to bathe as much as they can of themselves in it. Shouts towards the brief downpour fill the streets.

"We will never love each other again. We can never see each other again."

"I know," he says.

The night of her insistence on parting.

She sits, enclosed within herself, in the armour of her terrible conscience. He is unable to reach through it. Only his body is close to her.

"Never again. Whatever happens."

"Yes."

"I think he will go mad. Do you understand?"

He says nothing, abandoning the attempt to pull her within him.

An hour later they walk into a dry night. They can hear the gramophone songs in the distance from the Music for All cinema, its windows open for the heat. They will have to part before that closes up and people she might know emerge from there.

They are in the botanical garden, near the Cathedral of All Saints. She sees one tear and leans forward and licks it, taking it into her mouth. As she has taken the blood from his hand when he cut himself cooking for her. Blood. Tear. He feels everything is missing from his body, feels he contains smoke. All that is alive is the knowledge of future desire and want. What he would say he cannot say to this woman whose openness is like a wound, whose youth is not mortal yet. He cannot alter what he loves most in her, her lack of compromise, where the romance of the poems she loves still sits with ease in the real world. Outside these qualities he knows there is no order in the world.

This night of her insistence. Twenty-eighth of September. The rain in the trees already dried by hot moonlight. Not one cool drop to fall down upon him like a tear. This parting at Groppi Park. He has not asked if her husband is home in that high square of light, across the street.

He sees the tall row of traveller's palms above them, their outstretched wrists. The way her head and hair were above him, when she was his lover.

Now there is no kiss. Just one embrace. He untugs himself

from her and walks away, then turns. She is still there. He comes back within a few yards of her, one finger raised to make a point.

"I just want you to know. I don't miss you yet."

His face awful to her, trying to smile. Her head sweeps away from him and hits the side of the gatepost. He sees it hurt her, notices the wince. But they have separated already into themselves now, the walls up at her insistence. Her jerk, her pain, is accidental, is intentional. Her hand is near her temple.

"You will," she says.

From this point on in our lives, she had whispered to him earlier, we will either find or lose our souls.

How does this happen? To fall in love and be disassembled.

I was in her arms. I had pushed the sleeve of her shirt up to the shoulder so I could see her vaccination scar. I love this, I said. This pale aureole on her arm. I see the instrument scratch and then punch the serum within her and then release itself, free of her skin, years ago, when she was nine years old, in a school gymnasium.

VI

A Buried Plane

He glares out, each eye a path, down the long bed at the end of which is Hana. After she has bathed him she breaks the tip off an ampoule and turns to him with the morphine. An effigy. A bed. He rides the boat of morphine. It races in him, imploding time and geography the way maps compress the world onto a two-dimensional sheet of paper.

The long Cairo evenings. The sea of night sky, hawks in rows until they are released at dusk, arcing towards the last colour of the desert. A unison of performance like a handful of thrown seed.

In that city in 1936 you could buy anything—from a dog or a bird that came at one pitch of a whistle, to those terrible leashes that slipped over the smallest finger of a woman so she was tethered to you in a crowded market.

In the northeast section of Cairo was the great courtyard of religious students, and beyond it the Khan el Khalili bazaar. Above the narrow streets we looked down upon cats on the corrugated tin roofs who also looked down the next ten feet to the street and stalls. Above all this was our room. Windows open to minarets, feluccas, cats, tremendous noise. She spoke to me of her childhood gardens. When she couldn't sleep she drew her mother's garden for me, word by word, bed by bed, the December ice over the fish pond, the creak of rose trellises. She would take my wrist at the confluence of veins and guide it onto the hollow indentation at her neck.

March 1937, Uweinat. Madox is irritable because of the thinness in the air. Fifteen hundred feet above sea level and he is uncomfortable with even this minimal height. He is a desert man after all, having left his family's village of Marston Magna, Somerset, altered all customs and habits so he can have the proximity to sea level as well as regular dryness.

"Madox, what is the name of that hollow at the base of a woman's neck? At the front. *Here*. What is it, does it have an official name? That hollow about the size of an impress of your thumb?"

Madox watches me for a moment through the noon glare.

"Pull yourself together," he mutters.

Let me tell you a story," Caravaggio says to Hana. "There was a Hungarian named Almásy, who worked for the Germans during the war. He flew a bit with the Afrika Korps, but he was more valuable than that. In the 1930s he had been one of the great desert explorers. He knew every water hole and had helped map the Sand Sea. He knew all about the desert. He knew all about dialects. Does this sound familiar? Between the two wars he was always on expeditions out of Cairo. One was to search for Zerzura—the lost oasis. Then when war broke out he joined the Germans. In 1941 he became a guide for spies, taking them across the desert into Cairo. What I want to tell you is, I think the English patient is not English."

"Of course he is, what about all those flower beds in Gloucestershire?"

"Precisely. It's all a perfect background. Two nights ago, when we were trying to name the dog. Remember?"

"Yes."

"What were his suggestions?"

"He was strange that night."

"He was very strange, because I gave him an extra dose of morphine. Do you remember the names? He put out about eight names. Five of them were obvious jokes. Then three names. Cicero. Zerzura. Delilah."

"So?"

" 'Cicero' was a code name for a spy. The British unearthed him. A double then triple agent. He got away. 'Zerzura' is more complicated."

"I know about Zerzura. He's talked about it. He also talks about gardens."

"But it is mostly the desert now. The English garden is wearing thin. He's dying. I think you have the spy-helper Almásy upstairs."

They sit on the old cane hampers of the linen room looking at each other. Caravaggio shrugs. "It's possible."

"I think he is an Englishman," she says, sucking in her cheeks as she always does when she is thinking or considering something about herself.

"I know you love the man, but he's not an Englishman. In the early part of the war I was working in Cairo—the Tripoli Axis. Rommel's Rebecca spy—"

"What do you mean, 'Rebecca spy'?"

"In 1942 the Germans sent a spy called Eppler into Cairo before the battle of El Alamein. He used a copy of Daphne du Maurier's novel *Rebecca* as a code book to send messages back to Rommel on troop movements. Listen, the book became bedside reading with British Intelligence. Even I read it."

"You read a book?"

"Thank you. The man who guided Eppler through the desert into Cairo on Rommel's personal orders—from Tripoli all the way to Cairo—was Count Ladislaus de Almásy. This was a stretch of desert that, it was assumed, no one could cross.

"Between the wars Almásy had English friends. Great explorers. But when war broke out he went with the Germans. Rommel asked him to take Eppler across the desert into Cairo because it would have been too obvious by plane or parachute. He crossed the desert with the guy and delivered him to the Nile delta."

"You know a lot about this."

"I was based in Cairo. We were tracking them. From Gialo he led a company of eight men into the desert. They had to keep digging the trucks out of the sand hills. He aimed them towards Uweinat and its granite plateau so they could get water, take shelter in the caves. It was a halfway point. In the 1930s he had discovered caves with rock paintings there. But the plateau was crawling with Allies and he couldn't use the wells there. He struck out into the sand desert again. They raided British petrol dumps to fill up their tanks. In the Kharga Oasis they switched into British uniforms and hung British army number plates on their vehicles. When they were spotted from the air they hid in the wadis for as long as three days, completely still. Baking to death in the sand.

"It took them three weeks to reach Cairo. Almásy shook hands with Eppler and left him. This is where we lost him. He turned and went back into the desert alone. We think he crossed it again, back towards Tripoli. But that was the last time he was ever seen. The British picked up Eppler eventually and used the Rebecca code to feed false information to Rommel about El Alamein."

"I still don't believe it, David."

"The man who helped catch Eppler in Cairo was named Sansom."

"Delilah."

"Exactly."

"Maybe he's Sansom."

"I thought that at first. He was very like Almásy. A desert lover as well. He had spent his childhood in the Levant and knew the Bedouin. But the thing about Almásy was, he could fly. We are talking about someone who crashed in a plane. Here is this man, burned beyond recognition, who somehow ends up in the arms of the English at Pisa. Also, he can get away with sounding English. Almásy went to school in England. In Cairo he was referred to as the English spy."

She sat on the hamper watching Caravaggio. She said, "I think we should leave him be. It doesn't matter what side he was on, does it?"

Caravaggio said, "I'd like to talk with him some more. With more morphine in him. Talking it out. Both of us. Do you understand? To see where it will all go. Delilah. Zerzura. You will have to give him the altered shot."

"No, David. You're too obsessed. It doesn't matter who he is. The war's over."

"I will then. I'll cook up a Brompton cocktail. Morphine and alcohol. They invented it at Brompton Hospital in London for their cancer patients. Don't worry, it won't kill him. It absorbs fast into the body. I can put it together with what we've got. Give him a drink of it. Then put him back on straight morphine."

She watched him sitting on the hamper, clear-eyed, smiling. During the last stages of the war Caravaggio had become one of the numerous morphia thieves. He had sniffed out her medical supplies within hours of his arrival. The small tubes of morphine were now a source for him. Like toothpaste tubes for dolls, she had thought when she first saw them, finding them utterly quaint. Caravaggio carried two or three in his pocket all day long, slipping the fluid into his flesh. She had stumbled on him once vomiting from its excess, crouched and shaking in one of the dark corners of the villa, looking up and hardly recognizing her. She had tried speaking with him and he had stared back. He had found the metal supply box, torn it open with God knows what strength. Once when the sapper cut open the palm of his hand on an iron gate, Caravaggio broke the glass tip off with his teeth, sucked and spat the morphine onto the brown hand before Kip even knew what it was. Kip pushing him away, glaring in anger.

"Leave him alone. He's my patient."

"I won't damage him. The morphine and alcohol will take away the pain."

(3 cc's BROMPTON COCKTAIL. 3:00 P.M.)

Caravaggio slips the book out of the man's hands.

"When you crashed in the desert—where were you flying from?"

"I was leaving the Gilf Kebir. I had gone there to collect someone. In late August. Nineteen forty-two."

"During the war? Everyone must have left by then."

"Yes. There were just armies."

"The Gilf Kebir."

"Yes."

"Where is it?"

"Give me the Kipling book . . . here."

On the frontispiece of *Kim* was a map with a dotted line for the path the boy and the Holy One took. It showed just a portion of India—a darkly cross-hatched Afghanistan, and Kashmir in the lap of the mountains.

He traces his black hand along the Numi River till it enters the sea at 23°30′ latitude. He continues sliding his finger seven inches west, off the page, onto his chest; he touches his rib.

"Here. The Gilf Kebir, just north of the Tropic of Cancer. On the Egyptian–Libyan border."

What happened in 1942?

I had made the journey to Cairo and was returning from there. I was slipping between the enemy, remembering old maps, hitting the pre-war caches of petrol and water, driving towards Uweinat. It was easier now that I was alone. Miles from the Gilf Kebir, the truck exploded and I capsized, rolling automatically into the sand, not wanting a spark to touch me. In the desert one is always frightened of fire.

The truck exploded, probably sabotaged. There were spies among the Bedouin, whose caravans continued to drift like cities, carrying spice, rooms, government advisors wherever they went. At any given moment among the Bedouin in those days of the war, there were Englishmen as well as Germans.

Leaving the truck, I started walking towards Uweinat, where I knew there was a buried plane.

Wait. What do you mean, a buried plane?

Madox had an old plane in the early days, which he had shaved down to the essentials—the only "extra" was the closed bubble of cockpit, crucial for desert flights. During our times in the desert he had taught me to fly, the two of us walking around the guy-roped creature theorizing on how it hung or veered in the wind.

When Clifton's plane—*Rupert*—flew into our midst, the aging plane of Madox's was left where it was, covered with a tarpaulin, pegged down in one of the northeast alcoves of Uweinat. Sand collected over it gradually for the next few years. None of us thought we would see it again. It was another victim of the desert. Within a few months we would pass the northeast gully and see no contour of it. By now Clifton's plane, ten years younger, had flown into our story.

So you were walking towards it?

Yes. Four nights of walking. I had left the man in Cairo and turned back into the desert. Everywhere there was war. Suddenly there were "teams." The Bermanns, the Bagnolds, the Slatin Pashas—who had at various times saved each other's lives—had now split up into camps.

I walked towards Uweinat. I got there about noon and climbed up into the caves of the plateau. Above the well named Ain Dua.

"Caravaggio thinks he knows who you are," Hana said.

The man in the bed said nothing.

"He says you are not English. He worked with intelligence out of Cairo and Italy for a while. Till he was captured. My family knew Caravaggio before the war. He was a thief. He believed in 'the movement of things.' Some thieves are collectors, like some of the explorers you scorn, like some men with women or some women with men. But Caravaggio was not like that. He was too curious and generous to be a successful thief. Half the things he stole never came home. He thinks you are not English."

She watched his stillness as she spoke; it appeared that he was not listening carefully to what she was saying. Just his distant thinking. The way Duke Ellington looked and thought when he played "Solitude."

She stopped talking.

He reached the shallow well named Ain Dua. He removed all of his clothes and soaked them in the well, put his head and then his thin body into the blue water. His limbs exhausted from the four nights of walking. He left his clothes spread on the rocks and climbed up higher into the boulders, climbed out of the desert, which was now, in 1942, a vast battlefield, and went naked into the darkness of the cave.

He was among the familiar paintings he had found years earlier. Giraffes. Cattle. The man with his arms raised, in a plumed headdress. Several figures in the unmistakable posture of swimmers. Bermann had been right about the presence of an ancient lake. He walked farther into the coldness, into the Cave of Swimmers, where he had left her. She was still there.

She had dragged herself into a corner, had wrapped herself tight in the parachute material. He had promised to return for her.

He himself would have been happier to die in a cave, with its privacy, the swimmers caught in the rock around them. Bermann had told him that in Asian gardens you could look at rock and imagine water, you could gaze at a still pool and believe it had the hardness of rock. But she was a woman who had grown up within gardens, among moistness, with words like *trellis* and *hedgehog*. Her passion for the desert was temporary. She'd come to love its sternness because of him, wanting to understand his comfort in its solitude. She was always happier in rain, in bathrooms steaming with liquid air, in sleepy wetness, climbing back in from his window that rainy night in Cairo and putting on her clothes while still wet, in order to hold it all. Just as she loved family traditions and courteous ceremony and old memorized poems. She would have hated to die without a name. For her there was a line back to her ancestors that was tactile, whereas he had erased the path he had emerged from. He was amazed she had loved him in spite of such qualities of anonymity in himself.

She was on her back, positioned the way the mediaeval dead lie.

I approached her naked as I would have done in our South Cairo room, wanting to undress her, still wanting to love her.

What is terrible in what I did? Don't we forgive everything of a lover? We forgive selfishness, desire, guile. As long as we are the motive for it. You can make love to a woman with a broken arm, or a woman with fever. She once sucked blood from a cut on my hand as I had tasted and swallowed her menstrual blood. There are some European words you can never translate properly into another language. *Felhomaly.* The dusk of graves. With the connotation of intimacy there between the dead and the living.

I lifted her into my arms from the shelf of sleep. Clothing like cobweb. I disturbed all that.

I carried her out into the sun. I dressed. My clothes dry and brittle from the heat in the stones.

My linked hands made a saddle for her to rest on. As soon as I reached the sand I jostled her around so her body was facing back, over my shoulder. I was conscious of the airiness of her weight. I was used to her like this in my arms, she had spun around me in my room like a human reflection of the fan —her arms out, fingers like starfish.

We moved like this towards the northeast gully, where the plane was buried. I did not need a map. With me was the tank of petrol I had carried all the way from the capsized truck. Because three years earlier we had been impotent without it.

"What happened three years earlier?"

"She had been injured. In 1939. Her husband had crashed his plane. It had been planned as a suicide-murder by her husband that would involve all three of us. We were not even lovers at the time. I suppose information of the affair trickled down to him somehow."

"So she was too wounded to take with you."

"Yes. The only chance to save her was for me to try and reach help alone."

In the cave, after all those months of separation and anger, they had come together and spoken once more as lovers, rolling away the boulder they had placed between themselves for some social law neither had believed in.

In the botanical garden she had banged her head against the gatepost in determination and fury. Too proud to be a lover, a secret. There would be no compartments in her world. He had turned back to her, his finger raised, *I don't miss you yet.*

You will.

During their months of separation he had grown bitter and self-sufficient. He avoided her company. He could not stand her calmness when she saw him. He phoned her house and spoke to her husband and heard her laughter in the background. There was a public charm in her that tempted everyone. This was something he had loved in her. Now he began to trust nothing.

He suspected she had replaced him with another lover. He interpreted her every gesture to others as a code of promise. She gripped the front of Roundell's jacket once in a lobby and shook it, laughing at him as he muttered something, and he followed the innocent government aide for two days to see if there was more between them. He did not trust her last endearments to him anymore. She was with him or against him. She was against him. He couldn't stand even her tentative smiles at him. If she passed him a drink he would not drink it. If at a dinner she pointed to a bowl with a Nile lily floating in it he would not look at it. Just another fucking flower. She had a new group of intimates that excluded him and her husband. No one goes back to the husband. He knew that much about love and human nature.

He bought pale brown cigarette papers and glued them into sections of *The Histories* that recorded wars that were of no interest to him. He wrote down all her arguments against him. Glued into the book—giving himself only the voice of the watcher, the listener, the "he."

During the last days before the war he had gone for a last time to the Gilf Kebir to clear out the base camp. Her husband was supposed to pick him up. The husband they had both loved until they began to love each other.

Clifton flew up on Uweinat to collect him on the appointed day, buzzing the lost oasis so low the acacia shrubs dismantled their leaves in the wake of the plane, the Moth slipping into the depressions and cuts—while he stood on the high ridge signalling with blue tarpaulin. Then the plane pivoted down and came straight towards him, then crashed into the earth fifty yards away. A blue line of smoke uncoiling from the undercarriage. There was no fire.

A husband gone mad. Killing all of them. Killing himself and his wife—and him by the fact there was now no way out of the desert.

Only she was not dead. He pulled the body free, carrying it out of the plane's crumpled grip, this grip of her husband.

How did you hate me? she whispers in the Cave of Swimmers, talking through her pain of injuries. A broken wrist. Shattered ribs. You were terrible to me. That's when my husband suspected you. I still hate that about you—disappearing into deserts or bars.

You left *me* in Groppi Park.

Because you didn't want me as anything else.

Because you said your husband was going mad. Well, he went mad.

Not for a long time. I went mad before he did, you killed everything in me. Kiss me, will you. Stop defending yourself. Kiss me and call me by my name.

Their bodies had met in perfumes, in sweat, frantic to get under that thin film with a tongue or a tooth, as if they each could grip character there and during love pull it right off the body of the other.

Now there is no talcum on her arm, no rose water on her thigh.

You think you are an iconoclast, but you're not. You just move, or replace what you cannot have. If you fail at something you retreat into something else. Nothing changes you. How many women did you have? I left you because I knew I could never change you. You would stand in the room so still sometimes, so wordless sometimes, as if the greatest betrayal of yourself would be to reveal one more inch of your character.

In the Cave of Swimmers we talked. We were only two latitudes away from the safety of Kufra.

He pauses and holds out his hand. Caravaggio places a morphine tablet into the black palm, and it disappears into the man's dark mouth.

I crossed the dry bed of the lake towards Kufra Oasis, carrying nothing but robes against the heat and night cold, my Herodotus left behind with her. And three years later, in 1942, I walked with her towards the buried plane, carrying her body as if it was the armour of a knight.

In the desert the tools of survival are underground—troglodyte caves, water sleeping within a buried plant, weapons, a plane. At longitude 25, latitude 23, I dug down towards the tarpaulin, and Madox's old plane gradually emerged. It was night and even in the cold air I was sweating. I carried the naphtha lantern over to her and sat for a while, beside the silhouette of her nod. Two lovers and desert—starlight or moonlight, I don't remember. Everywhere else out there was a war.

The plane came out of the sand. There had been no food and I was weak. The tarp so heavy I couldn't dig it out but had simply to cut it away.

In the morning, after two hours' sleep, I carried her into the cockpit. I started the motor and it rolled into life. We moved and then slipped, years too late, into the sky.

The voice stops. The burned man looks straight ahead in his morphine focus.

The plane is now in his eye. The slow voice carries it with

effort above the earth, the engine missing turns as if losing a stitch, her shroud unfurling in the noisy air of the cockpit, noise terrible after his days of walking in silence. He looks down and sees oil pouring onto his knees. A branch breaks free of her shirt. Acacia and bone. How high is he above the land? How low is he in the sky?

The undercarriage brushes the top of a palm and he pivots up, and the oil slides over the seat, her body slipping down into it. There is a spark from a short, and the twigs at her knee catch fire. He pulls her back into the seat beside him. He thrusts his hands up against the cockpit glass and it will not shift. Begins punching the glass, cracking it, finally breaking it, and the oil and the fire slop and spin everywhere. How low is he in the sky? She collapses—acacia twigs, leaves, the branches that were shaped into arms uncoiling around him. Limbs begin disappearing in the suck of air. The odour of morphine on his tongue. Caravaggio reflected in the black lake of his eye. He goes up and down now like a well bucket. There is blood somehow all over his face. He is flying a rotted plane, the canvas sheetings on the wings ripping open in the speed. They are carrion. How far back had the palm tree been? How long ago? He lifts his legs out of the oil, but they are so heavy. There is no way he can lift them again. He is old. Suddenly. Tired of living without her. He cannot lie back in her arms and trust her to stand guard all day all night while he sleeps. He has no one. He is exhausted not from the desert but from solitude. Madox gone. The woman translated into leaves and twigs, the broken glass to the sky like a jaw above him.

He slips into the harness of the oil-wet parachute and pivots upside down, breaking free of glass, wind flinging his body back. Then his legs are free of everything, and he is in the air, bright, not knowing why he is bright until he realizes he is on fire.

Hana can hear the voices in the English patient's room and stands in the hall trying to catch what they are saying.

How is it?

Wonderful!

Now it's my turn.

Ahh! Splendid, splendid.

This is the greatest of inventions.

A remarkable find, young man.

When she enters she sees Kip and the English patient passing a can of condensed milk back and forth. The Englishman sucks at the can, then moves the tin away from his face to chew the thick fluid. He beams at Kip, who seems irritated that he does not have possession of it. The sapper glances at Hana and hovers by the bedside, snapping his fingers a couple of times, managing finally to pull the tin away from the dark face.

"We have discovered a shared pleasure. The boy and I. For me on my journeys in Egypt, for him in India."

"Have you ever had condensed-milk sandwiches?" the sapper asks.

Hana glances back and forth between the two of them.

Kip peers into the can. "I'll get another one," he says, and leaves the room.

Hana looks at the man in the bed.

"Kip and I are both international bastards—born in one place and choosing to live elsewhere. Fighting to get back to or get away from our homelands all our lives. Though

Kip doesn't recognize that yet. That's why we get on so well together."

In the kitchen Kip stabs two holes into the new can of condensed milk with his bayonet, which, he realizes, is now used more and more for only this purpose, and runs back upstairs to the bedroom.

"You must have been raised elsewhere," the sapper says. "The English don't suck it out that way."

"For some years I lived in the desert. I learned everything I knew there. Everything that ever happened to me that was important happened in the desert."

He smiles at Hana.

"One feeds me morphine. One feeds me condensed milk. We may have discovered a balanced diet!" He turns back to Kip.

"How long have you been a sapper?"

"Five years. Mostly in London. Then Italy. With the unexploded-bomb units."

"Who was your teacher?"

"An Englishman in Woolwich. He was considered eccentric."

"The best kind of teacher. That must have been Lord Suffolk. Did you meet Miss Morden?"

"Yes."

At no point does either of them attempt to make Hana comfortable in their conversation. But she wants to know about his teacher, and how he would describe him.

"What was he like, Kip?"

"He worked in Scientific Research. He was head of an experimental unit. Miss Morden, his secretary, was always with him, and his chauffeur, Mr. Fred Harts. Miss Morden would take notes, which he dictated as he worked on a bomb, while Mr. Harts helped with the instruments. He was a brilliant man. They were called the Holy Trinity. They were blown up, all three of them, in 1941. At Erith."

She looks at the sapper leaning against the wall, one foot up so the sole of his boot is against a painted bush. No expression of sadness, nothing to interpret.

Some men had unwound their last knot of life in her arms. In the town of Anghiari she had lifted live men to discover they were already being consumed by worms. In Ortona she had held cigarettes to the mouth of the boy with no arms. Nothing had stopped her. She had continued her duties while she secretly pulled her personal self back. So many nurses had turned into emotionally disturbed handmaidens of the war, in their yellow-and-crimson uniforms with bone buttons.

She watches Kip lean his head back against the wall and knows the neutral look on his face. She can read it.

VII

In Situ

Kirpal Singh stood where the horse's saddle would have lain across its back. At first he simply stood on the back of the horse, paused and waved to those he could not see but who he knew would be watching. Lord Suffolk watched him through binoculars, saw the young man wave, both arms up and swaying.

Then he descended, down into the giant white chalk horse of Westbury, into the whiteness of the horse, carved into the hill. Now he was a black figure, the background radicalizing the darkness of his skin and his khaki uniform. If the focus on the binoculars was exact, Lord Suffolk would see the thin line of crimson lanyard on Singh's shoulder that signalled his sapper unit. To them it would look like he was striding down a paper map cut out in the shape of an animal. But Singh was conscious only of his boots scuffing the rough white chalk as he moved down the slope.

Miss Morden, behind him, was also coming slowly down the hill, a satchel over her shoulder, aiding herself with a rolled umbrella. She stopped ten feet above the horse, unfurled the umbrella and sat within its shade. Then she opened up her notebooks.

"Can you hear me?" he asked.

"Yes, it's fine." She rubbed the chalk off her hands onto her skirt and adjusted her glasses. She looked up into the distance and, as Singh had done, waved to those she could not see.

Singh liked her. She was in effect the first Englishwoman he had really spoken with since he arrived in England. Most of his time had been spent in a barracks at Woolwich. In his three months there he had met only other Indians and English officers. A woman would reply to a question in the NAAFI canteen, but conversations with women lasted only two or three sentences.

He was the second son. The oldest son would go into the army, the next brother would be a doctor, a brother after that would become a businessman. An old tradition in his family. But all that had changed with the war. He joined a Sikh regiment and was shipped to England. After the first months in London he had volunteered himself into a unit of engineers that had been set up to deal with delayed-action and unexploded bombs. The word from on high in 1939 was naive: *"Unexploded bombs are considered the responsibility of the Home Office, who are agreed that they should be collected by A.R.P. wardens and police and delivered to convenient dumps, where members of the armed forces will in due course detonate them."*

It was not until 1940 that the War Office took over responsibility for bomb disposal, and then, in turn, handed it over to the Royal Engineers. Twenty-five bomb disposal units were set up. They lacked technical equipment and had in their possession only hammers, chisels and road-mending tools. There were no specialists.

A bomb is a combination of the following parts:
  1. A container or bomb case.
  2. A fuze.
  3. An initiating charge, or gaine.
  4. A main charge of high explosive.
  5. Superstructional fittings—fins, lifting lugs, kopfrings, etc.

Eighty percent of bombs dropped by airplanes over Britain were thin-walled, general-purpose bombs. They usually ranged from a hundred pounds to a thousand. A 2,000-pound bomb was called a "Hermann" or an "Esau." A 4,000-pound bomb was called a "Satan."

Singh, after long days of training, would fall asleep with diagrams and charts still in his hands. Half dreaming, he entered the maze of a cylinder alongside the picric acid and the gaine and the condensers until he reached the fuze deep within the main body. Then he was suddenly awake.

When a bomb hit a target, the resistance caused a trembler to activate and ignite the flash pellet in the fuze. The minute explosion would leap into the gaine, causing the penthrite wax to detonate. This set off the picric acid, which in turn caused the main filling of TNT, amatol and aluminized powder, to explode. The journey from trembler to explosion lasted a microsecond.

The most dangerous bombs were those dropped from low altitudes, which were not activated until they had landed. These unexploded bombs buried themselves in cities and fields and remained dormant until their trembler contacts were disturbed—by a farmer's stick, a car wheel's nudge, the bounce of a tennis ball against the casing—and then they would explode.

Singh was moved by lorry with the other volunteers to the research department in Woolwich. This was a time when the casualty rate in bomb disposal units was appallingly high, considering how few unexploded bombs there were. In 1940, after France had fallen and Britain was in a state of siege, it got worse.

By August the blitz had begun, and in one month there were suddenly 2,500 unexploded bombs to be dealt with.

Roads were closed, factories deserted. By September the number of live bombs had reached 3,700. One hundred new bomb squads were set up, but there was still no understanding of how the bombs worked. Life expectancy in these units was ten weeks.

"This was a Heroic Age of bomb disposal, a period of individual prowess, when urgency and a lack of knowledge and equipment led to the taking of fantastic risks. . . . It was, however, a Heroic Age whose protagonists remained obscure, since their actions were kept from the public for reasons of security. It was obviously undesirable to publish reports that might help the enemy to estimate the ability to deal with weapons."

In the car, driving down to Westbury, Singh had sat in front with Mr. Harts while Miss Morden rode in the back with Lord Suffolk. The khaki-painted Humber was famous. The mudguards were painted bright signal red—as all bomb disposal travel units were—and at night there was a blue filter over the left sidelight. Two days earlier a man walking near the famous chalk horse on the Downs had been blown up. When engineers arrived at the site they discovered that another bomb had landed in the middle of the historic location— in the stomach of the giant white horse of Westbury carved into the rolling chalk hills in 1778. Shortly after this event, all the chalk horses on the Downs—there were seven—had camouflage nets pegged down over them, not to protect them so much as stop them being obvious landmarks for bombing raids over England.

From the backseat Lord Suffolk chatted about the migration of robins from the war zones of Europe, the history of bomb disposal, Devon cream. He was introducing the customs of England to the young Sikh as if it was a recently discovered culture. In spite of being Lord Suffolk he lived in Devon, and

until war broke out his passion was the study of *Lorna Doone*
and how authentic the novel was historically and geographi-
cally. Most winters he spent puttering around the villages of
Brandon and Porlock, and he had convinced authorities that
Exmoor was an ideal location for bomb-disposal training.
There were twelve men under his command—made up of
talents from various units, sappers and engineers, and Singh
was one of them. They were based for most of the week at
Richmond Park in London, being briefed on new methods or
working on unexploded bombs while fallow deer drifted
around them. But on weekends they would go down to Exmoor, where they would continue training during the day and
afterwards be driven by Lord Suffolk to the church where
Lorna Doone was shot during her wedding ceremony. "Either
from this window or from that back door . . . shot right down
the aisle—into her shoulder. Splendid shot, actually, though
of course reprehensible. The villain was chased onto the moors
and had his muscles ripped from his body." To Singh it
sounded like a familiar Indian fable.

Lord Suffolk's closest friend in the area was a female aviator
who hated society but loved Lord Suffolk. They went shooting
together. She lived in a small cottage in Countisbury on a cliff
that overlooked the Bristol Channel. Each village they passed
in the Humber had its exotica described by Lord Suffolk.
"This is the very best place to buy blackthorn walking sticks."
As if Singh were thinking of stepping into the Tudor corner
store in his uniform and turban to chat casually with the
owners about canes. Lord Suffolk was the best of the
English, he later told Hana. If there had been no war he would
never have roused himself from Countisbury and his retreat,
called Home Farm, where he mulled along with the wine,
with the flies in the old back laundry, fifty years old, married
but essentially bachelor in character, walking the cliffs each

day to visit his aviator friend. He liked to fix things—old laundry tubs and plumbing generators and cooking spits run by a waterwheel. He had been helping Miss Swift, the aviator, collect information on the habits of badgers.

The drive to the chalk horse at Westbury was therefore busy with anecdote and information. Even in wartime he knew the best place to stop for tea. He swept into Pamela's Tea Room, his arm in a sling from an accident with guncotton, and shepherded in his clan—secretary, chauffeur and sapper —as if they were his children. How Lord Suffolk had persuaded the UXB Committee to allow him to set up his experimental bomb disposal outfit no one was sure, but with his background in inventions he probably had more qualifications than most. He was an autodidact, and he believed his mind could read the motives and spirit behind any invention. He had immediately invented the pocket shirt, which allowed fuzes and gadgets to be stored easily by a working sapper.

They drank tea and waited for scones, discussing the in situ defusing of bombs.

"I trust you, Mr. Singh, you know that, don't you?"

"Yes, sir." Singh adored him. As far as he was concerned, Lord Suffolk was the first real gentleman he had met in England.

"You know I trust you to do as well as I. Miss Morden will be with you to take notes. Mr. Harts will be farther back. If you need more equipment or more strength, blow on the police whistle and he will join you. He doesn't advise but he understands perfectly. If he won't do something it means he disagrees with you, and I'd take his advice. But you have total authority on the site. Here is my pistol. The fuzes are probably more sophisticated now, but you never know, you might be in luck."

Lord Suffolk was alluding to an incident that had made him

famous. He had discovered a method for inhibiting a delayed-action fuze by pulling out his army revolver and firing a bullet through the fuze head, so arresting the movement of the clock body. The method was abandoned when the Germans introduced a new fuze in which the percussion cap and not the clock was uppermost.

Kirpal Singh had been befriended, and he would never forget it. So far, half of his time during the war had taken place in the slipstream of this lord who had never stepped out of England and planned never to step out of Countisbury once the war ended. Singh had arrived in England knowing no one, distanced from his family in the Punjab. He was twenty-one years old. He had met no one but soldiers. So that when he read the notice asking for volunteers with an experimental bomb squad, even though he heard other sappers speak of Lord Suffolk as a madman, he had already decided that in a war you have to take control, and there was a greater chance of choice and life alongside a personality or an individual.

He was the only Indian among the applicants, and Lord Suffolk was late. Fifteen of them were led into a library and asked by the secretary to wait. She remained at the desk, copying out names, while the soldiers joked about the interview and the test. He knew no one. He walked over to a wall and stared at a barometer, was about to touch it but pulled back, just putting his face close to it. *Very Dry* to *Fair* to *Stormy*. He muttered the words to himself with his new English pronunciation. "Wery dry. *Very* dry." He looked back at the others, peered around the room and caught the gaze of the middle-aged secretary. She watched him sternly. An Indian boy. He smiled and walked towards the bookshelves. Again he touched nothing. At one point he put his nose close to a volume called *Raymond, or Life and Death* by Sir Oliver Hodge.

He found another, similar title. *Pierre, or the Ambiguities*. He turned and caught the woman's eyes on him again. He felt as guilty as if he had put the book in his pocket. She had probably never seen a turban before. The English! They expect you to fight for them but won't talk to you. Singh. And the ambiguities.

They met a very hearty Lord Suffolk during lunch, who poured wine for anyone who wanted it, and laughed loudly at every attempt at a joke by the recruits. In the afternoon they were all given a strange exam in which a piece of machinery had to be put back together without any prior information of what it was used for. They were allowed two hours but could leave as soon as the problem was solved. Singh finished the exam quickly and spent the rest of the time inventing other objects that could be made from the various components. He sensed he would be admitted easily if it were not for his race. He had come from a country where mathematics and mechanics were natural traits. Cars were never destroyed. Parts of them were carried across a village and readapted into a sewing machine or water pump. The backseat of a Ford was reupholstered and became a sofa. Most people in his village were more likely to carry a spanner or screwdriver than a pencil. A car's irrelevant parts thus entered a grandfather clock or irrigation pulley or the spinning mechanism of an office chair. Antidotes to mechanized disaster were easily found. One cooled an overheating car engine not with new rubber hoses but by scooping up cow shit and patting it around the condenser. What he saw in England was a surfeit of parts that would keep the continent of India going for two hundred years.

He was one of three applicants selected by Lord Suffolk. This man who had not even spoken to him (and had not laughed with him, simply because he had not joked) walked across the room and put his arm around his shoulder. The severe secretary turned out to be Miss Morden, and she bustled in with a tray that held two large glasses of sherry, handed one to Lord Suffolk and, saying, "I know you don't drink," took the other one for herself and raised her glass to him. "Congratulations, your exam was splendid. Though I was sure you would be chosen, even before you took it."

"Miss Morden is a splendid judge of character. She has a nose for brilliance and character."

"Character, sir?"

"Yes. It is not really necessary, of course, but we *are* going to be working together. We are very much a family here. Even before lunch Miss Morden had selected you."

"I found it quite a strain being unable to wink at you, Mr. Singh."

Lord Suffolk had his arm around Singh again and was walking him to the window.

"I thought, as we do not have to begin till the middle of next week, I'd have some of the unit come down to Home Farm. We can pool our knowledge in Devon and get to know each other. You can drive down with us in the Humber."

So he had won passage, free of the chaotic machinery of the war. He stepped into a family, after a year abroad, as if he were the prodigal returned, offered a chair at the table, embraced with conversations.

It was almost dark when they crossed the border from Somerset into Devon on the coastal road overlooking the Bristol Channel. Mr. Harts turned down the narrow path bordered with heather and rhododendrons, a dark blood colour in this last light. The driveway was three miles long.

Apart from the trinity of Suffolk, Morden and Harts, there were six sappers who made up the unit. They walked the moors around the stone cottage over the weekend. Miss Morden and Lord Suffolk and his wife were joined by the aviatrix for the Saturday-night dinner. Miss Swift told Singh she had always wished to fly overland to India. Removed from his barracks, Singh had no idea of his location. There was a map on a roller high up on the ceiling. Alone one morning he pulled the roller down until it touched the floor. *Countisbury and Area. Mapped by R. Fones. Drawn by desire of Mr. James Halliday.*

"Drawn by desire . . ." He was beginning to love the English.

He is with Hana in the night tent when he tells her about the explosion in Erith. A 250-kilogram bomb erupting as Lord Suffolk attempted to dismantle it. It also killed Mr. Fred Harts and Miss Morden and four sappers Lord Suffolk was training. May 1941. Singh had been with Suffolk's unit for a year. He was working in London that day with Lieutenant Blackler, clearing the Elephant and Castle area of a Satan bomb. They had worked together at defusing the 4,000-pound bomb and were exhausted. He remembered halfway through he looked up and saw a couple of bomb disposal officers pointing in his direction and wondered what that was about. It probably meant they had found another bomb. It was after ten at night and he was dangerously tired. There was another one waiting for him. He turned back to work.

When they had finished with the Satan he decided to save time and walked over to one of the officers, who had at first half turned away as if wanting to leave.

"Yes. Where is it?"

The man took his right hand, and he knew something was wrong. Lieutenant Blackler was behind him and the officer told them what had happened, and Lieutenant Blackler put his hands on Singh's shoulders and gripped him.

He drove to Erith. He had guessed what the officer was hesitating about asking him. He knew the man would not have come there just to tell him of the deaths. They were in a war, after all. It meant there was a second bomb somewhere in the vicinity, probably the same design, and this was the only chance to find out what had gone wrong.

He wanted to do this alone. Lieutenant Blackler would stay in London. They were the last two left of the unit, and it would have been foolish to risk both. If Lord Suffolk had failed, it meant there was something new. He wanted to do this alone, in any case. When two men worked together there had to be a base of logic. You had to share and compromise decisions.

He kept everything back from the surface of his emotions during the night drive. To keep his mind clear, they still had to be alive. Miss Morden drinking one large and stiff whisky before she got to the sherry. In this way she would be able to drink more slowly, appear more ladylike for the rest of the evening. "You don't drink, Mr. Singh, but if you did, you'd do what I do. One full whisky and then you can sip away like a good courtier." This was followed by her lazy, gravelly laugh. She was the only woman he was to meet in his life who carried two silver flasks with her. So she was still drinking, and Lord Suffolk was still nibbling at his Kipling cakes.

The other bomb had fallen half a mile away. Another SC-250kg. It looked like the familiar kind. They had defused hundreds of them, most by rote. This was the way the war progressed. Every six months or so the enemy altered something. You learned the trick, the whim, the little descant, and taught it to the rest of the units. They were at a new stage now.

He took no one with him. He would just have to remember each step. The sergeant who drove him was a man named

Hardy, and he was to remain by the jeep. It was suggested he wait till the next morning, but he knew they would prefer him to do it now. The 250-kilogram SC was too common. If there was an alteration they had to know quickly. He made them telephone ahead for lights. He didn't mind working tired, but he wanted proper lights, not just the beams of two jeeps.

When he arrived in Erith the bomb zone was already lit. In daylight, on an innocent day, it would have been a field. Hedges, perhaps a pond. Now it was an arena. Cold, he borrowed Hardy's sweater and put it on top of his. The lights would keep him warm, anyway. When he walked over to the bomb they were still alive in his mind. Exam.

With the bright light, the porousness of the metal jumped into precise focus. Now he forgot everything except distrust. Lord Suffolk had said you can have a brilliant chess player at seventeen, even thirteen, who might beat a grand master. But you can never have a brilliant bridge player at that age. Bridge depends on character. Your character and the character of your opponents. You must consider the character of your enemy. This is true of bomb disposal. It is two-handed bridge. You have one enemy. You have no partner. Sometimes for my exam I make them play bridge. People think a bomb is a mechanical object, a mechanical enemy. But you have to consider that somebody made it.

The wall of the bomb had been torn open in its fall to earth, and Singh could see the explosive material inside. He felt he was being watched, and refused to decide whether it was by Suffolk or the inventor of this contraption. The freshness of the artificial light had revived him. He walked around the bomb, peering at it from every angle. To remove the fuze, he would have to open the main chamber and get past the explosive. He unbuttoned his satchel and, with a universal key, carefully twisted off the plate at the back of the bomb case. Looking inside he saw that the fuze pocket had been knocked free of the case. This was good luck—or bad luck; he couldn't tell yet. The problem was that he didn't know if the mechanism was already at work, if it had already been triggered. He was on his knees, leaning over it, glad he was alone, back in the world of straightforward choice. Turn left or turn right. Cut this or cut that. But he was tired, and there was still anger in him.

He didn't know how long he had. There was more danger in waiting too long. Holding the nose of the cylinder firm with his boots, he reached in and ripped out the fuze pocket, and lifted it away from the bomb. As soon as he did this he began to shake. He had got it out. The bomb was essentially harmless now. He put the fuze with its tangled fringe of wires down on the grass; they were clear and brilliant in this light.

He started to drag the main case towards the truck, fifty yards away, where the men could empty it of the raw explosive. As he pulled it along, a third bomb exploded a quarter of a mile away and the sky lit up, making even the arc lights seem subtle and human.

An officer gave him a mug of Horlicks, which had some kind of alcohol in it, and he returned alone to the fuze pocket. He inhaled the fumes from the drink.

There was no longer serious danger. If he were wrong, the small explosion would take off his hand. But unless it was clutched to his heart at the moment of impact he wouldn't die. The problem was now simply the problem. The fuze. The new "joke" in the bomb.

He would have to reestablish the maze of wires into its original pattern. He walked back to the officer and asked him for the rest of the Thermos of the hot drink. Then he returned and sat down again with the fuze. It was about one-thirty in the morning. He guessed, he wasn't wearing a watch. For half an hour he just looked at it with a magnified circle of glass, a sort of monocle that hung off his buttonhole. He bent over and peered at the brass for any hint of other scratches that a clamp might have made. Nothing.

Later he would need distractions. Later, when there was a whole personal history of events and moments in his mind, he would need something equivalent to white sound to burn or bury everything while he thought of the problems in front of him. The radio or crystal set and its loud band music would come later, a tarpaulin to hold the rain of real life away from him.

But now he was aware of something in the far distance, like some reflection of lightning on a cloud. Harts and Morden and Suffolk were dead, suddenly just names. His eyes focused back onto the fuze box.

He began to turn the fuze upside down in his mind, considering the logical possibilities. Then turned it horizontal again. He unscrewed the gaine, bending over, his ear next to it so the scrape of brass was against him. No little clicks. It came apart in silence. Tenderly he separated the clockwork sections from the fuze and set them down. He picked up the fuze-pocket tube and peered down into it again. He saw nothing. He was about to lay it on the grass when he hesitated and brought it back up to the light. He wouldn't have noticed anything wrong except for the weight. And he would never have thought about the weight if he wasn't looking for the joke. All they did, usually, was listen or look. He tilted the tube carefully, and the weight slipped down toward the opening. It was a second gaine—a whole separate device—to foil any attempt at defusing.

He eased the device out towards him and unscrewed the gaine. There was a white-green flash and the sound of a whip from the device. The second detonator had gone off. He pulled it out and set it beside the other parts on the grass. He went back to the jeep.

"There was a second gaine," he muttered. "I was very lucky, being able to pull out those wires. Put a call in to headquarters and find out if there are other bombs."

He cleared the soldiers away from the jeep, set up a loose bench there and asked for the arc lights to be trained on it. He bent down and picked up the three components and placed them each a foot apart along the makeshift bench. He was cold now, and he breathed out a feather of his warmer body air. He looked up. In the distance some soldiers were still emptying out the main explosive. Quickly he wrote down a few notes and handed the solution for the new bomb to an officer. He didn't fully understand it, of course, but they would have this information.

When sunlight enters a room where there is a fire, the fire will go out. He had loved Lord Suffolk and his strange bits of information. But his absence here, in the sense that everything now depended on Singh, meant Singh's awareness swelled to all bombs of this variety across the city of London. He had suddenly a map of responsibility, something, he realized, that Lord Suffolk carried within his character at all times. It was this awareness that later created the need in him to block so much out when he was working on a bomb. He was one of those never interested in the choreography of power. He felt uncomfortable in the ferrying back and forth of plans and solutions. He felt capable only of reconnaissance, of locating a solution. When the reality of the death of Lord Suffolk came to him, he concluded the work he was assigned to and reenlisted into the anonymous machine of the army. He was on the troopship *Macdonald,* which carried a hundred other sappers towards the Italian campaign. Here they were used not just for bombs but for building bridges, clearing debris, setting up tracks for armoured rail vehicles. He hid there for the rest of the war. Few remembered the Sikh who had been with Suffolk's unit. In a year the whole unit was disbanded and forgotten, Lieutenant Blackler being the only one to rise in the ranks with his talent.

But that night as Singh drove past Lewisham and Blackheath towards Erith, he knew he contained, more than any other sapper, the knowledge of Lord Suffolk. He was expected to be the replacing vision.

He was still standing at the truck when he heard the whistle that meant they were turning off the arc lights. Within thirty seconds metallic light had been replaced with sulphur flares in the back of the truck. Another bomb raid. These lesser lights could be doused when they heard the planes. He sat down on the empty petrol can facing the three components he had removed from the SC-250kg, the hisses from the flares around him loud after the silence of the arc lights.

He sat watching and listening, waiting for them to click. The other men silent, fifty yards away. He knew he was for now a king, a puppet master, could order anything, a bucket of sand, a fruit pie for his needs, and those men who would not cross an uncrowded bar to speak with him when they were off duty would do what he desired. It was strange to him. As if he had been handed a large suit of clothes that he could roll around in and whose sleeves would drag behind him. But he knew he did not like it. He was accustomed to his invisibility. In England he was ignored in the various barracks, and he came to prefer that. The self-sufficiency and privacy Hana saw in him later were caused not just by his being a sapper in the Italian campaign. It was as much a result of being the anonymous member of another race, a part of the invisible world. He had built up defences of character against all that, trusting only those who befriended him. But that night in Erith he knew he was capable of having wires attached to him that influenced all around him who did not have his specific talent.

A few months later he had escaped to Italy, had packed the shadow of his teacher into a knapsack, the way he had seen the green-clothed boy at the Hippodrome do it on his first leave during Christmas. Lord Suffolk and Miss Morden had offered to take him to an English play. He had selected *Peter Pan,* and they, wordless, acquiesced and went with him to a screaming child-full show. There were such shadows of memory with him when he lay in his tent with Hana in the small hill town in Italy.

Revealing his past or qualities of his character would have been too loud a gesture. Just as he could never turn and inquire of her what deepest motive caused this relationship. He held her with the same strength of love he felt for those three strange English people, eating at the same table with them, who had watched his delight and laughter and wonder when the green boy raised his arms and flew into the darkness high above the stage, returning to teach the young girl in the earth-bound family such wonders too.

In the flare-lit darkness of Erith he would stop whenever planes were heard, and one by one the sulphur torches were sunk into buckets of sand. He would sit in the droning darkness, moving the seat so he could lean forward and place his ear close to the ticking mechanisms, still timing the clicks, trying to hear them under the throb of the German bombers above him.

Then what he had been waiting for happened. After exactly one hour, the timer tripped and the percussion cap exploded. Removing the main gaine had released an unseen striker that activated the second, hidden gaine. It had been set to explode sixty minutes later—long after a sapper would normally have assumed the bomb was safely defused.

This new device would change the whole direction of Allied bomb disposal. From now on, every delayed-action bomb would carry the threat of a second gaine. It would no longer be possible for sappers to deactivate a bomb by simply removing the fuze. Bombs would have to be neutralized with the fuze intact. Somehow, earlier on, surrounded by arc lights, and in his fury, he had withdrawn the sheared second fuze out of the booby trap. In the sulphureous darkness under the bombing raid he witnessed the white-green flash the size of his hand. One hour late. He had survived only with luck. He walked back to the officer and said, "I need another fuze to make sure."

They lit the flares around him again. Once more light poured into his circle of darkness. He kept testing the new fuzes for two more hours that night. The sixty-minute delay proved to be consistent.

He was in Erith most of that night. In the morning he woke up to find himself back in London. He could not remember being driven back. He woke up, went to a table and began to sketch the profile of the bomb, the gaines, the detonators, the whole ZUS-40 problem, from the fuze up to the locking rings. Then he covered the basic drawing with all the possible lines of attack to defuse it. Every arrow drawn exactly, the text written out clear the way he had been taught.

What he had discovered the night before held true. He had survived only through luck. There was no possible way to defuse such a bomb in situ without just blowing it up. He drew and wrote out everything he knew on the large blueprint sheet. At the bottom he wrote: *Drawn by desire of Lord Suffolk, by his student Lieutenant Kirpal Singh, 10 May 1941.*

He worked flat-out, crazily, after Suffolk's death. Bombs were altering fast, with new techniques and devices. He was barracked in Regent's Park with Lieutenant Blackler and three other specialists, working on solutions, blueprinting each new bomb as it came in.

In twelve days, working at the Directorate of Scientific Research, they came up with the answer. Ignore the fuze entirely. Ignore the first principle, which until then was "defuse the bomb." It was brilliant. They were all laughing and applauding and hugging each other in the officers' mess. They didn't have a clue what the alternative was, but they knew in the abstract they were right. The problem would not be solved by embracing it. That was Lieutenant Blackler's line. "If you are in a room with a problem don't talk to it." An offhand remark. Singh came towards him and held the statement from another angle. "Then we don't touch the fuze at all."

Once they came up with that, someone worked out the solution in a week. A steam sterilizer. One could cut a hole into the main case of a bomb, and then the main explosive could be emulsified by an injection of steam and drained away. That solved that for the time being. But by then he was on a ship to Italy.

"There is always yellow chalk scribbled on the side of bombs. Have you noticed that? Just as there was yellow chalk scribbled onto our bodies when we lined up in the Lahore courtyard.

"There was a line of us shuffling forward slowly from the street into the medical building and out into the courtyard as we enlisted. We were signing up. A doctor cleared or rejected our bodies with his instruments, explored our necks with his hands. The tongs slid out of Dettol and picked up parts of our skin.

"Those accepted filled up the courtyard. The coded results written onto our skin with yellow chalk. Later, in the lineup, after a brief interview, an Indian officer chalked more yellow onto the slates tied around our necks. Our weight, age, district, standard of education, dental condition and what unit we were best suited for.

"I did not feel insulted by this. I am sure my brother would have been, would have walked in fury over to the well, hauled up the bucket, and washed the chalk markings away. I was not like him. Though I loved him. Admired him. I had this side to my nature which saw reason in all things. I was the one who had an earnest and serious air at school, which he would imitate and mock. You understand, of course, I was far less serious than he was, it was just that I hated confrontation. It didn't stop me doing whatever I wished or doing things the way I wanted to. Quite early on I had discovered the over-looked space open to those of us with a silent life. I didn't argue with the policeman who said I couldn't cycle over a certain bridge or through a specific gate in the fort—I just stood there, still, until I was invisible, and then I went through. Like a cricket. Like a hidden cup of water. You understand? That is what my brother's public battles taught me.

"But to me my brother was always the hero in the family. I was in the slipstream of his status as firebrand. I witnessed his exhaustion that came after each protest, his body gearing up to respond to this insult or that law. He broke the tradition of our family and refused, in spite of being the oldest brother, to join the army. He refused to agree to any situation where the English had power. So they dragged him into their jails.

In the Lahore Central Prison. Later the Jatnagar jail. Lying back on his cot at night, his arm raised within plaster, broken by his friends to protect him, to stop him trying to escape. In jail he became serene and devious. More like me. He was not insulted when he heard I had signed up to replace him in the enlistment, no longer to be a doctor, he just laughed and sent a message through our father for me to be careful. He would never go to war against me or what I did. He was confident that I had the trick of survival, of being able to hide in silent places."

He is sitting on the counter in the kitchen talking with Hana. Caravaggio breezes through it on his way out, heavy ropes swathed over his shoulders, which are his own personal business, as he says when anyone asks him. He drags them behind him and as he goes out the door says, "The English patient wants to see you, boyo."

"Okay, boyo." The sapper hops off the counter, his Indian accent slipping over into the false Welsh of Caravaggio.

"My father had a bird, a small swift I think, that he kept beside him, as essential to his comfort as a pair of spectacles or a glass of water during a meal. In the house, even if he just was entering his bedroom he carried it with him. When he went to work the small cage hung off the bicycle's handlebars."

"Is your father still alive?"

"Oh, yes. I think. I've not had letters for some time. And it is likely that my brother is still in jail."

He keeps remembering one thing. He is in the white horse. He feels hot on the chalk hill, the white dust of it swirling up all around him. He works on the contraption, which is quite straightforward, but for the first time he is working alone. Miss Morden sits twenty yards above him, higher up the slope, taking notes on what he is doing. He knows that down and across the valley Lord Suffolk is watching through the glasses.

He works slowly. The chalk dust lifts, then settles on everything, his hands, the contraption, so he has to blow it off the fuze caps and wires continually to see the details. It is hot in the tunic. He keeps putting his sweating wrists behind himself to wipe them on the back of his shirt. All the loose and removed parts fill the various pockets across his chest. He is tired, checking things repetitively. He hears Miss Morden's voice. "Kip?" "Yes." "Stop what you're doing for a while, I'm coming down." "You'd better not, Miss Morden." "Of course I can." He does up the buttons on his various vest pockets and lays a cloth over the bomb; she clambers down into the white horse awkwardly and then sits next to him and opens up her satchel. She douses a lace handkerchief with the contents of a small bottle of eau de cologne and passes it to him. "Wipe your face with this. Lord Suffolk uses it to refresh himself." He takes it tentatively and at her suggestion dabs his forehead and neck and wrists. She unscrews the Thermos and pours each of them some tea. She unwraps oil paper and brings out strips of Kipling cake.

She seems to be in no hurry to go back up the slope, back to safety. And it would seem rude to remind her that she should return. She simply talks about the wretched heat and the fact that at least they have booked rooms in town with baths attached, which they can all look forward to. She begins a rambling story about how she met Lord Suffolk. Not a word about the bomb beside them. He had been slowing down, the way one, half asleep, continually rereads the same paragraph, trying to find a connection between sentences. She has pulled him out of the vortex of the problem. She packs up her satchel carefully, lays a hand on his right shoulder and returns to her position on the blanket above the Westbury horse. She leaves him some sunglasses, but he cannot see clearly enough through them so he lays them aside. Then he goes back to work. The scent of eau de cologne. He remembers he had smelled it once as a child. He had a fever and someone had brushed it onto his body.

VIII

The Holy Forest

KIP WALKS OUT of the field where he has been digging, his left hand raised in front of him as if he has sprained it.

He passes the scarecrow for Hana's garden, the crucifix with its hanging sardine cans, and moves uphill towards the villa. He cups the hand held in front of him with the other as if protecting the flame of a candle. Hana meets him on the terrace, and he takes her hand and holds it against his. The ladybird circling the nail on his small finger quickly crosses over onto her wrist.

She turns back into the house. Now her hand is held out in front of her. She walks through the kitchen and up the stairs.

The patient turns to face her as she comes in. She touches his foot with the hand that holds the ladybird. It leaves her, moving onto the dark skin. Avoiding the sea of white sheet, it begins to make the long trek towards the distance of the rest of his body, a bright redness against what seems like volcanic flesh.

In the library the fuze box is in midair, nudged off the counter by Caravaggio when he turned to Hana's gleeful yell in the hall. Before it reaches the floor Kip's body slides underneath it, and he catches it in his hand.

Caravaggio glances down to see the young man's face blowing out all the air quickly through his cheeks.

He thinks suddenly he owes him a life.

Kip begins to laugh, losing his shyness in front of the older man, holding up the box of wires.

Caravaggio will remember the slide. He could walk away, never see him again, and he would never forget him. Years from now on a Toronto street Caravaggio will get out of a taxi and hold the door open for an East Indian who is about to get into it, and he will think of Kip then.

Now the sapper just laughs up towards Caravaggio's face and up past that towards the ceiling.

"I know all about sarongs." Caravaggio waved his hand towards Kip and Hana as he spoke. "In the east end of Toronto I met these Indians. I was robbing a house and it turned out to belong to an Indian family. They woke from their beds and they were wearing these cloths, sarongs, to sleep in, and it intrigued me. We had lots to talk about and they eventually persuaded me to try it. I removed my clothes and stepped into one, and they immediately set upon me and chased me half naked into the night."

"Is that a true story?" She grinned.

"One of many!"

She knew enough about him to almost believe it. Caravaggio was constantly diverted by the human element during burglaries. Breaking into a house during Christmas, he would become annoyed if he noticed the Advent calendar had not been opened up to the date to which it should have been. He often had conversations with the various pets left alone in houses, rhetorically discussing meals with them, feeding them large helpings, and was often greeted by them with considerable pleasure if he returned to the scene of a crime.

She walks in front of the shelves in the library, eyes closed, and at random pulls out a book. She finds a clearing between two sections in a book of poetry and begins to write there.

He says Lahore is an ancient city. London is a recent town compared with Lahore. I say, Well, I come from an even newer country. He says they have always known about gunpowder. As far back as the seventeenth century, court paintings recorded fireworks displays.

He is small, not much taller than I am. An intimate smile up close that can charm anything when he displays it. A toughness to his nature he doesn't show. The Englishman says he's one of those warrior saints. But he has a peculiar sense of humour that is more rambunctious than his manner suggests. Remember "I'll rewire him in the morning." Ooh la la!

He says Lahore has thirteen gates—named for saints and emperors or where they lead to.

The word bungalow *comes from Bengali.*

At four in the afternoon they had lowered Kip into the pit in a harness until he was waist-deep in the muddy water, his body draped around the body of the Esau bomb. The casing from fin to tip ten feet high, its nose sunk into the mud by his feet. Beneath the brown water his thighs braced the metal casing, much the way he had seen soldiers holding women in the corner of NAAFI dance floors. When his arms tired he hung them upon the wooden struts at shoulder level, which were there to stop mud collapsing in around him. The sappers had dug the pit around the Esau and set up the wood-shaft walls before he had arrived on the site. In 1941, Esau bombs with a new Y fuze had started coming in; this was his second one.

It was decided during planning sessions that the only way around the new fuze was to immunize it. It was a huge bomb in ostrich posture. He had come down barefoot and he was already sinking slowly, being caught within the clay, unable to get a firm hold down there in the cold water. He wasn't wearing boots—they would have locked within the clay, and when he was pulleyed up later the jerk out of it could break his ankles.

He laid his left cheek against the metal casing, trying to think himself into warmth, concentrating on the small touch of sun that reached down into the twenty-foot pit and fell on the back of his neck. What he embraced could explode at any moment, whenever tumblers tremored, whenever the gaine was fired. There was no magic or X ray that would tell anyone when some small capsule broke, when some wire would stop wavering. Those small mechanical semaphores were like a heart murmur or a stroke within the man crossing the street innocently in front of you.

What town was he in? He couldn't even remember. He heard a voice and looked up. Hardy passed the equipment down in a satchel at the end of a rope, and it hung there while Kip began to insert the various clips and tools into the many pockets of his tunic. He was humming the song Hardy had been singing in the jeep on the way to the site—

> They're changing guard at Buckingham Palace—
> Christopher Robin went down with Alice.

He wiped the area of fuze head dry and began moulding a clay cup around it. Then he unstopped the jar and poured the liquid oxygen into the cup. He taped the cup securely onto the metal. Now he had to wait again.

There was so little space between him and the bomb he could feel the change in temperature already. If he were on dry land he could walk away and be back in ten minutes. Now he had to stand there beside the bomb. They were two suspicious creatures in an enclosed space. Captain Carlyle had been working in a shaft with frozen oxygen and the whole pit had suddenly burst into flames. They hauled him out fast, already unconscious in his harness.

Where was he? Lisson Grove? Old Kent Road?

Kip dipped cotton wool into the muddy water and touched it to the casing about twelve inches away from the fuze. It fell away, so it meant he had to wait longer. When the cotton wool stuck, it meant enough of the area around the fuze was frozen and he could go on. He poured more oxygen into the cup.

The growing circle of frost was a foot in radius now. A few more minutes. He looked at the clipping someone had taped onto the bomb. They had read it with much laughter that morning in the update kit sent to all bomb disposal units.

When is explosion reasonably permissible?

If a man's life could be capitalized as X, the risk at Y, and the estimated damage from explosion at V, then a logician might contend that if V is less than X over Y, the bomb should be blown up; but if V over Y is greater than X, an attempt should be made to avoid explosion in situ.

Who wrote such things?

He had by now been in the shaft with the bomb for more than an hour. He continued feeding in the liquid oxygen. At shoulder height, just to his right, was a hose pumping down normal air to prevent him from becoming giddy with oxygen. (He had seen soldiers with hangovers use the oxygen to cure headaches.) He tried the cotton wool again and this time it froze on. He had about twenty minutes. After that the battery temperature within the bomb would rise again. But for now the fuze was iced up and he could begin to remove it.

He ran his palms up and down the bomb case to detect any rips in the metal. The submerged section would be safe, but oxygen could ignite if it came into contact with exposed explosive. Carlyle's flaw. X over Y. If there were rips they would have to use liquid nitrogen.

"It's a two-thousand-pound bomb, sir. Esau." Hardy's voice from the top of the mud pit.

"Type-marked fifty, in a circle, B. Two fuze pockets, most likely. But we think the second one is probably not armed. Okay?"

They had discussed all this with each other before, but things were being confirmed, remembered for the final time.

"Put me on a microphone now and get back."

"Okay, sir."

Kip smiled. He was ten years younger than Hardy, and no Englishman, but Hardy was happiest in the cocoon of regimental discipline. There was always hesitation by the soldiers to call him "sir," but Hardy barked it out loud and enthusiastically.

He was working fast now to prise out the fuze, all the batteries inert.

"Can you hear me? Whistle. . . . Okay, I heard it. A last topping up with oxygen. Will let it bubble for thirty seconds. Then start. Freshen the frost. Okay, I'm going to remove the *dam*. . . . Okay, *dam* gone."

Hardy was listening to everything and recording it in case something went wrong. One spark and Kip would be in a shaft of flames. Or there could be a joker in the bomb. The next person would have to consider the alternatives.

"I'm using the quilter key." He had pulled it out of his breast pocket. It was cold and he had to rub it warm. He began to remove the locking ring. It moved easily and he told Hardy.

"They're changing guard at Buckingham Palace," Kip whistled. He pulled off the locking ring and the locating ring and let them sink into the water. He could feel them roll slowly at his feet. It would all take another four minutes.

"Alice is marrying one of the guard. 'A soldier's life is terrible hard,' says Alice!"

He was singing it out loud, trying to get more warmth into his body, his chest painfully cold. He kept trying to lean back far enough away from the frozen metal in front of him. And he had to keep moving his hands up to the back of his neck, where the sun still was, then rub them to free them of the muck and grease and frost. It was difficult to get the collet to grip the head. Then to his horror the fuze head broke away, came off completely.

"Wrong, Hardy. Whole fuze head snapped off. Talk back to me, okay? The main body of the fuze is jammed down there, I can't get to it. There's nothing exposed I can grip."

"Where is the frost at?" Hardy was right above him. It had been a few seconds but he had raced to the shaft.

"Six more minutes of frost."

"Come up and we'll blow it up."

"No, pass me down some more oxygen."

He raised his right hand and felt an icy canister being placed in it.

"I'm going to dribble the muck onto the area of exposed fuze —where the head separated—then I'll cut into the metal. Chip through till I can grip something. Get back now, I'll talk it through."

He could hardly keep his fury back at what had happened. The muck, which was their name for oxygen, was going all over his clothes, hissing as it hit the water. He waited for the frost to appear and then began to shear metal off with a chisel. He poured more on, waited and chiselled deeper. When nothing came off he ripped free a bit of his shirt, placed it between the metal and the chisel, and then banged the chisel dangerously with a mallet, chipping off fragments. The cloth of his shirt his only safety against a spark. What was more of a problem was the coldness on his fingers. They were no longer agile, they were inert as the batteries. He kept cutting sideways into the metal around the lost fuze head. Shaving it off in layers, hoping the freezing would accept this kind of surgery. If he cut down directly there was always a chance he would hit the percussion cap that flashed the gaine.

It took five more minutes. Hardy had not moved from the top of the pit, instead was giving him the approximate time left in the freezing. But in truth neither of them could be sure. Since the fuze head had broken off, they were freezing a different area, and the water temperature though cold to him was warmer than the metal.

Then he saw something. He did not dare chip the hole any bigger. The contact of the circuit quivering like a silver tendril. If he could reach it. He tried to rub warmth into his hands.

He breathed out, was still for a few seconds, and with the needle pliers cut the contact in two before he breathed in again. He gasped as the freeze burned part of his hand when he pulled it back out of the circuits. The bomb was dead.

"Fuze out. Gaine off. Kiss me." Hardy was already rolling up the winch and Kip was trying to clip on the halter; he could hardly do it with the burn and the cold, all his muscles cold. He heard the pulley jerk and just held tight onto the leather straps still half attached around him. He began to feel his brown legs being pulled from the grip of the mud, removed like an ancient corpse out of a bog. His small feet rising out of the water. He emerged, lifted out of the pit into the sunlight, head and then torso.

He hung there, a slow swivel under the tepee of poles that held the pulley. Hardy was now embracing him and unbuckling him simultaneously, letting him free. Suddenly he saw there was a large crowd watching from about twenty yards away, too close, far too close, for safety; they would have been destroyed. But of course Hardy had not been there to keep them back.

They watched him silently, the Indian, hanging onto Hardy's shoulder, scarcely able to walk back to the jeep with all the equipment—tools and canisters and blankets and the recording instruments still wheeling around, listening to the nothingness down in the shaft.

"I can't walk."

"Only to the jeep. A few yards more, sir. I'll pick up the rest."

They kept pausing, then walking on slowly. They had to go past the staring faces who were watching the slight brown man, shoeless, in the wet tunic, watching the drawn face that didn't recognize or acknowledge anything, any of them. All of them silent. Just stepping back to give him and Hardy room. At the jeep he started shaking. His eyes couldn't stand the glare off the windshield. Hardy had to lift him, in stages, into the passenger seat.

When Hardy left, Kip slowly pulled off his wet trousers and wrapped himself in the blanket. Then he sat there. Too cold and tired even to unscrew the Thermos of hot tea on the seat beside him. He thought: I wasn't even frightened down there. I was just angry—with my mistake, or the possibility that there was a joker. An animal reacting just to protect myself.

Only Hardy, he realized, keeps me human now.

When there is a hot day at the Villa San Girolamo they all wash their hair, first with kerosene to remove the possibility of lice, and then with water. Lying back, his hair spread out, eyes closed against the sun, Kip seems suddenly vulnerable. There is a shyness within him when he assumes this fragile posture, looking more like a corpse from a myth than anything living or human. Hana sits beside him, her dark brown hair already dry. These are the times he will talk about his family and his brother in jail.

He will sit up and flip his hair forward, and begin to rub the length of it with a towel. She imagines all of Asia through the gestures of this one man. The way he lazily moves, his quiet civilisation. He speaks of warrior saints and she now feels he is one, stern and visionary, pausing only in these rare times of sunlight to be godless, informal, his head back again on the table so the sun can dry his spread hair like grain in a fan-shaped straw basket. Although he is a man from Asia who has in these last years of war assumed English fathers, following their codes like a dutiful son.

"Ah, but my brother thinks me a fool for trusting the English." He turns to her, sunlight in his eyes. "One day, he says, I will open my eyes. Asia is still not a free continent, and he is appalled at how we throw ourselves into English wars. It is a battle of opinion we have always had. 'One day you will open your eyes,' my brother keeps saying."

The sapper says this, his eyes closed tight, mocking the metaphor. "Japan is a part of Asia, I say, and the Sikhs have been brutalized by the Japanese in Malaya. But my brother ignores that. He says the English are now hanging Sikhs who are fighting for independence."

She turns away from him, her arms folded. The feuds of the world. The feuds of the world. She walks into the daylight darkness of the villa and goes in to sit with the Englishman.

At night, when she lets his hair free, he is once more another constellation, the arms of a thousand equators against his pillow, waves of it between them in their embrace and in their turns of sleep. She holds an Indian goddess in her arms, she holds wheat and ribbons. As he bends over her it pours. She can tie it against her wrist. As he moves she keeps her eyes open to witness the gnats of electricity in his hair in the darkness of the tent.

He moves always in relation to things, beside walls, raised terrace hedges. He scans the periphery. When he looks at Hana he sees a fragment of her lean cheek in relation to the landscape behind it. The way he watches the arc of a linnet in terms of the space it gathers away from the surface of the earth. He has walked up Italy with eyes that tried to see everything except what was temporary and human.

The one thing he will never consider is himself. Not his twilit shadow or his arm reaching for the back of a chair or the reflection of himself in a window or how they watch him. In the years of war he has learned that the only thing safe is himself.

He spends hours with the Englishman, who reminds him of a fir tree he saw in England, its one sick branch, too weighted down with age, held up by a crutch made out of another tree. It stood in Lord Suffolk's garden on the edge of the cliff, overlooking the Bristol Channel like a sentinel. In spite of such infirmity he sensed the creature within it was noble, with a memory whose power rainbowed beyond ailment.

He himself has no mirrors He wraps his turban outside in his garden, looking about at the moss on trees. But he notices the swath scissors have made in Hana's hair. He is familiar with her breath when he places his face against her body, at the clavicle, where the bone lightens her skin. But if she asked him what colour her eyes are, although he has come to adore her, he will not, she thinks, be able to say. He will laugh and guess, but if she, black-eyed, says with her eyes shut that they are green, he will believe her. He may look intently at eyes but not register what colour they are, the way food already in his throat or stomach is just texture more than taste or specific object.

When someone speaks he looks at a mouth, not eyes and their colours, which, it seems to him, will always alter depending on the light of a room, the minute of the day. Mouths reveal insecurity or smugness or any other point on the spectrum of character. For him they are the most intricate aspect of faces. He's never sure what an eye reveals. But he can read how mouths darken into callousness, suggest tenderness. One can often misjudge an eye from its reaction to a simple beam of sunlight.

Everything is gathered by him as part of an altering harmony. He sees her in differing hours and locations that alter her voice or nature, even her beauty, the way the background power of the sea cradles or governs the fate of lifeboats.

They were in the habit of rising with daybreak and eating dinner in the last available light. Throughout the late evening there would be only one candle flaring into the darkness beside the English patient, or a lamp half filled with oil if Caravaggio had managed to forage any. But the corridors and other bedrooms hung in darkness, as if in a buried city. They became used to walking in darkness, hands out, touching the walls on either side with their fingertips.

"No more light. No more colour." Hana would sing the phrase to herself again and again. Kip's unnerving habit of leaping down the stairs one hand halfway down the rail had to be stopped. She imagined his feet travelling through air and hitting the returning Caravaggio in the stomach.

She had blown out the candle in the Englishman's room an hour earlier. She had removed her tennis shoes, her frock was unbuttoned at the neck because of summer heat, the sleeves unbuttoned as well and loose, high up at the arm. A sweet disorder.

On the main floor of the wing, apart from the kitchen, library and deserted chapel, was a glassed-in indoor courtyard. Four walls of glass with a glass door that let you into where there was a covered well and shelves of dead plants that at one time must have flourished in the heated room. This indoor courtyard reminded her more and more of a book opened to reveal pressed flowers, something to be glanced at during passing, never entered.

It was two a.m.

Each of them entered the villa from a different doorway,

Hana at the chapel entrance by the thirty-six steps and he at the north courtyard. As he stepped into the house he removed his watch and slid it into an alcove at chest level where a small saint rested. The patron of this villa hospital. She would not catch a glance of phosphorus. He had already removed his shoes and wore just trousers. The lamp strapped to his arm was switched off. He carried nothing else and just stood there for a while in darkness, a lean boy, a dark turban, the *kara* loose on his wrist against the skin. He leaned against the corner of the vestibule like a spear.

Then he was gliding through the indoor courtyard. He came into the kitchen and immediately sensed the dog in the dark, caught it and tied it with a rope to the table. He picked up the condensed milk from the kitchen shelf and returned to the glass room in the indoor courtyard. He ran his hands along the base of the door and found the small sticks leaning against it. He entered and closed the door behind him, at the last moment snaking his hand out to prop the sticks up against the door again. In case she had seen them. Then he climbed down into the well. There was a cross-plank three feet down he knew was firm. He closed the lid over himself and crouched there, imagining her searching for him or hiding herself. He began to suck at the can of condensed milk.

She suspected something like this from him. Having made her way to the library, she turned on the light on her arm and walked beside the bookcases that stretched from her ankles to unseen heights above her. The door was closed, so no light could reveal itself to anyone in the halls. He would be able to see the glow on the other side of the French doors only if he was outside. She paused every few feet, searching once again through the predominantly Italian books for the odd English one that she could present to the English patient. She had come to love these books dressed in their Italian spines, the frontispieces, the tipped-in colour illustrations with a covering of tissue, the smell of them, even the sound of the crack if you opened them too fast, as if breaking some minute unseen series of bones. She paused again. *The Charterhouse of Parma.*

"If I ever get out of my difficulties," he said to Clelia, "I shall pay a visit to the beautiful pictures at Parma, and then will you deign to remember the name: Fabrizio del Dongo."

Caravaggio lay on the carpet at the far end of the library. From his darkness it seemed that Hana's left arm was raw phosphorus, lighting the books, reflecting redness onto her dark hair, burning against the cotton of her frock and its puffed sleeve at her shoulder.

He came out of the well.

The three-foot diameter of light spread from her arm and then was absorbed into blackness, so it felt to Caravaggio that there was a valley of darkness between them. She tucked the book with the brown cover under her right arm. As she moved, new books emerged and others disappeared.

She had grown older. And he loved her more now than he loved her when he had understood her better, when she was the product of her parents. What she was now was what she herself had decided to become. He knew that if he had passed Hana on a street in Europe she would have had a familiar air but he wouldn't have recognized her. The night he had first come to the villa he had disguised his shock. Her ascetic face, which at first seemed cold, had a sharpness. He realized that during the last two months he had grown towards who she now was. He could hardly believe his pleasure at her translation. Years before, he had tried to imagine her as an adult but had invented someone with qualities moulded out of her community. Not this wonderful stranger he could love more deeply because she was made up of nothing he had provided.

She was lying on the sofa, had twisted the lamp inward so she could read, and had already fallen deep into the book. At some point later she looked up, listening, and quickly switched off the light.

Was she conscious of him in the room? Caravaggio was aware of the noisiness of his breath and the difficulty he was having breathing in an ordered, demure way. The light went on for a moment and then was quickly shut off again.

Then everything in the room seemed to be in movement but Caravaggio. He could hear it all around him, surprised he wasn't touched. The boy was in the room. Caravaggio walked over to the sofa and placed his hand down towards Hana. She was not there. As he straightened up, an arm went around his neck and pulled him down backwards in a grip. A light glared harshly into his face, and there was a gasp from them both as they fell towards the floor. The arm with the light still holding him at the neck. Then a naked foot emerged into the light, moved past Caravaggio's face and stepped onto the boy's neck beside him. Another light went on.

"Got you. *Got you.*"

The two bodies on the floor looked up at the dark outline of Hana above the light. She was singing it, "*I got you, I got you. I used Caravaggio—who really does have a bad wheeze! I knew he would be here. He was the trick.*"

Her foot pressed down harder onto the boy's neck. "Give up. *Confess.*"

Caravaggio began to shake within the boy's grip, sweat already all over him, unable to struggle out. The glare of light from both lamps now on him. He somehow had to climb and crawl out of this terror. *Confess.* The girl was laughing. He needed to calm his voice before he spoke, but they were hardly listening, excited at their adventure. He worked his way out of the boy's loosening grip and, not saying a word, left the room.

They were in darkness again. "Where are you?" she asks. Then moves quickly. He positions himself so she bangs into his chest, and in this way slips her into his arms. She puts her hand to his neck, then her mouth to his mouth. "Condensed milk! During our contest? Condensed milk?" She puts her mouth at his neck, the sweat of it, tasting him where her bare foot had been. "I want to see you." His light goes on and he sees her, her face streaked with dirt, her hair spiked up in a swirl from perspiration. Her grin towards him.

He puts his thin hands up into the loose sleeves of her dress and cups her shoulders with his hands. If she swerves now, his hands go with her. She begins to lean, puts all her weight into her fall backwards, trusting him to come with her, trusting his hands to break the fall. Then he will curl himself up, his feet in the air, just his hands and arms and his mouth on her, the rest of his body the tail of a mantis. The lamp is still strapped against the muscle and sweat of his left arm. Her face slips into the light to kiss and lick and taste. His forehead towelling itself in the wetness of her hair.

Then he is suddenly across the room, the bounce of his sapper lamp all over the place, in this room he has spent a week sweeping of all possible fuzes so it is now cleared. As if the room has now finally emerged from the war, is no longer a zone or territory. He moves with just the lamp, swaying his arm, revealing the ceiling, her laughing face as he passes her standing on the back of the sofa looking down at the glisten of his slim body. The next time he passes her he sees she is leaning down and wiping her arms on the skirt of her dress. "But I got you, I got you," she chants. "I'm the Mohican of Danforth Avenue."

Then she is riding on his back and her light swerves into the spines of books in the high shelves, her arms rising up and down as he spins her, and she dead-weights forward, drops and catches his thighs, then pivots off and is free of him, lying back on the old carpet, the smell of the past ancient rain still in it, the dust and grit on her wet arms. He bends down to her, she reaches out and clicks off his light. "I won, right?" He still has said nothing since he came into the room. His head goes into that gesture she loves which is partly a nod, partly a shake of possible disagreement. He cannot see her for the glare. He turns off her light so they are equal in darkness.

There is the one month in their lives when Hana and Kip sleep beside each other. A formal celibacy between them. Discovering that in lovemaking there can be a whole civilisation, a whole country ahead of them. The love of the idea of him or her. I don't want to be fucked. I don't want to fuck you. Where he had learned it or she had who knows, in such youth. Perhaps from Caravaggio, who had spoken to her during those evenings about his age, about the tenderness towards every cell in a lover that comes when you discover your mortality. This was, after all, a mortal age. The boy's desire completed itself only in his deepest sleep while in the arms of Hana, his orgasm something more to do with the pull of the moon, a tug of his body by the night.

All evening his thin face lay against her ribs. She reminded him of the pleasure of being scratched, her fingernails in circles raking his back. It was something an ayah had taught him years earlier. All comfort and peace during childhood, Kip remembered, had come from her, never from the mother he loved or from his brother or father, whom he played with. When he was scared or unable to sleep it was the ayah who recognized his lack, who would ease him into sleep with her hand on his small thin back, this intimate stranger from South India who lived with them, helped run a household, cooked and served them meals, brought up her own children within the shell of the household, having comforted his older brother too in earlier years, probably knowing the character of all of the children better than their real parents did.

It was a mutual affection. If Kip had been asked whom he loved most he would have named his ayah before his mother. Her comforting love greater than any blood love or sexual love for him. All through his life, he would realize later, he was drawn outside the family to find such love. The platonic intimacy, or at times the sexual intimacy, of a stranger. He would be quite old before he recognized that about himself, before he could ask even himself that question of whom he loved most.

Only once did he feel he had given her back any comfort, though she already understood his love for her. When her mother died he had crept into her room and held her suddenly old body. In silence he lay beside her mourning in her small servant's room where she wept wildly and formally. He watched as she collected her tears in a small glass cup held against her face. She would take this, he knew, to the funeral. He was behind her hunched-over body, his nine-year-old hands on her shoulders, and when she was finally still, just now and then a shudder, he began to scratch her through the sari, then pulled it aside and scratched her skin—as Hana now received this tender art, his nails against the million cells of her skin, in his tent, in 1945, where their continents met in a hill town.

IX

The Cave of Swimmers

I PROMISED to tell you how one falls in love.

A young man named Geoffrey Clifton had met a friend at Oxford who had mentioned what we were doing. He contacted me, got married the next day, and two weeks later flew with his wife to Cairo. They were on the last days of their honeymoon. That was the beginning of our story.

When I met Katharine she was married. A married woman. Clifton climbed out of the plane and then, unexpected, for we had planned the expedition with just him in mind, she emerged. Khaki shorts, bony knees. In those days she was too ardent for the desert. I liked his youth more than the eagerness of his new young wife. He was our pilot, messenger, reconnaissance. He was the New Age, flying over and dropping codes of long coloured ribbon to advise us where we should be. He shared his adoration of her constantly. Here were four men and one woman and her husband in his verbal joy of honeymoon. They went back to Cairo and returned a month later, and it was almost the same. She was quieter this time but he was still the youth. She would squat on some petrol cans, her jaw cupped in her hands, her elbows on her knees, staring at some constantly flapping tarpaulin, and Clifton would be singing her praises. We tried to joke him out of it, but to wish him more modest would have been against him and none of us wanted that.

After that month in Cairo she was muted, read constantly, kept more to herself, as if something had occurred or she realized suddenly that wondrous thing about the human being, it can change. She did not have to remain a socialite who had married an adventurer. She was discovering herself. It was painful to watch, because Clifton could not see it, her self-education. She read everything about the desert. She could talk about Uweinat and the lost oasis, had even hunted down marginal articles.

I was a man fifteen years older than she, you understand. I had reached that stage in life where I identified with cynical villains in a book. I don't believe in permanence, in relationships that span ages. I was fifteen years older. But she was smarter. She was hungrier to change than I expected.

What altered her during their postponed honeymoon on the Nile estuary outside Cairo? We had seen them for a few days —they had arrived two weeks after their Cheshire wedding. He had brought his bride along, as he couldn't leave her and he couldn't break the commitment to us. To Madox and me. We would have devoured him. So her bony knees emerged from the plane that day. That was the burden of our story. Our situation.

Clifton celebrated the beauty of her arms, the thin lines of her ankles. He described witnessing her swim. He spoke about the new bidets in the hotel suite. Her ravenous hunger at breakfast.

To all that, I didn't say a word. I would look up sometimes as he spoke and catch her glance, witnessing my unspoken exasperation, and then her demure smile. There was some irony. I was the older man. I was the man of the world, who

had walked ten years earlier from Dakhla Oasis to the Gilf
Kebir, who charted the Farafra, who knew Cyrenaica and had
been lost more than twice in the Sand Sea. She met me when
I had all those labels. Or she could twist a few degrees and see
the labels on Madox. Yet apart from the Geographical Society
we were unknown; we were the thin edge of a cult she had
stumbled onto because of this marriage.

The words of her husband in praise of her meant nothing.
But I am a man whose life in many ways, even as an explorer,
has been governed by words. By rumours and legends. Charted
things. Shards written down. The tact of words. In the desert
to repeat something would be to fling more water into the
earth. Here nuance took you a hundred miles.

Our expedition was about forty miles from Uweinat, and
Madox and I were to leave alone on a reconnaissance. The
Cliftons and the others were to remain behind. She had consumed all her reading and asked me for books. I had nothing
but maps with me. "That book you look at in the evenings?"
"Herodotus. Ahh. You want that?" "I don't presume. If it is
private." "I have my notes within it. And cuttings. I need it
with me." "It was forward of me, excuse me." "When I return
I shall show it to you. It is unusual for me to travel without
it."

All this occurred with much grace and courtesy. I explained
it was more a commonplace book, and she bowed to that. I was
able to leave without feeling in any way selfish. I acknowledged her graciousness. Clifton was not there. We were alone.
I had been packing in my tent when she had approached me.
I am a man who has turned my back on much of the social
world, but sometimes I appreciate the delicacy of manner.

We returned a week later. Much had happened in terms of
findings and piecings together. We were in good spirits. There

was a small celebration at the camp. Clifton was always one to celebrate others. It was catching.

She approached me with a cup of water. "Congratulations, I heard from Geoffrey already—" "Yes!" "Here, drink this." I put out my hand and she placed the cup in my palm. The water was very cold after the stuff in the canteens we had been drinking. "Geoffrey has planned a party for you. He's writing a song and wants me to read a poem, but I want to do something else." "Here, take the book and look through it." I pulled it from my knapsack and handed it to her.

After the meal and herb teas Clifton brought out a bottle of cognac he had hidden from everyone till this moment. The whole bottle was to be drunk that night during Madox's account of our journey, Clifton's funny song. Then she began to read from *The Histories*—the story of Candaules and his queen. I always skim past that story. It is early in the book and has little to do with the places and period I am interested in. But it is of course a famous story. It was also what she had chosen to talk about.

> *This Candaules had become passionately in love with his own wife; and having become so, he deemed that his wife was fairer by far than all other women. To Gyges, the son of Daskylus (for he of all his spearmen was the most pleasing to him), he used to describe the beauty of his wife, praising it above all measure.*

"Are you listening, Geoffrey?"
"Yes, my darling."

> *He said to Gyges: "Gyges, I think that you do not believe me when I tell you of the beauty of my wife, for it happens that men's ears are less apt of belief than their eyes. Contrive therefore means by which you may look upon her naked."*

There are several things one can say. Knowing that eventually I will become her lover, just as Gyges will be the queen's lover and murderer of Candaules. I would often open Herodotus for a clue to geography. But Katharine had done that as a window to her life. Her voice was wary as she read. Her eyes only on the page where the story was, as if she were sinking within quicksand while she spoke.

"I believe indeed that she is of all women the fairest and I entreat you not to ask of me that which it is not lawful for me to do." But the King answered him thus: "Be of good courage, Gyges, and have no fear, either of me, that I am saying these words to try you, or of my wife, lest any harm may happen to you from her. For I will contrive it so from the first that she shall not perceive that she has been seen by you."

This is a story of how I fell in love with a woman, who read me a specific story from Herodotus. I heard the words she spoke across the fire, never looking up, even when she teased her husband. Perhaps she was just reading it to him. Perhaps there was no ulterior motive in the selection except for themselves. It was simply a story that had jarred her in its familiarity of situation. But a path suddenly revealed itself in real life. Even though she had not conceived it as a first errant step in any way. I am sure.

"I will place you in the room where we sleep, behind the open door; and after I have gone in, my wife will also come to lie down. Now there is a seat near the entrance of the room and on this she lays her garments as she takes them off one by one; and so you will be able to gaze at her at full leisure."

But Gyges is witnessed by the queen when he leaves the bedchamber. She understands then what has been done by her husband; and though ashamed, she raises no outcry . . . she holds her peace.

It is a strange story. Is it not, Caravaggio? The vanity of a man to the point where he wishes to be envied. Or he wishes to be believed, for he thinks he is not believed. This was in no way a portrait of Clifton, but he became a part of this story. There is something very shocking but human in the husband's act. Something makes us believe it.

The next day the wife calls in Gyges and gives him two choices.

"There are now two ways open to you, and I will give you the choice which of the two you will prefer to take. Either you must slay Candaules and possess both me and the King-dom of Lydia, or you must yourself here on the spot be slain, so that you mayest not in future, by obeying Candaules in all things, see that which you should not. Either he must die who formed this design, or you who have looked upon me naked."

So the king is killed. A New Age begins. There are poems written about Gyges in iambic trimeters. He was the first of the barbarians to dedicate objects at Delphi. He reigned as King of Lydia for twenty-eight years, but we still remember him as only a cog in an unusual love story.

She stopped reading and looked up. Out of the quicksand. She was evolving. So power changed hands. Meanwhile, with the help of an anecdote, I fell in love.

Words, Caravaggio. They have a power.

When the Cliftons were not with us they were based in Cairo. Clifton doing other work for the English, God knows what, an uncle in some government office. All this was before the war. But at that time the city had every nation swimming in it, meeting at Groppi's for the soirée concerts, dancing into the night. They were a popular young couple with honour between them, and I was on the periphery of Cairo society. They lived well. A ceremonial life that I would slip into now and then. Dinners, garden parties. Events I would not normally have been interested in but now went to because she was there. I am a man who fasts until I see what I want.

How do I explain her to you? With the use of my hands? The way I can arc out in the air the shape of a mesa or rock? She had been part of the expedition for almost a year. I saw her, conversed with her. We had each been continually in the presence of the other. Later, when we were aware of mutual desire, these previous moments flooded back into the heart, now suggestive, that nervous grip of an arm on a cliff, looks that had been missed or misinterpreted.

I was at that time seldom in Cairo, there about one month in three. I worked in the Department of Egyptology on my own book, *Récentes Explorations dans le Désert Libyque,* as the days progressed, coming closer and closer to the text as if the desert were there somewhere on the page, so I could even smell the ink as it emerged from the fountain pen. And simultaneously struggled with her nearby presence, more obsessed if truth be known with her possible mouth, the tautness behind the knee, the white plain of stomach, as I wrote my brief book, seventy pages long, succinct and to the point, complete with maps of travel. I was unable to remove her body from the page. I wished to dedicate the monograph to her, to her voice, to her body that I imagined rose white out of a bed like a long bow, but it was a book I dedicated to a king. Believing such an obsession would be mocked, patronized by her polite and embarrassed shake of the head.

I began to be doubly formal in her company. A characteristic of my nature. As if awkward about a previously revealed nakedness. It is a European habit. It was natural for me—having translated her strangely into my text of the desert—now to step into metal clothing in her presence.

> *The wild poem is a substitute*
> *For the woman one loves or ought to love,*
> *One wild rhapsody a fake for another.*

On Hassanein Bey's lawn—the grand old man of the 1923 expedition—she walked over with the government aide Roundell and shook my hand, asked him to get her a drink, turned back to me and said, "I want you to ravish me." Roundell returned. It was as if she had handed me a knife. Within a month I was her lover. In that room over the souk, north of the street of parrots.

I sank to my knees in the mosaic-tiled hall, my face in the curtain of her gown, the salt taste of these fingers in her mouth. We were a strange statue, the two of us, before we began to unlock our hunger. Her fingers scratching against the sand in my thinning hair. Cairo and all her deserts around us.

Was it desire for her youth, for her thin adept boyishness? Her gardens were the gardens I spoke of when I spoke to you of gardens.

There was that small indentation at her throat we called the Bosphorus. I would dive from her shoulder into the Bosphorus. Rest my eye there. I would kneel while she looked down on me quizzical as if I were a planetary stranger. She of the quizzical look. Her cool hand suddenly against my neck on a Cairo bus. Taking a closed taxi and our quick-hand love between the Khedive Ismail Bridge and the Tipperary Club. Or the sun through her fingernails on the third-floor lobby at the museum when her hand covered my face.

As far as we were concerned there was only one person to avoid being seen by.

But Geoffrey Clifton was a man embedded in the English machine. He had a family genealogy going back to Canute. The machine would not necessarily have revealed to Clifton, married only eighteen months, his wife's infidelity, but it began to encircle the fault, the disease in the system. It knew every move she and I made from the first day of the awkward touch in the porte cochère of the Semiramis Hotel.

I had ignored her remarks about her husband's relatives. And Geoffrey Clifton was as innocent as we were about the great English web that was above us. But the club of body-guards watched over her husband and kept him protected. Only Madox, who was an aristocrat with a past of regimental associations, knew about such discreet convolutions. Only Madox, with considerable tact, warned me about such a world.

I carried Herodotus, and Madox—a saint in his own mar-riage—carried *Anna Karenina*, continually rereading the story of romance and deceit. One day, far too late to avoid the machinery we had set in motion, he tried to explain Clifton's world in terms of Anna Karenina's brother. Pass me my book. Listen to this.

Half Moscow and Petersburg were relations or friends of Oblonsky. He was born into the circle of people who were, or who became, the great ones of this earth. A third of the official world, the older men, were his father's friends and had known him from the time he was a baby in petticoats. . . . Conse-quently, the distributors of the blessings of this world were all friends of his. They could not pass over one of their own. . . . It was only necessary not to raise objections or be envious, not to quarrel or take offence, which in accordance with his nat-ural kindliness he never did.

I have come to love the tap of your fingernail on the syringe, Caravaggio. The first time Hana gave me morphine in your company you were by the window, and at the tap of her nail your neck jerked towards us. I know a comrade. The way a lover will always recognize the camouflage of other lovers.

Women want everything of a lover. And too often I would sink below the surface. So armies disappear under sand. And there was her fear of her husband, her belief in her honour, my old desire for self-sufficiency, my disappearances, her suspicions of me, my disbelief that she loved me. The paranoia and claustrophobia of hidden love.

"I think you have become inhuman," she said to me.

"I'm not the only betrayer."

"I don't think you care—that this has happened among us. You slide past everything with your fear and hate of ownership, of owning, of being owned, of being named. You think this is a virtue. I think you are inhuman. If I leave you, who will you go to? Would you find another lover?"

I said nothing.

"Deny it, damn you."

She had always wanted words, she loved them, grew up on them. Words gave her clarity, brought reason, shape. Whereas I thought words bent emotions like sticks in water.

She returned to her husband.

From this point on, she whispered, we will either find or lose our souls.

Seas move away, why not lovers? The harbours of Ephesus, the rivers of Heraclitus disappear and are replaced by estuaries of silt. The wife of Candaules becomes the wife of Gyges. Libraries burn.

What had our relationship been? A betrayal of those around us, or the desire of another life?

She climbed back into her house beside her husband, and I retired to the zinc bars.

> *I'll be looking at the moon,*
> *but I'll be seeing you.*

That old Herodotus classic. Humming and singing that song again and again, beating the lines thinner to bend them into one's own life. People recover from secret loss variously. I was seen by one of her retinue sitting with a spice trader. She had once received from him a pewter thimble that held saffron. One of the ten thousand things.

And if Bagnold—having seen me sitting by the saffron trader—brought up the incident during dinner at the table where she sat, how did I feel about that? Did it give me some comfort that she would remember the man who had given her a small gift, a pewter thimble she hung from a thin dark chain around her neck for two days when her husband was out of town? The saffron still in it, so there was the stain of gold on her chest.

How did she hold this story about me, pariah to the group after some scene or other where I had disgraced myself, Bagnold laughing, her husband who was a good man worrying about me, and Madox getting up and walking to a window and looking out towards the south section of the city. The conversation perhaps moved to other sightings. They were mapmakers, after all. But did she climb down into the well we helped dig together and hold herself, the way I desired myself towards her with my hand?

We each now had our own lives, armed by the deepest treaty with the other.

"What are you doing?" she said running into me on the street. "Can't you see you are driving us all *mad*."

To Madox I had said I was courting a widow. But she was not a widow yet. When Madox returned to England she and I were no longer lovers. "Give my greetings to your Cairo widow," Madox murmured. "Would've liked to have met her." Did he know? I always felt more of a deceiver with him, this friend I had worked with for ten years, this man I loved more than any other man. It was 1939, and we were all leaving this country, in any case, to the war.

And Madox returned to the village of Marston Magna, Somerset, where he had been born, and a month later sat in the congregation of a church, heard the sermon in honour of war, pulled out his desert revolver and shot himself.

I, Herodotus of Halicarnassus, set forth my history, that time may not draw the colour from what Man has brought into being, nor those great and wonderful deeds manifested by both Greeks and Barbarians . . . together with the reason they fought one another.

Men had always been the reciters of poetry in the desert. And Madox—to the Geographical Society—had spoken beautiful accounts of our traversals and coursings. Bermann blew theory into the embers. And I? I was the skill among them. The mechanic. The others wrote out their love of solitude and meditated on what they found there. They were never sure of what I thought of it all. "Do you like that moon?" Madox asked me after he'd known me for ten years. He asked it tentatively, as if he had breached an intimacy. For them I was a bit too cunning to be a lover of the desert. More like Odysseus. Still, I was. Show me a desert, as you would show another man a river, or another man the metropolis of his childhood.

When we parted for the last time, Madox used the old farewell. "May God make safety your companion." And I strode away from him saying, "There is no God." We were utterly unlike each other.

Madox said Odysseus never wrote a word, an intimate book. Perhaps he felt alien in the false rhapsody of art. And my own monograph, I must admit, had been stern with accuracy. The fear of describing her presence as I wrote caused me to burn down all sentiment, all rhetoric of love. Still, I described the desert as purely as I would have spoken of her. Madox asked me about the moon during our last days together before the war began. We parted. He left for England, the probability of the oncoming war interrupting everything, our slow un-earthing of history in the desert. Good-bye, Odysseus, he said grinning, knowing I was never that fond of Odysseus, less fond of Aeneas, but we had decided Bagnold was Aeneas. But I was not that fond of Odysseus either. Good-bye, I said.

I remember he turned back, laughing. He pointed his thick finger to the spot by his Adam's apple and said, "This is called the vascular sizood." Giving that hollow at her neck an official name. He returned to his wife in the village of Marston Magna, took only his favourite volume of Tolstoy, left all of his compasses and maps to me. Our affection left unspoken.

And Marston Magna in Somerset, which he had evoked for me again and again in our conversations, had turned its green fields into an aerodrome. The planes burned their exhaust over Arthurian castles. What drove him to the act I do not know. Maybe it was the permanent noise of flight, so loud to him now after the simple drone of the Gypsy Moth that had putted over our silences in Libya and Egypt. Someone's war was slashing apart his delicate tapestry of companions. I was Odysseus, I understood the shifting and temporary vetoes of war. But he was a man who made friends with difficulty. He was a man who knew two or three people in his life, and they had turned out now to be the enemy.

He was in Somerset alone with his wife, who had never met

us. Small gestures were enough for him. One bullet ended the war.

It was July 1939. They caught a bus from their village into Yeovil. The bus had been slow and so they had been late for the service. At the back of the crowded church, in order to find seats they decided to sit separately. When the sermon began half an hour later, it was jingoistic and without any doubt in its support of the war. The priest intoned blithely about battle, blessing the government and the men about to enter the war. Madox listened as the sermon grew more impassioned. He pulled out the desert pistol, bent over and shot himself in the heart. He was dead immediately. A great silence. Desert silence. Planeless silence. They heard his body collapse against the pew. Nothing else moved. The priest frozen in a gesture. It was like those silences when a glass funnel round a candle in church splits and all faces turn. His wife walked down the centre aisle, stopped at his row, muttered something, and they let her in beside him. She knelt down, her arms enclosing him.

How did Odysseus die? A suicide, wasn't it? I seem to recall that. Now. Maybe the desert spoiled Madox. That time when we had nothing to do with the world. I keep thinking of the Russian book he always carried. Russia has always been closer to my country than to his. Yes, Madox was a man who died because of nations.

I loved his calmness in all things. I would argue furiously about locations on a map, and his reports would somehow speak of our "debate" in reasonable sentences. He wrote calmly and joyfully about our journeys when there was joy to describe, as if we were Anna and Vronsky at a dance. Still, he was a man who never entered those Cairo dance halls with me. And I was the man who fell in love while dancing.

He moved with a slow gait. I never saw him dance. He was a man who wrote, who interpreted the world. Wisdom grew out of being handed just the smallest sliver of emotion. A glance could lead to paragraphs of theory. If he witnessed a new knot among a desert tribe or found a rare palm, it would charm him for weeks. When we came upon messages on our travels—any wording, contemporary or ancient, Arabic on a mud wall, a note in English written in chalk on the fender of a jeep—he would read it and then press his hand upon it as if to touch its possible deeper meanings, to become as intimate as he could with the words.

He holds out his arm, the bruised veins horizontal, facing up, for the raft of morphine. As it floods him he hears Caravaggio drop the needle into the kidney-shaped enamel tin. He sees the grizzled form turn its back to him and then reappear, also caught, a citizen of morphia with him.

There are days when I come home from arid writing when all that can save me is "Honeysuckle Rose" by Django Reinhardt and Stéphane Grappelly performing with the Hot Club of France. 1935. 1936. 1937. Great jazz years. The years when it floated out of the Hôtel Claridge on the Champs-Élysées and into the bars of London, southern France, Morocco, and then slid into Egypt, where the rumour of such rhythms was introduced in a hush by an unnamed Cairo dance band. When I went back into the desert, I took with me the evenings of dancing to the 78 of "Souvenirs" in the bars, the women pacing like greyhounds, leaning against you while you muttered into their shoulders during "My Sweet." Courtesy of the Société Ultraphone Française record company. 1938. 1939. There was the whispering of love in a booth. There was war around the corner.

During those final nights in Cairo, months after the affair was over, we had finally persuaded Madox into a zinc bar for his farewell. She and her husband were there. One last night. One last dance. Almásy was drunk and attempting an old dance step he had invented called the Bosphorus hug, lifting Katharine Clifton into his wiry arms and traversing the floor until he fell with her across some Nile-grown aspidistras.

Who is he speaking as now? Caravaggio thinks.

Almásy was drunk and his dancing seemed to the others a brutal series of movements. In those days he and she did not seem to be getting on well. He swung her from side to side as if she were some anonymous doll, and smothered with drink his grief at Madox's leaving. He was loud at the tables with us. When Almásy was like this we usually dispersed, but this was Madox's last night in Cairo and we stayed. A bad Egyptian violinist mimicking Stéphane Grappelly, and Almásy like a planet out of control. "To us—the planetary strangers," he lifted his glass. He wanted to dance with everyone, men and women. He clapped his hands and announced, "Now for the Bosphorus hug. You, Bernhardt? Hetherton?" Most pulled back. He turned to Clifton's young wife, who was watching him in a courteous rage, and she went forward as he beckoned and then slammed into her, his throat already at her left shoulder on that naked plateau above the sequins. A maniac's tango ensued till one of them lost the step. She would not back down from her anger, refused to let him win by her walking away and returning to the table. Just staring hard at him when he pulled his head back, not solemn but with an attacking face. His mouth muttering at her when he bent his face down, swearing the lyrics of "Honeysuckle Rose," perhaps.

In Cairo between expeditions no one ever saw much of Almásy. He seemed either distant or restless. He worked in the museum during the day and frequented the South Cairo market bars at night. Lost in another Egypt. It was only for Madox they had all come here. But now Almásy was dancing with Katharine Clifton. The line of plants brushed against her slimness. He pivoted with her, lifting her up, and then fell. Clifton stayed in his seat, half watching them. Almásy lying across her and then slowly trying to get up, smoothing back his blond hair, kneeling over her in the far corner of the room. He had at one time been a man of delicacy.

It was past midnight. The guests there were not amused, except for the easily amused regulars, accustomed to these ceremonies of the desert European. There were women with long tributaries of silver hanging off their ears, women in sequins, little metal droplets warm from the bar's heat that Almásy in the past had always been partial towards, women who in their dancing swung the jagged earrings of silver against his face. On other nights he danced with them, carrying their whole frame by the fulcrum of rib cage as he got drunker. Yes, they were amused, laughing at Almásy's stomach as his shirt loosened, not charmed by his weight, which leaned on their shoulders as he paused during the dance, collapsing at some point later during a schottische onto the floor.

It was important during such evenings to *proceed* into the plot of the evening, while the human constellations whirled and skidded around you. There was no thought or forethought. The evening's field notes came later, in the desert, in the landforms between Dakhla and Kufra. Then he would remember that doglike yelp at which he looked around for a dog on the dance floor and realized, now regarding the compass disc floating on oil, that it may have been a woman he had stepped on. Within sight of an oasis he would pride himself on

his dancing, waving his arms and his wristwatch up to the
sky.

Cold nights in the desert. He plucked a thread from the
horde of nights and put it into his mouth like food. This was
during the first two days of a trek out, when he was in the
zone of limbo between city and plateau. After six days had
passed he would never think about Cairo or the music or the
streets or the women; by then he was moving in ancient time,
had adapted into the breathing patterns of deep water. His
only connection with the world of cities was Herodotus, his
guidebook, ancient and modern, of supposed lies. When he
discovered the truth to what had seemed a lie, he brought out
his glue pot and pasted in a map or news clipping or used a
blank space in the book to sketch men in skirts with faded
unknown animals alongside them. The early oasis dwellers
had not usually depicted cattle, though Herodotus claimed
they had. They worshipped a pregnant goddess and their rock
portraits were mostly of pregnant women.

Within two weeks even the idea of a city never entered his
mind. It was as if he had walked under the millimetre of haze
just above the inked fibres of a map, that pure zone between
land and chart between distances and legend between nature
and storyteller. Sandford called it geomorphology. The place
they had chosen to come to, to be their best selves, to be
unconscious of ancestry. Here, apart from the sun compass
and the odometer mileage and the book, he was alone, his own
invention. He knew during these times how the mirage
worked, the fata morgana, for he was within it.

He awakens to discover Hana washing him. There is a bureau
at waist level. She leans over, her hands bringing water from
the porcelain basin to his chest. When she finishes she runs

her wet fingers through her hair a few times, so it turns damp and dark. She looks up and sees his eyes are open, and smiles.

When he opens his eyes again, Madox is there, looking ragged, weary, carrying the morphinic injection, having to use both hands because there are no thumbs. How does he give it to himself? he thinks. He recognizes the eye, the habit of the tongue fluttering at the lip, the clearness of the man's brain catching all he says. Two old coots.

Caravaggio watches the pink in the man's mouth as he talks. The gums perhaps the light iodine colour of the rock paintings discovered in Uweinat. There is more to discover, to divine out of this body on the bed, nonexistent except for a mouth, a vein in the arm, wolf-grey eyes. He is still amazed at the clarity of discipline in the man, who speaks sometimes in the first person, sometimes in the third person, who still does not admit that he is Almásy.

"Who was talking, back then?"

" 'Death means you are in the third person.' "

All day they have shared the ampoules of morphine. To unthread the story out of him, Caravaggio travels within the code of signals. When the burned man slows down, or when Caravaggio feels he is not catching everything—the love affair, the death of Madox—he picks up the syringe from the kidney-shaped enamel tin, breaks the glass tip off an ampoule with the pressure of a knuckle and loads it. He is blunt about all this now with Hana, having ripped the sleeve off his left arm completely. Almásy wears just a grey singlet, so his black arm lies bare under the sheet.

Each swallow of morphine by the body opens a further door, or he leaps back to the cave paintings or to a buried plane or lingers once more with the woman beside him under a fan, her cheek against his stomach.

Caravaggio picks up the Herodotus. He turns a page, comes

over a dune to discover the Gilf Kebir, Uweinat, Gebel Kissu. When Almásy speaks he stays alongside him reordering the events. Only desire makes the story errant, flickering like a compass needle. And this is the world of nomads in any case, an apocryphal story. A mind travelling east and west in the disguise of sandstorm.

On the floor of the Cave of Swimmers, after her husband had crashed their plane, he had cut open and stretched out the parachute she had been carrying. She lowered herself onto it, grimacing with the pain of her injuries. He placed his fingers gently into her hair, searching for other wounds, then touched her shoulders and her feet.

Now in the cave it was her beauty he did not want to lose, the grace of her, these limbs. He knew he already had her nature tight in his fist.

She was a woman who translated her face when she put on makeup. Entering a party, climbing into a bed, she had painted on blood lipstick, a smear of vermilion over each eye.

He looked up to the one cave painting and stole the colours from it. The ochre went into her face, he daubed blue around her eyes. He walked across the cave, his hands thick with red, and combed his fingers through her hair. Then all of her skin, so her knee that had poked out of the plane that first day was saffron. The pubis. Hoops of colour around her legs so she would be immune to the human. There were traditions he had discovered in Herodotus in which old warriors celebrated their loved ones by locating and holding them in whatever world made them eternal—a colourful fluid, a song, a rock drawing.

It was already cold in the cave. He wrapped the parachute around her for warmth. He lit one small fire and burned the acacia twigs and waved smoke into all the corners of the cave. He found he could not speak directly to her, so he spoke formally, his voice against the bounce of the cave walls. *I'm going for help now, Katharine. Do you understand? There is another plane nearby, but there is no petrol. I might meet a caravan or a jeep, which means I will be back sooner. I don't know.* He pulled out the copy of Herodotus and placed it beside her. It was September 1939. He walked out of the cave, out of the flare of firelight, down through darkness and into the desert full of moon.

He climbed down the boulders to the base of the plateau and stood there.

No truck. No plane. No compass. Only moon and his shadow. He found the old stone marker from the past that located the direction of El Taj, north-northwest. He memorized the angle of his shadow and started walking. Seventy miles away was the souk with the street of clocks. Water in a skin bag he had filled from the *ain* hung from his shoulder and sloshed like a placenta.

There were two periods of time when he could not move. At noon, when the shadow was under him, and at twilight, between sunset and the appearance of the stars. Then everything on the disc of the desert was the same. If he moved, he might err as much as ninety degrees off his course. He waited for the live chart of stars, then moved forward reading them every hour. In the past, when they had had desert guides, they would hang a lantern from a long pole and the rest of them would follow the bounce of light above the star reader.

A man walks as fast as a camel. Two and a half miles an hour. If lucky, he would come upon ostrich eggs. If unlucky, a sandstorm would erase everything. He walked for three days without any food. He refused to think about her. If he got to El Taj he would eat *abra,* which the Goran tribes made out of colocynth, boiling the pips to get rid of bitterness and then crushing it along with dates and locusts. He would walk through the street of clocks and alabaster. May God make safety your companion, Madox had said. Good-bye. A wave. There is God only in the desert, he wanted to acknowledge that now. Outside of this there was just trade and power, money and war. Financial and military despots shaped the world.

He was in broken country, had moved from sand to rock. He refused to think about her. Then hills emerged like mediaeval castles. He walked till he stepped with his shadow into the shadow of a mountain. Mimosa shrubs. Colocynths. He yelled out her name into the rocks. *For echo is the soul of the voice exciting itself in hollow places.*

Then there was El Taj. He had imagined the street of mirrors for most of his journey. When he got to the outskirts of the settlements, English military jeeps surrounded him and took him away, not listening to his story of the woman injured at Uweinat, just seventy miles away, listening in fact to nothing he said.

"Are you telling me the English did not believe you? No one listened to you?"

"No one listened."

"Why?"

"I didn't give them a right name."

"Yours?"

"I gave them mine."

"Then what—"

"*Hers*. Her name. The name of her husband."

"What did you say?"

He says nothing.

"Wake up! What did you say?"

"I said she was my *wife*. I said *Katharine*. Her husband was dead. I said she was badly injured, in a cave in the Gilf Kebir, at Uweinat, north of the Ain Dua well. She needed water. She needed food. I would go back with them to guide them. I said all I wanted was a jeep. One of their damn jeeps . . . Perhaps I seemed like one of those mad desert prophets after the journey, but I don't think so. The war was beginning already. They were just pulling spies in out of the desert. Everyone with a foreign name who drifted into these small oasis towns was suspect. She was just seventy miles away and they wouldn't listen. Some stray English outfit in El Taj. I must have gone berserk then. They were using these wicker prisons, size of a shower. I was put into one and moved by truck. I was flailing around in there until I fell off onto the street, still in it. I was yelling Katharine's name. Yelling the Gilf Kebir. Whereas the only name I should have yelled, dropped like a calling card into their hands, was Clifton's.

"They hauled me up into the truck again. I was just another possible second-rate spy. Just another international bastard."

Caravaggio wants to rise and walk away from this villa, the country, the detritus of a war. He is just a thief. What Caravaggio wants is his arms around the sapper and Hana or, better, people of his own age, in a bar where he knows everyone, where he can dance and talk with a woman, rest his head on her shoulder, lean his head against her brow, whatever, but he knows first he must get out of this desert, its architecture of morphine. He needs to pull away from the invisible road to El Taj. This man he believes to be Almásy has used him and the morphine to return to his own world, for his own sadness. It no longer matters which side he was on during the war.

But Caravaggio leans forward.

"I need to know something."

"What?"

"I need to know if you murdered Katharine Clifton. That is, if you murdered Clifton, and in so doing killed her."

"No. I never even imagined that."

"The reason I ask is that Geoffrey Clifton was with British Intelligence. He was not just an innocent Englishman, I'm afraid. Your friendly boy. As far as the English were concerned, he was keeping an eye on your strange group in the Egyptian–Libyan desert. They knew the desert would some-day be a theatre of war. He was an aerial photographer. His death perturbed them, still does. They still raise the question. And Intelligence knew about your affair with his wife, from the beginning. Even if Clifton didn't. They thought his death may have been engineered as protection, hoisting up the draw-bridge. They were waiting for you in Cairo, but of course you turned back into the desert. Later, when I was sent to Italy, I lost the last part of your story. I didn't know what had hap-pened to you."

"So you have run me to earth."

"I came because of the girl. I knew her father. The last person I expected to find here in this shelled nunnery was Count Ladislaus de Almásy. Quite honestly, I've become more fond of you than most of the people I worked with."

The rectangle of light that had drifted up Caravaggio's chair was framing his chest and head so that to the English patient the face seemed a portrait. In muted light his hair appeared dark, but now the wild hair lit up, bright, the bags under his eyes washed out in the pink late daylight.

He had turned the chair around so he could lean forward on its back, facing Almásy. Words did not emerge easily from Caravaggio. He would rub his jaw, his face creasing up, the eyes closed, to think in darkness, and only then would he blurt out something, tearing himself away from his own thoughts. It was this darkness that showed in him as he sat in the rhomboid frame of light, hunched over a chair beside Almásy's bed. One of the two older men in this story.

"I can talk with you, Caravaggio, because I feel we are both mortal. The girl, the boy, they are not mortal yet. In spite of what they have been through. Hana was greatly distressed when I first met her."

"Her father was killed in France."

"I see. She would not talk about it. She was distant from everybody. The only way I could get her to communicate was to ask her to read to me. . . . Do you realize neither of us has children?"

Then pausing, as if considering a possibility.

"Do you have a wife?" Almásy asked.

Caravaggio sat in the pink light, his hands over his face to erase everything so he could think precisely, as if this was one more gift of youth that did not come so easily to him any longer.

"You must talk to me, Caravaggio. Or am I just a book? Something to be read, some creature to be tempted out of a loch and shot full of morphine, full of corridors, lies, loose vegetation, pockets of stones."

"Thieves like us were used a great deal during this war. We were legitimized. We stole. Then some of us began to advise. We could read through the camouflage of deceit more naturally than official intelligence. We created double bluffs. Whole campaigns were being run by this mixture of crooks and intellectuals. I was all over the Middle East, that's where I first heard about you. You were a mystery, a vacuum on their charts. Turning your knowledge of the desert into German hands."

"Too much happened at El Taj in 1939, when I was rounded up, imagined to be a spy."

"So that's when you went over to the Germans."

Silence.

"And you still were unable to get back to the Cave of Swimmers and Uweinat?"

"Not till I volunteered to take Eppler across the desert."

"There is something I must tell you. To do with 1942, when you guided the spy into Cairo . . ."

"Operation Salaam."

"Yes. When you were working for Rommel."

"A brilliant man. . . . What were you going to tell me?"

"I was going to say, when you came through the desert avoiding Allied troops, travelling with Eppler—it *was* heroic. From Gialo Oasis all the way to Cairo. Only you could have gotten Rommel's man into Cairo with his copy of *Rebecca*."

"How did you know that?"

"What I want to say is that they did not just discover Eppler in Cairo. They knew about the whole journey. A German code had been broken long before, but we couldn't let Rommel know that or our sources would have been discovered. So we had to wait till Cairo to capture Eppler.

"We watched you all the way. All through the desert. And because Intelligence had your name, knew you were involved, they were even more interested. They wanted you as well. You were supposed to be killed. . . . If you don't believe me, you left Gialo and it took you twenty days. You followed the buried-well route. You couldn't get near Uweinat because of Allied troops, and you avoided Abu Ballas. There were times when Eppler had desert fever and you had to look after him, care for him, though you say you didn't like him. . . .

"Planes supposedly 'lost' you, but you were being tracked very carefully. You were not the spies, we were the spies. Intelligence thought you had killed Geoffrey Clifton over the woman. They had found his grave in 1939, but there was no sign of his wife. You had become the enemy not when you sided with Germany but when you began your affair with Katharine Clifton."

"I see."

"After you left Cairo in 1942, we lost you. They were supposed to pick you up and kill you in the desert. But they lost you. Two days out. You must have been haywire, not rational, or we would have found you. We had mined the hidden jeep. We found it exploded later, but there was nothing of you. You were gone. That must have been your great journey, not the one to Cairo. When you must have been mad."

"Were you there in Cairo with them tracking me?"

"No, I saw the files. I was going into Italy and they thought you might be there."

"Here."

"Yes."

The rhomboid of light moved up the wall leaving Caravaggio in shadow. His hair dark again. He leaned back, his shoulder against the foliage.

"I suppose it doesn't matter," Almásy murmured.

"Do you want morphine?"

"No. I'm putting things into place. I was always a private man. It is difficult to realize I was so *discussed*."

"You were having an affair with someone connected with Intelligence. There were some people in Intelligence who knew you personally."

"Bagnold probably."

"Yes."

"Very English Englishman."

"Yes."

Caravaggio paused.

"I have to talk to you about one last thing."

"I know."

"What happened to Katharine Clifton? What happened just

before the war to make you all come to the Gilf Kebir again? After Madox left for England."

I was supposed to make one more journey to the Gilf Kebir, to pack up the last of the base camp at Uweinat. Our life there was over. I thought nothing more would happen between us. I had not met her as a lover for almost a year. A war was preparing itself somewhere like a hand entering an attic window. And she and I had already retreated behind our own walls of previous habit, into seeming innocence of relationship. We no longer saw each other very much.

During the summer of 1939 I was to go overland to the Gilf Kebir with Gough, pack up the base camp, and Gough would leave by truck. Clifton would fly in and pick me up. Then we would disperse, out of the triangle that had grown up among us.

When I heard the plane, saw it, I was already climbing down the rocks of the plateau. Clifton was always prompt.

There is a way a small cargo plane will come down to land, slipping from the level of horizon. It tips its wings within desert light and then sound stops, it drifts to earth. I have never fully understood how planes work. I have watched them approach me in the desert and I have come out of my tent always with fear. They dip their wings across the light and then they enter that silence.

The Moth came skimming over the plateau. I was waving the blue tarpaulin. Clifton dropped altitude and roared over me, so low the acacia shrubs lost their leaves. The plane veered to the left and circled, and sighting me again realigned itself and came straight towards me. Fifty yards away from me it suddenly tilted and crashed. I started running towards it.

I thought he was alone. He was supposed to be alone. But when I got there to pull him out, she was beside him. He was dead. She was trying to move the lower part of her body, looking straight ahead. Sand had come in through the cockpit window and had filled her lap. There didn't seem to be a mark on her. Her left hand had gone forward to cushion the collapse of their flight. I pulled her out of the plane Clifton had called *Rupert* and carried her up into the rock caves. Into the Cave of Swimmers, where the paintings were. Latitude 23°30' on the map, longitude 25°15'. I buried Geoffrey Clifton that night.

Was I a curse upon them? For her? For Madox? For the desert raped by war, shelled as if it were just sand? The Barbarians versus the Barbarians. Both armies would come through the desert with no sense of what it was. *The deserts of Libya*. Remove politics, and it is the loveliest phrase I know. *Libya*. A sexual, drawn-out word, a coaxed well. The *b* and the *y*. Madox said it was one of the few words in which you heard the tongue turn a corner. Remember Dido in the deserts of Libya? *A man shall be as rivers of water in a dry place.* . . .

I do not believe I entered a cursed land, or that I was ensnared in a situation that was evil. Every place and person was a gift to me. Finding the rock paintings in the Cave of Swimmers. Singing "burdens" with Madox during expeditions. Katharine's appearance among us in the desert. The way I would walk towards her over the red polished concrete floor and sink to my knees, her belly against my head as if I were a boy. The gun tribe healing me. Even the four of us, Hana and you and the sapper.

Everything I have loved or valued has been taken away from me.

I stayed with her. I discovered three of her ribs were broken. I kept waiting for her wavering eye, for her broken wrist to bend, for her still mouth to speak.

How did you hate me? she whispered. You killed almost everything in me.

Katharine . . . you didn't—

Hold me. Stop defending yourself. Nothing changes you.

Her glare was permanent. I could not move out of the target of that gaze. I will be the last image she sees. The jackal in the cave who will guide and protect her, who will never deceive her.

There are a hundred deities associated with animals, I tell her. There are the ones linked to jackals—Anubis, Duamutef, Wepwawet. These are creatures who guide you into the afterlife—as my early ghost accompanied you, those years before we met. All those parties in London and Oxford. Watching you. I sat across from you as you did schoolwork, holding a large pencil. I was there when you met Geoffrey Clifton at two a.m. in the Oxford Union Library. Everybody's coats were strewn on the floor and you in your bare feet like some heron picking your way among them. He is watching you but I am watching you too, though you miss my presence, ignore me. You are at an age when you see only good-looking men. You are not yet aware of those outside your sphere of grace. The jackal is not used much at Oxford as an escort. Whereas I am the man who fasts until I see what I want. The wall behind you is covered in books. Your left hand holds a long loop of pearls that hangs from your neck. Your bare feet picking their way through. You are looking for something. You were more plump in those days, though aptly beautiful for university life.

There are three of us in the Oxford Union Library, but you find only Geoffrey Clifton. It will be a whirlwind romance. He has some job with archaeologists in North Africa, of all places. "A strange old coot I'm working with." Your mother is quite delighted at your adventure.

But the spirit of the jackal, who was the "opener of the ways," whose name was Wepwawet or Almásy, stood in the room with the two of you. My arms folded, watching your attempts at enthusiastic small talk, a problem as you both were drunk. But what was wonderful was that even within the drunkenness of two a.m., each of you somehow recognized the more permanent worth and pleasure of the other. You may have arrived with others, will perhaps cohabit this night with others, but both of you have found your fates.

At three a.m. you feel you must leave, but you are unable to find one shoe. You hold the other in your hand, a rose-coloured slipper. I see one half buried near me and pick it up. The sheen of it. They are obviously favourite shoes, with the indentation of your toes. Thank you, you say accepting it, as you leave, not even looking at my face.

I believe this. When we meet those we fall in love with, there is an aspect of our spirit that is historian, a bit of a pedant, who imagines or remembers a meeting when the other had passed by innocently, just as Clifton might have opened a car door for you a year earlier and ignored the fate of his life. But all parts of the body must be ready for the other, all atoms must jump in one direction for desire to occur.

I have lived in the desert for years and I have come to believe in such things. It is a place of pockets. The trompe l'oeil of time and water. The jackal with one eye that looks back and one that regards the path you consider taking. In his jaws are pieces of the past he delivers to you, and when all of that time is fully discovered it will prove to have been already known.

Her eyes looked at me, tired of everything. A terrible weariness. When I pulled her from the plane her stare had tried to receive all things around her. Now the eyes were guarded, as if protecting something inside. I moved closer, and sat on my heels. I leaned forward and put my tongue against the right blue eye, a taste of salt. Pollen. I carried that taste to her mouth. Then the other eye. My tongue against the fine porousness of the eyeball, wiping off the blue; when I moved back there was a sweep of white across her gaze. I parted the lips on her mouth, this time I let the fingers go in deeper and prised the teeth apart, the tongue was "withdrawn," and I had to pull it forward, there was a thread, a breath of death in her. It was almost too late. I leaned forward and with my tongue carried the blue pollen to her tongue. We touched this way once. Nothing happened. I pulled back, took a breath and then went forward again. As I met the tongue there was a twitch within it.

Then the terrible snarl, violent and intimate, came out of her upon me. A shudder through her whole body like a path of electricity. She was flung from the propped position against the painted wall. The creature had entered her and it leapt and fell against me. There seemed to be less and less light in the cave. Her neck flipping this way and that.

I know the devices of a demon. I was taught as a child about the demon lover. I was told about a beautiful temptress who came to a young man's room. And he, if he were wise, would demand that she turn around, because demons and witches have no back, only what they wish to present to you. What had I done? What animal had I delivered into her? I had been speaking to her I think for over an hour. Had I been her demon lover? Had I been Madox's demon friend? This country—had I charted it and turned it into a place of war?

It is important to die in holy places. That was one of the secrets of the desert. So Madox walked into a church in Somerset, a place he felt had lost its holiness, and he committed what he believed was a holy act.

When I turned her around, her whole body was covered in bright pigment. Herbs and stones and light and the ash of acacia to make her eternal. The body pressed against sacred colour. Only the eye blue removed, made anonymous, a naked map where nothing is depicted, no signature of lake, no dark cluster of mountain as there is north of the Borkou-Ennedi-Tibesti, no lime-green fan where the Nile rivers enter the open palm of Alexandria, the edge of Africa.

And all the names of the tribes, the nomads of faith who walked in the monotone of the desert and saw brightness and faith and colour. The way a stone or found metal box or bone can become loved and turn eternal in a prayer. Such glory of this country she enters now and becomes part of. We die containing a richness of lovers and tribes, tastes we have swallowed, bodies we have plunged into and swum up as if rivers of wisdom, characters we have climbed into as if trees, fears we have hidden in as if caves. I wish for all this to be marked on my body when I am dead. I believe in such cartography— to be marked by nature, not just to label ourselves on a map like the names of rich men and women on buildings. We are communal histories, communal books. We are not owned or monogamous in our taste or experience. All I desired was to walk upon such an earth that had no maps.

I carried Katharine Clifton into the desert, where there is the communal book of moonlight. We were among the rumour of wells. In the palace of winds.

Almásy's face fell to the left, staring at nothing—Caravaggio's knees perhaps.

"Do you want some morphine now?"

"No."

"Can I get you something?"

"Nothing."

X

August

CARAVAGGIO CAME DOWN the stairs through darkness and into the kitchen. Some celery on the table, some turnips whose roots were still muddy. The only light came from a fire Hana had recently started. She had her back to him and had not heard his steps into the room. His days at the villa had loosened his body and freed his tenseness, so he seemed bigger, more sprawled out in his gestures. Only his silence of movement remained. Otherwise there was an easy inefficiency to him now, a sleepiness to his gestures.

He dragged out the chair so she would turn, realize he was in the room.

"Hello, David."

He raised his arm. He felt that he had been in deserts for too long.

"How is he?"

"Asleep. Talked himself out."

"Is he what you thought he was?"

"He's fine. We can let him be."

"I thought so. Kip and I are both sure he is English. Kip thinks the best people are eccentrics, he worked with one."

"I think Kip is the eccentric myself. Where is he, anyway?"

"He's plotting something on the terrace, doesn't want me out there. Something for my birthday." Hana stood up from her crouch at the grate, wiping her hand on the opposite forearm.

"For your birthday I'm going to tell you a small story," he said.

She looked at him.

"Not about Patrick, okay?"

"A little about Patrick, mostly about you."

"I still can't listen to those stories, David."

"Fathers die. You keep on loving them in any way you can. You can't hide him away in your heart."

"Talk to me when the morphia wears off."

She came up to him and put her arms around him, reached up and kissed his cheek. His embrace tightened around her, his stubble like sand against her skin. She loved that about him now; in the past he had always been meticulous. The parting in his hair like Yonge Street at midnight, Patrick had said. Caravaggio had in the past moved like a god in her presence. Now, with his face and his trunk filled out and this greyness in him, he was a friendlier human.

Tonight dinner was being prepared by the sapper. Caravaggio was not looking forward to it. One meal in three was a loss as far as he was concerned. Kip found vegetables and presented them barely cooked, just briefly boiled into a soup. It was to be another purist meal, not what Caravaggio wished for after a day such as this when he had been listening to the man upstairs. He opened the cupboard beneath the sink. There, wrapped in damp cloth, was some dried meat, which Caravaggio cut and put into his pocket.

"I can get you off the morphine, you know. I'm a good nurse."

"You're surrounded by madmen. . . ."

"Yes, I think we are all mad."

When Kip called them, they walked out of the kitchen and

onto the terrace, whose border, with its low stone balustrade, was ringed with light.

It looked to Caravaggio like a string of small electric candles found in dusty churches, and he thought the sapper had gone too far in removing them from a chapel, even for Hana's birthday. Hana walked slowly forward with her hands over her face. There was no wind. Her legs and thighs moved through the skirt of her frock as if it were thin water. Her tennis shoes silent on the stone.

"I kept finding dead shells wherever I was digging," the sapper said.

They still didn't understand. Caravaggio bent over the flutter of lights. They were snail shells filled with oil. He looked along the row of them; there must have been about forty.

"Forty-five," Kip said, "the years so far of this century. Where I come from, we celebrate the age as well as ourselves."

Hana moved alongside them, her hands in her pockets now, the way Kip loved to see her walk. So relaxed, as if she had put her arms away for the night, now in simple armless movement.

Caravaggio was diverted by the startling presence of three bottles of red wine on the table. He walked over and read the labels and shook his head, amazed. He knew the sapper wouldn't drink any of it. All three had already been opened. Kip must have picked his way through some etiquette book in the library. Then he saw the corn and the meat and the potatoes. Hana slid her arm into Kip's and came with him to the table.

They ate and drank, the unexpected thickness of the wine like meat on their tongues. They were soon turning silly in their toasts to the sapper—"the great forager"—and to the English patient. They toasted each other, Kip joining in with his beaker of water. This was when he began to talk about himself. Caravaggio pressing him on, not always listening, sometimes standing up and walking around the table, pacing and pacing with pleasure at all this. He wanted these two married, longed to force them verbally towards it, but they seemed to have their own strange rules about their relationship. What was he doing in *this* role. He sat down again. Now and then he noticed the death of a light. The snail shells held only so much oil. Kip would rise and refill them with pink paraffin.

"We must keep them lit till midnight."

They talked then about the war, so far away. "When the war with Japan is over, everyone will finally go home," Kip said. "And where will *you* go?" Caravaggio asked. The sapper rolled his head, half nodding, half shaking it, his mouth smiling. So Caravaggio began to talk, mostly to Kip.

The dog cautiously approached the table and laid its head on Caravaggio's lap. The sapper asked for other stories about Toronto as if it were a place of peculiar wonders. Snow that drowned the city, iced up the harbour, ferryboats in the summer where people listened to concerts. But what he was really interested in were the clues to Hana's nature, though she was evasive, veering Caravaggio away from stories that involved some moment of her life. She wanted Kip to know her only in the present, a person perhaps more flawed or more compassionate or harder or more obsessed than the girl or young woman she had been then. In her life there was her mother Alice her father Patrick her stepmother Clara and Caravaggio. She had already admitted these names to Kip as if they were her credentials, her dowry. They were faultless and needed no discussion. She used them like authorities in a book she could refer to on the right way to boil an egg, or the correct way to slip garlic into a lamb. They were not to be questioned.

And now—because he was quite drunk—Caravaggio told the story of Hana's singing the "Marseillaise," which he had told her before. "Yes, I have heard the song," said Kip, and he attempted a version of it. "No, you have to sing it *out*," said Hana, "you have to sing it standing up!"

She stood up, pulled her tennis shoes off and climbed onto the table. There were four snail lights flickering, almost dying, on the table beside her bare feet.

"This is for you. This is how you must learn to sing it, Kip. This is for *you*."

She sang up into darkness beyond their snail light, beyond the square of light from the English patient's room and into the dark sky waving with shadows of cypress. Her hands came out of their pockets.

Kip had heard the song in the camps, sung by groups of men, often during strange moments, such as before an impromptu soccer match. And Caravaggio when he had heard it in the last few years of the war never really liked it, never liked to listen to it. In his heart he had Hana's version from many years before. Now he listened with a pleasure because she was singing again, but this was quickly altered by the way she sang. Not the passion of her at sixteen but echoing the tentative circle of light around her in the darkness. She was singing it as if it was something scarred, as if one couldn't ever again bring all the hope of the song together. It had been altered by the five years leading to this night of her twenty-first birthday in the forty-fifth year of the twentieth century. Singing in the voice of a tired traveller, alone against everything. A new testament. There was no certainty to the song anymore, the singer could only be one voice against all the mountains of power. That was the only sureness. The one voice was the single unspoiled thing. A song of snail light. Caravaggio realized she was singing with and echoing the heart of the sapper.

In the tent there have been nights of no talk and nights full of talk. They are never sure what will occur, whose fraction of past will emerge, or whether touch will be anonymous and silent in their darkness. The intimacy of her body or the body of her language in his ear—as they lie upon the air pillow he insists on blowing up and using each night. He has been charmed by this Western invention. He dutifully releases the air and folds it into three each morning, as he has done all the way up the landmass of Italy.

In the tent Kip nestles against her neck. He dissolves to her scratching fingernails across his skin. Or he has his mouth against her mouth, his stomach against her wrist.

She sings and hums. She thinks him, in this tent's darkness, to be half bird—a quality of feather within him, the cold iron at his wrist. He moves sleepily whenever he is in such darkness with her, not quite quick as the world, whereas in daylight he glides through all that is random around him, the way colour glides against colour.

But at night he embraces torpor. She cannot see his order and discipline without seeing his eyes. There isn't a key to him. Everywhere she touches braille doorways. As if organs, the heart, the rows of rib, can be seen under the skin, saliva across her hand now a colour. He has mapped her sadness more than any other. Just as she knows the strange path of love he has for his dangerous brother. "To be a wanderer is in our blood. That is why jailing is most difficult for his nature and he would kill himself to get free."

During the verbal nights, they travel his country of five

rivers. The Sutlej, Jhelum, Ravi, Chenab, Beas. He guides her into the great gurdwara, removing her shoes, watching as she washes her feet, covers her head. What they enter was built in 1601, desecrated in 1757 and built again immediately. In 1830 gold and marble were applied. "If I took you before morning you would see first of all the mist over the water. Then it lifts to reveal the temple in light. You will already be hearing the hymns of the saints—Ramananda, Nanak and Kabir. Singing is at the centre of worship. You hear the song, you smell the fruit from the temple gardens—pomegranates, oranges. The temple is a haven in the flux of life, accessible to all. It is the ship that crossed the ocean of ignorance."

They move through the night, they move through the silver door to the shrine where the Holy Book lies under a canopy of brocades. The *ragis* sing the Book's verses accompanied by musicians. They sing from four in the morning till eleven at night. The Granth Sahib is opened at random, a quotation selected, and for three hours, before the mist lifts off the lake to reveal the Golden Temple, the verses mingle and sway out with unbroken reading.

Kip walks her beside a pool to the tree shrine where Baba Gujhaji, the first priest of the temple, is buried. A tree of superstitions, four hundred and fifty years old. "My mother came here to tie a string onto a branch and beseeched the tree for a son, and when my brother was born returned and asked to be blessed with another. There are sacred trees and magic water all over the Punjab."

Hana is quiet. He knows the depth of darkness in her, her lack of a child and of faith. He is always coaxing her from the edge of her fields of sadness. A child lost. A father lost.

"I have lost someone like a father as well," he has said. But she knows this man beside her is one of the charmed, who has grown up an outsider and so can switch allegiances, can replace loss. There are those destroyed by unfairness and those who are not. If she asks him he will say he has had a good life —his brother in jail, his comrades blown up, and he risking himself daily in this war.

In spite of the kindnesses in such people they were a terrible unfairness. He could be all day in a clay pit dismantling a bomb that might kill him at any moment, could come home from the burial of a fellow sapper, his energy saddened, but whatever the trials around him there was always solution and light. But she saw none. For him there were the various maps of fate, and at Amritsar's temple all faiths and classes were welcome and ate together. She herself would be allowed to place money or a flower onto the sheet spread upon the floor and then join in the great permanent singing.

She wished for that. Her inwardness was a sadness of nature. He himself would allow her to enter any of his thirteen gates of character, but she knew that if he were in danger he would never turn to face her. He would create a space around himself and concentrate. This was his craft. Sikhs, he said, were brilliant at technology. "We have a mystical closeness . . . what is it?" "Affinity." "Yes, affinity, with machines."

He would be lost among them for hours, the beat of music within the crystal set whacking away at his forehead and into his hair. She did not believe she could turn fully to him and be his lover. He moved at a speed that allowed him to replace loss. That was his nature. She would not judge it in him. What right did she have. Kip stepping out each morning with his satchel hanging off his left shoulder and walking the path away from the Villa San Girolamo. Each morning she watched him, seeing his freshness towards the world perhaps for the last time. After a few minutes he would look up into the shrapnel-torn cypresses, whose middle branches had been shelled away. Pliny must have walked down a path like this, or Stendahl, because passages in *The Charterhouse of Parma* had occurred in this part of the world too.

Kip would look up, the arch of the high wounded trees over him, the path in front of him mediaeval, and he a young man of the strangest profession his century had invented, a sapper, a military engineer who detected and disarmed mines. Each morning he emerged from the tent, bathed and dressed in the garden, and stepped away from the villa and its surroundings, not even entering the house—maybe a wave if he saw her— as if language, humanity, would confuse him, get, like blood, into the machine he had to understand. She would see him forty yards from the house, in a clearing of the path.

It was the moment he left them all behind. The moment the drawbridge closed behind the knight and he was alone with just the peacefulness of his own strict talent. In Siena there was that mural she had seen. A fresco of a city. A few yards outside the city walls the artist's paint had crumbled away, so there was not even the security of art to provide an orchard in the far acres for the traveller leaving the castle. That was where, she felt, Kip went during the day. Each morning he would step from the painted scene towards dark bluffs of chaos. The knight. The warrior saint. She would see the khaki uniform flickering through the cypresses. The Englishman had called him *fato profugus*—fate's fugitive. She guessed that these days began for him with the pleasure of lifting his eyes up to the trees.

They had flown the sappers into Naples at the beginning of October 1943, selecting the best from the engineering corps that were already in southern Italy, Kip among the thirty men who were brought into the booby-trapped city.

The Germans in the Italian campaign had choreographed one of the most brilliant and terrible retreats in history. The advance of the Allies, which should have taken a month, took a year. There was fire in their path. Sappers rode the mudguards of trucks as the armies moved forward, their eyes searching for fresh soil disturbances that signalled land mines or glass mines or shoe mines. The advance impossibly slow. Farther north in the mountains, partisan bands of Garibaldi communist groups, who wore identifying red handkerchiefs, were also wiring explosives over the roads which detonated when German trucks passed over them.

The scale of the laying of mines in Italy and in North Africa cannot be imagined. At the Kismaayo–Afmadu road junction, 260 mines were found. There were 300 at the Omo River Bridge area. On June 30, 1941, South African sappers laid 2,700 Mark 11 mines in Mersa Matruh in one day. Four months later the British cleared Mersa Matruh of 7,806 mines and placed them elsewhere.

Mines were made out of everything. Forty-centimetre galvanized pipes were filled with explosives and left along military paths. Mines in wooden boxes were left in homes. Pipe mines were filled with gelignite, metal scraps and nails. South African sappers packed iron and gelignite into four-gallon petrol cans that could then destroy armoured cars.

It was worst in the cities. Bomb disposal units, barely trained, were shipped out from Cairo and Alexandria. The Eighteenth Division became famous. During three weeks in October 1941, they dismantled 1,403 high-explosive bombs.

Italy was worse than Africa, the clockwork fuzes nightmarishly eccentric, the spring-activated mechanisms different from the German ones that units had been trained in. As sappers entered cities they walked along avenues where corpses were strung from trees or the balconies of buildings. The Germans often retaliated by killing ten Italians for every German killed. Some of the hanging corpses were mined and had to be blown up in midair.

The Germans evacuated Naples on October 1, 1943. During an Allied raid the previous September, hundreds of citizens had walked away and begun living in the caves outside the city. The Germans in their retreat bombed the entrance to the caves, forcing the citizens to stay underground. A typhus epidemic broke out. In the harbour scuttled ships were freshly mined underwater.

The thirty sappers walked into a city of booby traps. There were delayed-action bombs sealed into the walls of public buildings. Nearly every vehicle was rigged. The sappers became permanently suspicious of any object placed casually in a room. They distrusted everything they saw on a table unless it was placed facing "four o'clock." Years after the war a sapper putting a pen on a table would position it with the thicker end facing four o'clock.

Naples continued as a war zone for six weeks and Kip was there with the unit for the whole period. After two weeks they discovered the citizens in the caves. Their skin dark with shit and typhus. The procession of them back into the city hospitals was one of ghosts.

Four days later the central post office blew up, and seventy-two were killed or wounded. The richest collection of mediae-val records in Europe had already burned in the city archives.

On the twentieth of October, three days before electricity was to be restored, a German turned himself in. He told authorities that there were thousands of bombs hidden in the harbour section of the city that were wired to the dormant electrical system. When power was turned on, the city would dissolve in flames. He was interrogated more than seven times, in differing stages of tact and violence—at the end of which the authorities were still uncertain about his confession. This time an entire area of the city was evacuated. Children and the old, those almost dead, those pregnant, those who had been brought out of the caves, animals, valuable jeeps, wounded soldiers out of the hospitals, mental patients, priests and monks and nuns out of the abbeys. By dusk on the evening of October 22, 1943, only twelve sappers remained behind.

The electricity was to be turned on at three p.m. the next day. None of the sappers had ever been in an empty city before, and these were to be the strangest and most disturbing hours of their lives.

During the evenings thunderstorms roll over Tuscany. Lightning drops towards any metal or spire that rises up out of the landscape. Kip always returns to the villa along the yellow path between the cypresses around seven in the evening, which is when the thunder, if there is going to be thunder, begins. The mediaeval experience.

He seems to like such temporal habits. She or Caravaggio will see his figure in the distance, pausing in his walk home to look back towards the valley to see how far away the rain is from him. Hana and Caravaggio return to the house. Kip continues his half-mile uphill walk on the path that curls slowly to the right and then slowly to the left. There is the noise of his boots on the gravel. The wind reaches him in bursts, hitting the cypresses broadside so they tilt, entering the sleeves of his shirt.

For the next ten minutes he walks, never sure if the rain will overtake him. He will hear the rain before he feels it, a clicking on the dry grass, on the olive leaves. But for now he is in the great refreshing wind of the hill, in the foreground of the storm.

If the rain reaches him before he gets to the villa, he continues walking at the same pace, snaps the rubber cape over his haversack and walks on within it.

In his tent he hears the pure thunder. Sharp cracks of it overhead, a coach-wheel sound as it disappears into the mountains. A sudden sunlight of lightning through the tent wall, always, it seems to him, brighter than sunlight, a flash of contained phosphorus, something machinelike, to do with the new word he has heard in the theory rooms and through his crystal set, which is "nuclear." In the tent he unwinds the wet turban, dries his hair and weaves another around his head.

The storm rolls out of Piedmont to the south and to the east. Lightning falls upon the steeples of the small alpine chapels whose tableaux reenact the Stations of the Cross or the Mysteries of the Rosary. In the small towns of Varese and Varallo, larger-than-life terra-cotta figures carved in the 1600s are revealed briefly, depicting biblical scenes. The bound arms of the scourged Christ pulled back, the whip coming down, the baying dog, three soldiers in the next chapel tableau raising the crucifix higher towards the painted clouds.

The Villa San Girolamo, located where it is, also receives such moments of light—the dark halls, the room the Englishman lies in, the kitchen where Hana is laying a fire, the shelled chapel—all lit suddenly, without shadow. Kip will walk with no qualms under the trees in his patch of garden during such storms, the dangers of being killed by lightning pathetically minimal compared with the danger of his daily life. The naive Catholic images from those hillside shrines that he has seen are with him in the half-darkness, as he counts the seconds between lightning and thunder. Perhaps this villa is a similar tableau, the four of them in private movement, momentarily lit up, flung ironically against this war.

The twelve sappers who remained behind in Naples fanned out into the city. All through the night they have broken into sealed tunnels, descended into sewers, looking for fuze lines that might be linked with the central generators. They are to drive away at two p.m., an hour before the electricity is to be turned on.

A city of twelve. Each in separate parts of the town. One at the generator, one at the reservoir, still diving—the authorities most certain destruction will be caused by flooding. How to mine a city. It is unnerving mostly because of the silence. All they hear of the human world are barking dogs and bird songs that come from apartment windows above the streets. When the time comes, he will go into one of the rooms with a bird. Some human thing in this vacuum. He passes the Museo Archeologico Nazionale, where the remnants of Pompeii and Herculaneum are housed. He has seen the ancient dog frozen in white ash.

The scarlet sapper light strapped to his left arm is turned on as he walks, the only source of light on the Strada Carbonara. He is exhausted from the night search, and now there seems little to do. Each of them has a radiophone, but it is to be used only for an emergency discovery. It is the terrible silence in the empty courtyards and the dry fountains that makes him most tired.

At one p.m. he traces his way towards the damaged Church of San Giovanni a Carbonara, where he knows there is a chapel of the Rosary. He had been walking through the church a few evenings earlier when lightning filled the darkness, and he had seen large human figures in the tableau. An angel and a woman in a bedroom. Darkness replaced the brief scene and he sat in a pew waiting, but there was to be no more revelation.

He enters that corner of the church now, with the terracotta figures painted the colour of white humans. The scene depicts a bedroom where a woman is in conversation with an angel. The woman's curly brown hair reveals itself under the loose blue cape, the fingers of her left hand touching her breastbone. When he steps forward into the room he realizes everything is larger than life. His own head is no higher than the shoulder of the woman. The angel's raised arm reaches fifteen feet in height. Still, for Kip, they are company. It is an inhabited room, and he walks within the discussion of these creatures that represent some fable about mankind and heaven.

He slips his satchel from his shoulder and faces the bed. He wants to lie on it, hesitating only because of the presence of the angel. He has already walked around the ethereal body and noticed the dusty light bulbs attached to its back beneath the dark coloured wings, and he knows in spite of his desire that he could not sleep easily in the presence of such a thing. There are three pairs of stage slippers, a set designer's subtlety, peeking out from under the bed. It is about one-forty.

He spreads his cape on the floor, flattens the satchel into a pillow and lies down on the stone. Most of his childhood in Lahore he slept on a mat on the floor of his bedroom. And in truth he has never gotten accustomed to the beds of the West. A pallet and an air pillow are all he uses in his tent, whereas in England when staying with Lord Suffolk he sank claustrophobically into the dough of a mattress, and lay there captive and awake until he crawled out to sleep on the carpet.

He stretches out beside the bed. The shoes too, he notices, are larger than life. The feet of Amazonians slip into them. Above his head the tentative right arm of the woman. Beyond his feet the angel. Soon one of the sappers will turn on the city's electricity, and if he is going to explode he will do so in the company of these two. They will die or be secure. There is nothing more he can do, anyway. He has been up all night on a final search for caches of dynamite and time cartridges. Walls will crumble around him or he will walk through a city of light. At least he has found these parental figures. He can relax in the midst of this mime of conversation.

He has his hands under his head, interpreting a new toughness in the face of the angel he didn't notice before. The white flower it holds has fooled him. The angel too is a warrior. In the midst of this series of thoughts his eyes close and he gives in to tiredness.

He is sprawled out with a smile on his face, as if relieved finally to be sleeping, the luxuriousness of such a thing. The palm of his left hand facedown on the concrete. The colour of his turban echoes that of the lace collar at the neck of Mary.

At her feet the small Indian sapper, in uniform, beside the six slippers. There seems to be no time here. Each of them has selected the most comfortable of positions to forget time. So we will be remembered by others. In such smiling comfort when we trust our surroundings. The tableau now, with Kip at the feet of the two figures, suggests a debate over his fate. The raised terra-cotta arm a stay of execution, a promise of some great future for this sleeper, childlike, foreign-born. The three of them almost at the point of decision, agreement.

Under the thin layer of dust the angel's face has a powerful joy. Attached to its back are the six light bulbs, two of which are defunct. But in spite of that the wonder of electricity suddenly lights its wings from underneath, so that their blood-red and blue and goldness the colour of mustard fields shine animated in the late afternoon.

Wherever Hana is now, in the future, she is aware of the line of movement Kip's body followed out of her life. Her mind repeats it. The path he slammed through among them. When he turned into a stone of silence in their midst. She recalls everything of that August day—what the sky was like, the objects on the table in front of her going dark under the thunder.

She sees him in the field, his hands clasped over his head, then realizes this is a gesture not of pain but of his need to hold the earphones tight against his brain. He is a hundred yards away from her in the lower field when she hears a scream emerge from his body which had never raised its voice among them. He sinks to his knees, as if unbuckled. Stays like that and then slowly gets up and moves in a diagonal towards his tent, enters it, and closes the flaps behind him. There is the dry crackle of thunder and she sees her arms darken.

Kip emerges from the tent with the rifle. He comes into the Villa San Girolamo and sweeps past her, moving like a steel ball in an arcade game, through the doorway and up the stairs three steps at a time, his breath metronomed, the hit of his boots against the vertical sections of stairs. She hears his feet along the hallway as she continues to sit at the table in the kitchen, the book in front of her, the pencil, these objects frozen and shadowed in the pre-storm light.

He enters the bedroom. He stands at the foot of the bed where the English patient lies.

Hello, sapper.

The rifle stock is against his chest, its sling braced against his triangled arm.

What was going on outside?

Kip looks condemned, separate from the world, his brown face weeping. The body turns and fires into the old fountain, and the plaster explodes dust onto the bed. He pivots back so the rifle points at the Englishman. He begins to shudder, and then everything in him tries to control that.

Put down the gun, Kip.

He slams his back against the wall and stops his shaking. Plaster dust in the air around them.

I sat at the foot of this bed and listened to you, Uncle. These last months. When I was a kid I did that, the same thing. I believed I could fill myself up with what older people taught me. I believed I could carry that knowledge, slowly altering it, but in any case passing it beyond me to another.

I grew up with traditions from my country, but later, more often, from *your* country. Your fragile white island that with customs and manners and books and prefects and reason somehow converted the rest of the world. You stood for precise behaviour. I knew if I lifted a teacup with the wrong finger I'd be banished. If I tied the wrong kind of knot in a tie I was out. Was it just ships that gave you such power? Was it, as my brother said, because you had the histories and printing presses?

You and then the Americans converted us. With your missionary rules. And Indian soldiers wasted their lives as heroes so they could be *pukkah*. You had wars like cricket. How did you fool us into this? Here . . . listen to what you people have done.

He throws the rifle on the bed and moves towards the Englishman. The crystal set is at his side, hanging off his belt. He unclips it and puts the earphones over the black head of the patient, who winces at the pain on his scalp. But the sapper leaves them on him. Then he walks back and picks up the rifle. He sees Hana at the door.

One bomb. Then another. Hiroshima. Nagasaki.

He swerves the rifle towards the alcove. The hawk in the valley air seems to float intentionally into the V sight. If he closes his eyes he sees the streets of Asia full of fire. It rolls across cities like a burst map, the hurricane of heat withering bodies as it meets them, the shadow of humans suddenly in the air. This tremor of Western wisdom.

He watches the English patient, earphones on, the eyes focused inwards, listening. The rifle sight moves down the thin nose to the Adam's apple, above the collarbone. Kip stops breathing. Braced at exact right angles to the Enfield rifle. No waver.

Then the Englishman's eyes look back at him.

Sapper.

Caravaggio enters the room and reaches for him, and Kip wheels the butt of the rifle into his ribs. A swat from the paw of an animal. And then, as if part of the same movement, he is back in the braced right-angle position of those in firing squads, drilled into him in various barracks in India and England. The burned neck in his sights.

Kip, talk to me.

Now his face is a knife. The weeping from shock and horror contained, seeing everything, all those around him, in a different light. Night could fall between them, fog could fall, and the young man's dark brown eyes would reach the new revealed enemy.

My brother told me. Never turn your back on Europe. The deal makers. The contract makers. The map drawers. Never trust Europeans, he said. Never shake hands with them. But we, oh, we were easily impressed—by speeches and medals and your ceremonies. What have I been doing these last few years? Cutting away, defusing, limbs of evil. For what? For *this* to happen?

What is it? Jesus, tell us!

I'll leave you the radio to swallow your history lesson. Don't move again, Caravaggio. All those speeches of civilisation from kings and queens and presidents . . . such voices of abstract order. Smell it. Listen to the radio and smell the celebration in it. In my country, when a father breaks justice in two, you kill the father.

You don't know who this man is.

The rifle sight unwavering at the burned neck. Then the sapper swerves it up towards the man's eyes.

Do it, Almásy says.

The eyes of the sapper and the patient meet in this half-dark room crowded now with the world.

He nods to the sapper.

Do it, he says quietly.

Kip ejects the cartridge and catches it as it begins to fall. He throws the rifle onto the bed, a snake, its venom collected. He sees Hana on the periphery.

The burned man untugs the earphones off his head and slowly places them down in front of him. Then his left hand reaches up and pulls away the hearing aid, and drops it to the floor.

Do it, Kip. I don't want to hear any more.

He closes his eyes. Slips into darkness, away from the room.

The sapper leans against the wall, his hands folded, head down. Caravaggio can hear air being breathed in and out of his nostrils, fast and hard, a piston.

He isn't an Englishman.

American, French, I don't care. When you start bombing the brown races of the world, you're an Englishman. You had King Leopold of Belgium and now you have fucking Harry Truman of the USA. You all learned it from the English.

No. Not him. Mistake. Of all people he is probably on your side.

He would say that doesn't matter, Hana says.

Caravaggio sits down in the chair. He is always, he thinks, sitting in this chair. In the room there is the thin squawking from the crystal set, the radio still speaking in its underwater voice. He cannot bear to turn and look at the sapper or look towards the blur of Hana's frock. He knows the young soldier is right. They would never have dropped such a bomb on a white nation.

The sapper walks out of the room, leaving Caravaggio and Hana by the bed. He has left the three of them to their world, is no longer their sentinel. In the future, if and when the patient dies, Caravaggio and the girl will bury him. Let the dead bury the dead. He has never been sure what that meant. Those few callous words in the Bible.

They will bury everything except the book. The body, the sheets, his clothes, the rifle. Soon he will be alone with Hana. And the motive for all this on the radio. A terrible event emerging out of the shortwave. A new war. The death of a civilisation.

Still night. He can hear nighthawks, their faint cries, the muted thud of wings as they turn. The cypress trees rise over his tent, still on this windless night. He lies back and stares into the dark corner of the tent. When he closes his eyes he sees fire, people leaping into rivers into reservoirs to avoid flame or heat that within seconds burns everything, whatever they hold, their own skin and hair, even the water they leap into. The brilliant bomb carried over the sea in a plane, passing the moon in the east, towards the green archipelago. And released.

He has not eaten food or drunk water, is unable to swallow anything. Before light failed he stripped the tent of all military objects, all bomb disposal equipment, stripped all insignia off his uniform. Before lying down he undid the turban and combed his hair out and then tied it up into a topknot and lay back, saw the light on the skin of the tent slowly disperse, his eyes holding onto the last blue of light, hearing the drop of wind into windlessness and then hearing the swerve of the hawks as their wings thudded. And all the delicate noises of the air.

He feels all the winds of the world have been sucked into Asia. He steps away from the many small bombs of his career towards a bomb the size, it seems, of a city, so vast it lets the living witness the death of the population around them. He knows nothing about the weapon. Whether it was a sudden assault of metal and explosion or if boiling air scoured itself towards and through anything human. All he knows is, he feels he can no longer let anything approach him, cannot eat the food or even drink from a puddle on a stone bench on the terrace. He does not feel he can draw a match out of his bag and fire the lamp, for he believes the lamp will ignite everything. In the tent, before the light evaporated, he had brought out the photograph of his family and gazed at it. His name is Kirpal Singh and he does not know what he is doing here.

He stands now under the trees in the August heat, unturbanned, wearing only a *kurta*. He carries nothing in his hands, just walks alongside the outline of hedges, his bare feet on the grass or on terrace stone or in the ash of an old bonfire. His body alive in its sleeplessness, standing on the edge of a great valley of Europe.

In the early morning she sees him standing beside the tent. During the evening she had watched for some light among the trees. Each of them in the villa had eaten alone that night, the Englishman eating nothing. Now she sees the sapper's arm sweep out and the canvas walls collapse on themselves like a sail. He turns and comes towards the house, climbs the steps onto the terrace and disappears.

In the chapel he moves past the burned pews towards the apse, where under a tarpaulin weighted down with branches is the motorbike. He begins dragging the covering off the machine. He crouches down by the bike and begins nuzzling oil into the sprockets and cogs.

When Hana comes into the roofless chapel he is sitting there leaning his back and head against the wheel.

Kip.

He says nothing, looking through her.

Kip, it's *me*. What did we have to do with it?

He is a stone in front of her.

She kneels down to his level and leans forward into him, the side of her head against his chest, holding herself like that.

A beating heart.

When his stillness doesn't alter she rolls back onto her knees.

The Englishman once read me something, from a book: "Love is so small it can tear itself through the eye of a needle."

He leans to his side away from her, his face stopping a few inches from a rain puddle.

A boy and a girl.

While the sapper unearthed the motorcycle from under the tarpaulin, Caravaggio leaned forward on the parapet, his chin against his forearm. Then he felt he couldn't bear the mood of the house and walked away. He wasn't there when the sapper gunned the motorbike to life and sat on it while it half bucked, alive under him, and Hana stood nearby.

Singh touched her arm and let the machine roll away, down the slope, and only then revved it to life.

Halfway down the path to the gate, Caravaggio was waiting for him, carrying the gun. He didn't even lift it formally towards the motorbike when the boy slowed down, as Caravaggio walked into his path. Caravaggio came up to him and put his arms around him. A great hug. The sapper felt the stubble against his skin for the first time. He felt drawn in, gathered into the muscles. "I shall have to learn how to miss you," Caravaggio said. Then the boy pulled away and Caravaggio walked back to the house.

The machine broke into life around him. The smoke of the Triumph and dust and fine gravel fell away through the trees. The bike leapt the cattle grid at the gates, and then he was weaving down out of the village, passing the smell of gardens on either side of him that were tacked onto the slopes in their treacherous angle.

His body slipped into a position of habit, his chest parallel with, almost touching, the petrol tank, his arms horizontal in the shape of least resistance. He went south, avoiding Florence completely. Through Greve, across to Montevarchi and Ambra, small towns ignored by war and invasion. Then, as the new hills appeared, he began to climb the spine of them towards Cortona.

He was travelling against the direction of the invasion, as if rewinding the spool of war, the route no longer tense with military. He took only roads he knew, seeing the familiar castle towns from a distance. He lay static on the Triumph as it burned under him in its tear along the country roads. He carried little, all weapons left behind. The bike hurled through each village, not slowing for town or memory of war. *"The earth shall reel to and fro like a drunkard, and shall be removed like a cottage."*

She opened up his knapsack. There was a pistol wrapped in oilskin, so that its smell was released when she uncovered it. Toothbrush and tooth powder, pencil sketches in a notebook, including a drawing of her—she was sitting on the terrace and he had been looking down from the Englishman's room. Two turbans, a bottle of starch. One sapper lamp with its leather straps, to be worn in emergencies. She flicked it on and the knapsack filled with crimson light.

In the side pockets she found pieces of equipment to do with bomb disposal, which she didn't wish to touch. Wrapped up in another small piece of cloth was the metal spile she had given him, which was used for tapping maple sugar out of a tree in her country.

From within the collapsed tent she unearthed a portrait that must have been of his family. She held the photograph in her palm. A Sikh and his family.

An older brother who was only eleven in this picture. Kip beside him, eight years old. *"When the war came my brother sided with whoever was against the English."*

There was also a small handbook that had a map of bombs. And a drawing of a saint accompanied by a musician.

She packed everything back in except the photograph, which she held in her free hand. She carried the bag through the trees, walked across the loggia and brought it into the house.

Each hour or so he slowed to a stop, spat into the goggles and wiped dust off with the sleeve of his shirt. He looked into the map again. He would go to the Adriatic, then south. Most of the troops were at the northern borders.

He climbed into Cortona, the high-pitched gunning of the bike all around him. He rode the Triumph up the steps to the door of the church and then walked in. A statue was there, bandaged in scaffold. He wanted to get closer to the face, but he had no rifle telescope and his body felt too stiff to climb up the construction pipes. He wandered around underneath like somebody unable to enter the intimacy of a home. He walked the bike down the church steps, and then coasted down through the shattered vineyards and went on to Arezzo.

At Sansepolcro he took a winding road into the mountains, into their mist, so he had to slow to minimal speed. The Bocca Trabaria. He was cold but locked the weather out of his mind. Finally the road rose above the whiteness, the mist a bed behind him. He skirted Urbino where the Germans had burned all the field horses of the enemy. They had fought here in this region for a month; now he slid through in minutes, recognizing only the Black Madonna shrines. The war had made all the cities and towns similar.

He came down towards the coast. Into Gabicce Mare, where he had seen the Virgin emerge from the sea. He slept on the hill, overlooking cliff and water, near where the statue had been taken. That was the end of his first day.

Dear Clara—Dear Maman,

Maman is a French word, Clara, a circular word, suggesting cuddles, a personal word that can be even shouted in public. Something as comforting and as eternal as a barge. Though you, in spirit, I know are still a canoe. Can swerve one around and enter a creek in seconds. Still independent. Still private. Not a barge responsible for all around you. This is my first letter in years, Clara, and I am not used to the formality of them. I have spent the last few months living with three others, and our talk has been slow, casual. I am not used to talking in any way but that now.

The year is 194-. What? For a second I forget. But I know the month and the day. One day after we heard the bombs were dropped in Japan, so it feels like the end of the world. From now on I believe the personal will forever be at war with the public. If we can rationalize this we can rationalize anything.

Patrick died in a dove-cot in France. In France in the seventeenth and eighteenth centuries they built them huge, larger than most houses. Like this.

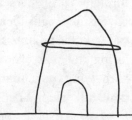

The horizontal line one-third of the way down was called the rat ledge—to stop rats running up the brick, so the doves would be safe. Safe as a dove-cot. A sacred place. Like a church in many ways. A comforting place. Patrick died in a comforting place.

At five a.m. he kicked the Triumph to life, and the rear wheel threw gravel in a skirt. He was still in darkness, still unable to distinguish sea in the vista beyond the cliff. For the journey from here to the south he had no maps, but he could recognize the war roads and follow the coast route. When sunlight came he was able to double his speed. The rivers were still ahead of him.

Around two in the afternoon he reached Ortona, where the sappers had laid the Bailey bridges, nearly drowning in the storm in mid-river. It began to rain and he stopped to put on a rubber cape. He walked around the machine in the wetness. Now, as he travelled, the sound in his ears changed. The *shush shush* replacing the whine and howl, the water flung onto his boots from the front wheel. Everything he saw through the goggles was grey. He would not think of Hana. In all the silence within the bike's noise he did not think of her.

When her face appeared he erased it, pulled the handlebars so he would swerve and have to concentrate. If there were to be words they would not be hers; they would be names on this map of Italy he was riding through.

He feels he carries the body of the Englishman with him in this flight. It sits on the petrol tank facing him, the black body in an embrace with his, facing the past over his shoulder, facing the countryside they are flying from, that receding palace of strangers on the Italian hill which shall never be rebuilt. *"And my words which I have put in thy mouth shall not depart out of thy mouth. Nor out of the mouth of thy seed. Nor out of the mouth of thy seed's seed."*

The voice of the English patient sang Isaiah into his ear as he had that afternoon when the boy had spoken of the face on the chapel ceiling in Rome. "There are of course a hundred Isaiahs. Someday you will want to see him as an old man—in southern France the abbeys celebrate him as bearded and old, but the power is still there in his look." The Englishman had sung out into the painted room. *"Behold, the Lord will carry thee away with a mighty captivity, and He will surely cover thee. He will surely violently turn and toss thee like a ball into a large country."*

He was riding deeper into thick rain. Because he had loved the face on the ceiling he had loved the words. As he had believed in the burned man and the meadows of civilisation he tended. Isaiah and Jeremiah and Solomon were in the burned man's bedside book, his holy book, whatever he had loved glued into his own. He had passed his book to the sapper, and the sapper had said we have a Holy Book too.

The rubber lining on the goggles had cracked during the past months and the rain now began filling each pocket of air in front of his eyes. He would ride without them, the *shush*

shush a permanent sea in his ears, and his crouched body stiff, cold, so there was only the idea of heat from this machine he rode so intimately, the white spray of it as he slid through villages like a slipping star, a half-second of visitation when one could make a wish. *"For the heavens shall vanish away like smoke and the earth shall wax old like a garment. And they that dwell therein shall die in like manner. For the moth shall eat them up like a garment, and the worms shall eat them like wool."* A secret of deserts from Uweinat to Hiroshima.

He was removing the goggles as he came out of the curve and onto the bridge over the Ofanto River. And with his left arm up holding the goggles free he began to skid. He dropped them and calmed the bike but was not prepared for the iron bounce onto the lip of the bridge, the bike lying down to the right underneath him. He was suddenly sliding with it along the skin of rainwater down the centre of the bridge, blue sparks from the scratching metal around his arms and face.

Heavy tin flew off and shouldered past him. Then he and the bike veered to the left, there was no side to the bridge, and they hurtled out parallel to the water, he and the bike sideways, his arms flung back above his head. The cape released itself away from him, from whatever was machine and mortal, part of the element of air.

The motorbike and the soldier stilled in midair, then pivoted down into the water, the metal body between his legs as they slammed into it, jarring a white path through it, disappearing, the rain too entering the river. *"He will toss thee like a ball into a large country."*

How did Patrick end up in a dove-cot, Clara? His unit had left him, burned and wounded. So burned the buttons of his shirt were part of his skin, part of his dear chest. That I kissed and you kissed. And how was my father burned? He who could swerve like an eel, or like your canoe, as if charmed, from the real world. In his sweet and complicated innocence. He was the most unverbal of men, and I am always surprised women liked him. We tend to like a verbal man around us. We are the rationalists, the wise, and he was often lost, uncertain, unspoken.

He was a burned man and I was a nurse and I could have nursed him. Do you understand the sadness of geography? I could have saved him or at least been with him till the end. I know a lot about burning. How long was he alone with doves and rats? With the last stages of blood and life in him? Doves over him. The flutter when they thrashed around him. Unable to sleep in the darkness. He always hated darkness. And he was alone, without lover or kin.

I am sick of Europe, Clara. I want to come home. To your small cabin and pink rock in Georgian Bay. I will take a bus up to Parry Sound. And from the mainland send a message over the shortwave radio out towards the Pancakes. And wait for you, wait to see the silhouette of you in a canoe coming to rescue me from this place we all entered, betraying you. How did you become so smart? How did you become so determined? How were you not fooled like us? You that demon for pleasure who became so wise. The purest among us, the darkest bean, the greenest leaf.

Hana

The sapper's bare head comes out of the water, and he gasps in all the air above the river.

Caravaggio has made a one-strand bridge with hemp rope down to the roof of the next villa. The rope is tightened at this end round the waist of the statue of Demetrius and then secured to the well. The rope barely higher than the tops of the two olive trees along his path. If he loses his balance he will fall into the rough dusty arms of the olive.

He steps onto it, his socked feet gripping the hemp. How valuable is that statue? he once asked Hana casually, and she told him the English patient had said all statues of Demetrius were worthless.

She seals the letter and stands up, moves across the room to close the window, and at that moment lightning slips through the valley. She sees Caravaggio in midair halfway across the gorge that lies like a deep scar alongside the villa. She stands there as if in one of her dreams, then climbs into the window alcove and sits there looking out.

Every time there is lightning, rain freezes in the suddenly lit night. She sees the buzzard hawks flung up into the sky, looks for Caravaggio.

He is halfway across when he smells the rain, and then it begins to fall all over his body, clinging to him, and suddenly there is the greater weight of his clothes.

She puts her cupped palms out of the window and combs the rain into her hair.

The villa drifts in darkness. In the hallway by the English patient's bedroom the last candle burns, still alive in the night.

Whenever he opens his eyes out of sleep, he sees the old wavering yellow light.

For him now the world is without sound, and even light seems an unneeded thing. He will tell the girl in the morning he wants no candle flame to accompany him while he sleeps.

Around three a.m. he feels a presence in the room. He sees, for a pulse of a moment, a figure at the foot of his bed, against the wall or painted onto it perhaps, not quite discernible in the darkness of foliage beyond the candlelight. He mutters something, something he had wanted to say, but there is silence and the slight brown figure, which could be just a night shadow, does not move. A poplar. A man with plumes. A swimming figure. And he would not be so lucky, he thinks, to speak to the young sapper again.

He stays awake in any case this night, to see if the figure moves towards him. Ignoring the tablet that brings painlessness, he will remain awake till the light dies out and the smell of candle smoke drifts into his room and into the girl's room farther down the hall. If the figure turns around there will be paint on his back, where he slammed in grief against the mural of trees. When the candle dies out he will be able to see this.

His hand reaches out slowly and touches his book and returns to his dark chest. Nothing else moves in the room.

Now where does he sit as he thinks of her? These years later. A stone of history skipping over the water, bouncing up so she and he have aged before it touches the surface again and sinks.

Where does he sit in his garden thinking once again he should go inside and write a letter or go one day down to the telephone depot, fill out a form and try to contact her in another country. It is this garden, this square patch of dry cut grass that triggers him back to the months he spent with Hana and Caravaggio and the English patient north of Florence in the Villa San Girolamo. He is a doctor, has two children and a laughing wife. He is permanently busy in this city. At six p.m. he removes his white lab coat. Underneath he wears dark trousers and a short-sleeved shirt. He closes up the clinic, where all the paperwork has weights of various kinds—stones, inkpots, a toy truck his son no longer plays with—to keep it from being blown away by the fan. He climbs onto his bicycle and pedals the four miles home, through the bazaar. Whenever he can he swerves his bicycle over to the shadowed part of the street. He has reached an age when he suddenly realizes that the sun of India exhausts him.

He glides under the willows by the canal and then stops at a small neighbourhood of houses, removes his cycle clips and carries the bicycle down the steps into the small garden his wife has nurtured.

And something this evening has brought the stone out of the water and allowed it to move back within the air towards the hill town in Italy. It was perhaps the chemical burn on the arm of the girl he treated today. Or the stone stairway, where brown weeds grow ardently along the steps. He had been carrying his bicycle and was halfway up the steps before he remembered. This had been on the way to work, so the trigger of memory was postponed when he got to the hospital and ran into seven hours of constant patients and administration. Or it might have been the burn on the young girl's arm.

He sits in the garden. And he watches Hana, her hair longer, in her own country. And what does she do? He sees her always, her face and body, but he doesn't know what her profession is or what her circumstances are, although he sees her reactions to people around her, her bending down to children, a white fridge door behind her, a background of noiseless tram cars. This is a limited gift he has somehow been given, as if a camera's film reveals her, but only her, in silence. He cannot discern the company she moves among, her judgement; all he can witness is her character and the lengthening of her dark hair, which falls again and then again into her eyes.

She will, he realizes now, always have a serious face. She has moved from being a young woman into having the angular look of a queen, someone who has made her face with her desire to be a certain kind of person. He still likes that about her. Her smartness, the fact that she did not inherit that look or that beauty, but that it was something searched for and that it will always reflect a present stage of her character. It seems every month or two he witnesses her this way, as if these moments of revelation are a continuation of the letters she wrote to him for a year, getting no reply, until she stopped sending them, turned away by his silence. His character, he supposed.

Now there are these urges to talk with her during a meal and return to that stage they were most intimate at in the tent or in the English patient's room, both of which contained the turbulent river of space between them. Recalling the time, he is just as fascinated at himself there as he is with her—boyish and earnest, his lithe arm moving across the air towards the girl he has fallen in love with. His wet boots are by the Italian door, the laces tied together, his arm reaches for her shoulder, there is the prone figure on the bed.

During the evening meal he watches his daughter struggling with her cutlery, trying to hold the large weapons in her small hands. At this table all of their hands are brown. They move with ease in their customs and habits. And his wife has taught them all a wild humour, which has been inherited by his son. He loves to see his son's wit in this house, how it surprises him constantly, going beyond even his and his wife's knowledge and humour—the way he treats dogs on the streets, imitating their stroll, their look. He loves the fact that this boy can almost guess the wishes of dogs from the variety of expressions at a dog's disposal.

And Hana moves possibly in the company that is not her choice. She, at even this age, thirty-four, has not found her own company, the ones she wanted. She is a woman of honour and smartness whose wild love leaves out luck, always taking risks, and there is something in her brow now that only she can recognize in a mirror. Ideal and idealistic in that shiny dark hair! People fall in love with her. She still remembers the lines of poems the Englishman read out loud to her from his commonplace book. She is a woman I don't know well enough to hold in my wing, if writers have wings, to harbour for the rest of my life.

And so Hana moves and her face turns and in a regret she

lowers her hair. Her shoulder touches the edge of a cupboard and a glass dislodges. Kirpal's left hand swoops down and catches the dropped fork an inch from the floor and gently passes it into the fingers of his daughter, a wrinkle at the edge of his eyes behind his spectacles.

Acknowledgements

While some of the characters who appear in this book are based on historical figures, and while many of the areas described—such as the Gilf Kebir and its surrounding desert—exist, and were explored in the 1930s, it is important to stress that this story is a fiction and that the portraits of the characters who appear in it are fictional, as are some of the events and journeys.

I would like to thank the Royal Geographical Society, London, for allowing me to read archival material and to glean from their *Geographical Journals* the world of explorers and their journeys—often beautifully recorded by their writers. I have quoted a passage from Hassanein Bey's article "Through Kufra to Darfur" (1924), describing sandstorms, and I have drawn from him and other explorers to evoke the desert of the 1930s. I would like to acknowledge information drawn from Dr. Richard A. Bermann's "Historical Problems of the Libyan Desert" (1934) and R. A. Bagnold's review of Almásy's monograph on his explorations in the desert.

Many books were important to me in my research. *Unexploded Bomb* by Major A. B. Hartley was especially useful in re-creating the construction of bombs and in describing the British bomb disposal units at the start of World War II. I have quoted directly from his book (the italicized lines in the "In Situ" section) and have based some of Kirpal Singh's methods of defusing on actual techniques that Hartley records. Information found in the patient's notebook on the nature of certain winds is drawn from Lyall Watson's wonderful book *Heaven's Breath*, direct quotes appearing in quotation marks. The section from the Candaules-Gyges story in Herodotus's *Histories* is from the 1890 translation by G. C. Mc-Cauley (Macmillan). Other quotations from Herodotus use the David Grene translation (University of Chicago Press). The line in italics on page 21 is by Christopher Smart; the lines in italics on page 144 are from John Milton's *Paradise Lost;* the line Hana remembers on page 288 is by Anne Wilkinson. I would also like to acknowledge Alan Moorehead's *The Villa Diana*, which discusses the life of Poliziano in Tuscany. Other important books were Mary McCarthy's *The Stones of Florence;* Leonard Mosley's *The Cat and the Mice;* G. W. L. Nicholson's *The Canadians in Italy 1943–5* and *Canada's Nursing Sisters; The Marshall Cavendish Encyclopaedia of World War II;* F. Yeats-Brown's

Acknowledgements

Martial India; and three other books on the Indian military: *The Tiger Strikes* and *The Tiger Kills,* published in 1942 by the Directorate of Public Relations, New Delhi, India, and *A Roll of Honor.*

Thanks to the English department at Glendon College, York University, the Villa Serbelloni, the Rockefeller Foundation, and the Metropolitan Toronto Reference Library.

I would like to thank the following for their generous help: Elisabeth Dennys, who let me read her letters written from Egypt during the war; Sister Margaret at the Villa San Girolamo; Michael Williamson at the National Library of Canada, Ottawa; Anna Jardine; Rodney Dennys; Linda Spalding; Ellen Levine. And Lally Marwah, Douglas LePan, David Young and Donya Peroff.

Finally a special thanks to Ellen Seligman, Liz Calder and Sonny Mehta.

Grateful acknowledgement is made to
the following for permission to reprint
previously published material:

Famous Music Corporation: Excerpt from "When I Take My Sugar to Tea" by Sammy Fain, Irving Kahal and Pierre Norman. Copyright 1931 by Famous Music Corporation. Copyright renewed 1958 by Famous Music Corporation. Reprinted by permission.

Alfred A. Knopf, Inc.: Excerpt from "Arrival at the Waldorf" by Wallace Stevens from *The Collected Poems of Wallace Stevens.* Copyright 1954 by Wallace Stevens. Reprinted by permission.

Macmillan Publishing Company: Excerpts from *Unexploded Bomb: A History of Bomb Disposal* by Major A. B. Hartley. Copyright © 1958 by Major A. B. Hartley. Copyright renewed. Published in 1958 by Cassell & Co., London, and in 1959 by W. W. Norton & Co., New York. Reprinted by permission of Macmillan Publishing Company.

Edward B. Marks Music Company: Excerpt from "Manhattan" by Lorenz Hart and Richard Rodgers. Copyright 1925 by Edward B. Marks Music Company. Copyright renewed. Used by permission. All rights reserved.

Penguin USA: Excerpts from "Buckingham Palace" from *When We Were Very Young* by A. A. Milne. Copyright 1924 by E. P. Dutton. Copyright renewed 1952 by A. A. Milne. Reprinted by permission of Dutton Children's Books, a division of Penguin Books USA Inc.

The Royal Geographical Society: Excerpt from article by John Ball, Director of Desert Surveys in Egypt (1927), from *The Geographical Journal,* Vol. LXX, pp.